Danger Point

Danger Point

by Douglas J. Bourg

2:30 a.m., South Central Los Angeles, 2004.

It is late, dark and raining. We are chasing some dickhead who had just fired shots into a crowd of people leaving a concert, only two blocks away. We were cruising in our patrol car, having just barely cleared back on duty from dinner when we see a car fitting the description of the suspected shooter's. We light up the car and the asshole takes off up the street, weaving in and out of traffic. This homeboy takes the light up ahead, running the red and smacks into a car coming from the other direction. He skids to a stop, jumps out of his car and runs down an alley, into the night. I leap out of the car and draw my weapon as I yell at my partner to try to head this clown off before he actually kills someone.

The rain is coming down in sheets. The alley is dark - the city being slow to replace broken streetlights – and all I can make out is the shadow of my guy up ahead. To my right, out of the corner of my eye, I see a second figure step out of a doorway. He has a gun in his right hand and raises it toward me. Instinctively I turn, aim and fire my weapon. The figure hits the ground with a soft thud. I look around the alley but the first shooter is nowhere to be seen. I run over to the doorway to see if this guy is still alive and if I should be calling the paramedics, or the coroner. He is lying on his side, his breathing labored, but he's still alive. My stomach drops as I realize he's just a kid – no more than twelve or thirteen years old – holding a pellet gun. His breathing becomes more labored and then, it just stops.

I sit bolt upright in my bed, my heart racing, bathed in a cold sweat, alone in my room, with my guilt.

Chapter 1

San Clemente, CA, Summer 2013

It is dawn and the sunlight that peaks over the mountains is a light orange, the water is inky black and slick as glass. The first wave set of the day is six-foot and clean. I paddle hard, jump to my feet, make the drop, then crank a sweeping turn off the bottom, drive up off the lip, make a slashing cutback and duck into a clean A-frame, the tube, for three or four seconds. Once again I feel whole, cleansed of my guilt. The Doc says I'm making progress but some days it sure doesn't feel like it.

My name is Robert Paladin, but my friends call me Bobby. I'm an ex-pro surfer, ex-cop, and now I work construction full-time for my best friend. I still love to surf when the waves are good. I catch a couple more waves and realize that I'm going to be late for work. Again.

I head in. Standing beside my restored '67 VW van, I pull my wetsuit down to my waist. I see a pair of middle-aged women on their morning walk staring at me. I wrap a towel around my waist before I peel the wetsuit off all the way. I pull on my jeans, put on my shirt and shoes, hop into the van, and haul ass to work. Lucky for me the jobsite is only ten minutes away.

As I pull up in front of the job I can see the boss, DJ, waving his clipboard in the air as he makes some point with the crew. He's on a roll already, tearing everyone a new one, and I'm late again, great.

"Where the hell have you been?" DJ says as he turns to look at me. "It's eight fifteen and work starts at eight a.m., Bobby, not eight ten and not eight fifteen. Eight a.m. Got it?"

"Good morning, DJ." I say with a smile, hoping my natural charm will save my ass. "I'll work through my lunch to make up the time, okay?"

DJ looks over at me and finally gives me the grin I first saw as he was beating me at a game of marbles when I was five years old and he was six.

"Your hair's still wet. How was the surf at Cotton's? I heard that you were on fire this morning. I would have liked to have been out there, too, but some of us have to work."

"It was killer." I reply with a smile. I don't want to push my luck, so I hustle over to my tool box, get my gear and go to work.

DJ's construction company is building a house right across the street from T-Street Beach, where he and I started surfing when we were kids. We surfed seven days a week, rain or shine. Then we joined the Shorecliff's Middle School Surf Team, San Clemente High School Surf Team, the NSSA National Team, and finally we both tried to go pro. I made it but DJ didn't. At the time, I was worried it would mess up our friendship, but DJ went to work for his dad's company and learned the craft of building fine custom homes. He took over the family business when his dad died of a heart attack at fifty-six years old and has never looked back.

Later in the day, after we finally set the last of the custom wood beams in the living room, we clean up and I head back to the beach. The surf is good, but not great, and at least the water isn't crowded. I paddle out, catch a few then head home to eat. I'll try to get a good night's sleep tonight, hopefully without the dream about the kid.

Just like DJ and pro-surfing, I try never to look back either, because what I see scares me. Badly.

Chapter 2

I wake-up to someone ringing my doorbell and banging on my front door. The clock on the bedside table reads 3:30 a.m. This cannot be good. I walk into the front room and push back the side curtain just far enough to see someone in a uniform. An Orange County Sheriff's uniform and another man I can't see clearly are standing on my front porch. I can't imagine why the cops would be here. With a sick feeling, I open the door.

"What's up, guys?" I ask. "Am I in some kind of trouble?"

"No sir," says the uniformed officer standing in front of me. "We just need to ask you some questions. May we come in?"

"Sure." I realize I'm in my boxers and say, "Have a seat while I pull
on some clothes."

They turn into the living room as I head back to my bedroom. I put on the jeans and t-shirt I left on the floor last night, then return to the living room.

The guy in uniform is in my recliner and the man I did not see clearly at the door is sitting on the edge of my sofa, his hands on his knees. He's in plain clothes. That probably means he's a detective. The uniformed officer's name plate on his chest identifies him simply as Mason, but the man sitting on my couch looks familiar to me. I take a closer look and say, "Murphy, is that you?"

His terse, "Yes," is not the kind of welcome you would expect from an old friend.

"Don't you remember me?" I ask. "Bobby Paladin. I was a couple of years behind you at San Clemente High. You worked for my dad at the hardware store."

"Yeah, I remember you," he says a little scornfully, "Weren't you with the LAPD?"

The uniformed sheriff looks over at him. "You know this guy?"

"We've met."

"So I take it you're not here for a reunion." I say to Murphy.

He shakes his head, "No. We found a body on the Frasier Construction site down on T-Street. We went by DJ's house but no one was home. I remembered you and DJ were close, so we came by to ask you if you might be able to help us identify the victim. Here's a picture of the guy."

"Somebody was killed on the jobsite? How would I know anything?" I take the picture from him, "I'm just one of the carpenters working on the house. I left the job at four yesterday afternoon and went surfing." I look down at the picture in my hands. Shock runs through me. The gray face of the body lying flat on the floor is familiar. I look up.

"It looks like Ricky Weaver."

Detective Murphy gives a short nod.

"I can't believe this." I say. "I didn't even know Ricky was back in town. The last I heard he had retired and was living somewhere in Mexico. Cabo San Lucas, I think. I haven't seen him in years."

It's funny to call someone Ricky when they grew up to be six foot six, but Richard just never fit him. He, DJ and I were fixtures on the beach as teenagers. Inseparable for a while, but surfing, girls, jobs and life came along and Ricky grew apart from the group.

I look at the picture again. "I need a drink. Is that okay?" I just can't believe this could be Ricky.

They nod as I turn to the bar that I have set up on my grandmother's antique sideboard. I pour two fingers of Crown Royal into a tumbler. I look at the glass, and then pour in some more. My hands are shaking. I sit down on the other sofa and run my hand through my hair. I pull myself together enough to ask, "Can you tell me what happened to him?"

Officer Mason says, "We got a call around 11:30 last night. A couple of kids were looking for a place to make out and smoke some dope, so they snuck into the job site at T-Street. The sliding glass door was left unlocked and when they were entering the house, one of the girls tripped over a body lying just inside the doorway. She's pretty freaked out. I'll bet she never smokes dope again." He manages a little smile. "Anyway, the body was fully dressed and there was blood everywhere. It looks like a suicide."

Murphy interrupts him and says, "We found your phone number and address on a scrap of paper in his pocket. He had no wallet, no ID, no money, just your name and phone number. Strange, don't you think?" He stares directly at me. I just look down at my glass.

"I don't know what to tell you, Murph. As I said, I haven't heard from Ricky or seen him in, like, two or three years, maybe longer. I know his parents are dead. I have no idea how to reach anyone else in his family. They all moved away a long time ago."

Officer Mason and Murphy take turns asking me more questions, and I answer in a daze. I just don't know enough to be able to help them. Finally Murphy hands me his card and says, "Give me a call if you think of anything else that might help. Sorry about waking you up with such bad news."
I close the door behind them as they step into the warm night. I stand there with my drink empty in my trembling hand. Subconsciously I put my hand into my pocket and find a card that I

7

don't remember being there yesterday. I flip it over and read:
Bobby, I need to see you ASAP. I am in big trouble. I will catch up with you at the Red Fox Lounge at 7 tomorrow morning. Ricky.

Ricky must have slid it into my jeans while I was surfing.
I think back to the sunny, summer days, the water glassy, when Ricky, DJ and I were surfing and hanging out. Ricky left town right after graduation from high school when his dad got him a job as an assistant project manager with the big international construction company that Mr. Weaver worked for. From then on, Ricky would pop up now and again, always with a big smile, a fist full of hundreds and ready to party. But just as quickly as he had arrived, he was gone again, off to work who knows where?

If Ricky was close enough to have put this card into my pocket while I was surfing at State Park last night, why didn't he just hang around and wait to talk to me when I was done?

Chapter 3

After the cops leave, I know I'm not going to get any more sleep tonight. Since I'm already up and dressed, I walk into the bathroom, lift up my t-shirt and rub some deodorant under my arms. I throw some cold water on my face and run a comb through my hair. I should brush my teeth, but instead I make some instant coffee and pour it in my travel cup. I climb into my van and drive over to the job site.

I arrive just as the Crime Scene Investigation van pulls away. I feel like I'm watching a television show. The bath-robed neighbors are huddled in their driveways, coffee cups in hand, wondering how this kind of crime could happen on their street, as though paying a few million dollars for a house should protect them from the dark side of life. As the CSI van pulls away, I see Murphy and a couple of uniforms standing around talking. I catch his eye and he leans toward the sheriff guarding the entrance to the site and says something. The sheriff nods at me and lifts the crime scene tape. I follow Murphy as he walks away from the rest of the sheriffs and we stand alone at the end of the patio, looking down at the pier.

"What an incredible view," Murph says. "Nothing I could ever afford on a cop's salary, that's for sure. You and DJ are lucky you get to work on these rich people's houses."

I nod and ask, "What do you think happened?"

"Well," he says, turning away from the view and looking at me with those intense blue eyes of his, "There's no sign of a struggle, just Rick sprawled out near the patio door opening. There was a knife lying on the ground right next to him. His carotid artery had been severed and he bled out. Not a deep cut, but deep enough to do the job, so it looks like he did it himself. He reeked of booze and there was blood all over his right hand, but there was blood everywhere," He pauses and looks toward the house. "We'll have to wait for the autopsy to confirm suicide."

I turn around and look toward the patio door opening. There's a dark brown stain on the concrete and a man and woman in white coveralls are inspecting it. They seem to be assessing what will be needed to clean it up.

We turn toward a commotion over at the job gate, and I see DJ pulling out his wallet and showing the cop his ID. He's trying to get into the job site. Murphy yells over to the cop, who lets DJ pass through. DJ stalks up to us, red in the face and blustering.

"What the hell is going on?" He asks me. "Why are the cops here? Why the hell are you here so early for a change? What the hell is that over there? Is that blood!? Holy shit, is that blood!?"

I know better than to try to placate DJ when he's like this, and he has every reason to be upset. "DJ, it's Ricky's blood," I say quietly.

DJ stops talking and stares at me in shock. "Ricky? Ricky Weaver?"

Murphy tells DJ what he knows about what happened last night, but it isn't much. I sip my coffee. Instant coffee is bad enough but cold instant coffee makes me want to chain myself to a Starbucks like it was a redwood scheduled for destruction.

Finally Murphy has answered all of DJ's questions. He's not sure about a lot of things – like when we'll be able to get back to work and who's going to contact the homeowners and when - but he promises to get us answers today. Murphy gives us both his most direct stare before he says, "This stays between the three of us, okay? I don't want to hear anything about this from anyone else, including a newspaper, especially a newspaper." He points his finger at me and says, "Stay out of this, Bobby. I don't need an ex-cop looking over my shoulder, trying to second guess me or the department's investigation, comprendé?" That must be the only word he remembers from our high-school Spanish class.

With that, Murphy climbs into his car and drives away. DJ and I turn to look at each other.

"Shit, closing down the job is going to put us way behind schedule." DJ says, "I hope Murphy gets back to me soon so I can notify the clients about the delay. I hope the cops call them and I don't have to do it. Shit. This is bad, really bad."

"There's nothing more that we can do here now, DJ. Do you want to get wet? It might take some pressure off." I say.

Looking out at the set waves, stacking up one behind another, DJ says, "No time. I have to stay here and explain to the sub-contractors that the job has been shut down." I can see DJ's wheels are turning, "I can use you over at the remodel job in San Juan Capistrano. I have a lot of pick-up work that needs to be done. What do you think?"

I think about Ricky's card in my pocket and ask him, "Can I have a couple of days off DJ? I need to take some time to think about what happened and why. I can use the work, that's for sure, but I won't be able to concentrate right now." He nods and I get in my van and drive away as the first news truck pulls up. It is definitely time for me to get the hell out of here. DJ can deal with the press.

As I drive away, I think about the possibility of Ricky killing himself. The shock is starting to wear off and I'm thinking a little more clearly. I knew Ricky, and knew he was too much of a coward to kill himself. I remember the day we got drunk in Venice Beach and wanted to get tattoos. When Ricky saw the blood poking up from a guy getting a tattoo, all two hundred and twenty pounds of him hit the floor of the tattoo parlor. He had fainted from watching someone get a Tweety Bird tattoo. He just wasn't the kind of person who would kill himself, especially with a knife.

Chapter 4

Detective Dwayne Murphy is grabbing lunch at Café Calypso in downtown San Clemente. He hasn't eaten since dinner last night. The death of Rick Weaver makes him think back to his youth and despite the seriousness of the investigation, he can't help smiling at the memories he had of San Clemente in the late 1970s and early 1980s. He wasn't in the same year as DJ, Ricky and Bobby, but he knew them from around town, the beach and from school. He lost track of them while he got on with his own life.

He'd left San Clemente after high school to join the San Francisco Police Department, where he finished first in his class at the police academy. After that, he was assigned to a patrol car with a long-time veteran, who showed him the ropes and taught him how to stay alive on the seedy streets of San Francisco. After a few years on patrol, he was recruited to join the S.W.A.T. Team. He rose to the position of Team Leader, where he was awarded the Medal of Valor for saving the lives of thirty people who had been taken hostage during a bank robbery gone bad. He got married and he and his wife wanted kids, but Murphy wanted them to have the same kind of childhood that he had. So, after talking it over with his wife, Debbie, they decided to come back to his home town, to San Clemente, where he applied and was accepted by the Orange County Sherriff's Department as a Homicide Detective.

Murphy remembered that during the 1980s, the three, Bobby Paladin, Rick Weaver and DJ Frasier, were joined at the hip. But eventually they all went their separate ways. DJ and Bobby were invited to join the qualifying pro surf tour. Bobby won three surf contests in a row their first year, and he was invited to join the professional tour. He used to see Bobby's name in the paper all the time. After almost dying at the Pipeline Masters on the pro tour, Bobby had a brief career as a cop with the L.A.P.D. He didn't know for sure why Bobby quit the police department, but he had heard the rumors. Bobby had been back in town for quite a while now, working construction and surfing; apparently, he was through with being a cop. At least, that is what Murphy hoped.

DJ finally gave up his pro surfing dream after Bobby qualified, and he didn't. After that, DJ went into the family construction business. Not that taking over your Dad's well-established business was considered settling. Murphy knew that Bobby and DJ were still tight, but it appeared that Rick was not around as much anymore. His background information on Rick said that he went to work for a large company that had plenty of interests in Saudi Arabia, Kuwait and other places.

Now these three had all ended up in the same place at the same time again, with one big difference. One of them was dead, and on DJ Frasier's jobsite. Too much of a coincidence and he didn't believe in coincidence.

His phone rings. "Murphy," he says distractedly. He listens for a minute, frowns then shuts his phone. He stuffs the end of his sandwich into his mouth and swallows the last of his coffee before he jumps in his car and heads back to the office. Who knows when he'll get another chance to eat again?

****

At dusk I'm sitting on my deck, watching the sun sink lower in the sky, down behind Catalina Island and thinking. Ricky, back in town after all these years, leaving me that note, wanting to meet up with me at the Red Fox Lounge, and then killing himself? It doesn't make sense. Ricky was my lifeline at one time and if he needed help now he knew I would be there for him. So had he tried to reach out to me then just gave up? No, Ricky was stronger than that. I remember all he'd done for me in the past.

A few months after shooting that child, I left the Los Angeles Police department on a disability pension and found myself slipping into my own personal hell. I know now that I hadn't come

14

to terms with what had happened, and that I'd lost my edge as a cop. How could I pull a gun on a perp again without second guessing what I was doing? But how would the second guessing protect me, my partner or an innocent person? Thoughts went around and around in my head and kept me distracted at work. That's when the police shrink stepped in and told my commander I was no longer fit for duty.

Once away from the force, I started drinking nonstop, snorting cocaine, not eating, just trying to keep the voices in my head quiet. Worst of all, I had given up on life. Unknown to me, an old friend, John G., was keeping an eye on me and contacted Ricky, who stepped in and saved my life. DJ, Ricky and I were at this sponsor's party house at Pipeline and this slick guy walked over with one of the sponsor's models on each arm. He introduced himself to us as John Gomez but said to just call him John G. We had been warned about him from the rules committee, he was known for throwing crazy parties where there were booze and drugs flowing freely. The sponsors were trying to clean up the image of pro-surfing, but John G. seemed cool to us.

When Ricky found me I was living at The Alagodon Motel, a real dump. I had leased out my house to earn extra drug money and I was sharing the room with cockroaches, ants and my own puke. I was drinking all day and snorting coke all night. I was a mess and I didn't care. I don't remember the first few days after he arrived, but Ricky got me into a drug and alcohol treatment program. And that was the start.

When I'd been in rehab for a couple of weeks, Ricky notified the tenants who were renting my house in San Clemente that the lease would not be renewed. That gave them time to find someplace else while I completed treatment. When they moved out, Ricky helped me move back in to my house. But most important of all, Ricky convinced me to get help, real help, to heal my mind and help me find peace with myself. When I was strong enough, he called DJ and asked him to hire me and to teach me a trade, and DJ did just that. Ricky had helped me further by getting me to go A.A.

meetings and learning to stay clean. Then one day he was gone again and I haven't heard from him in a few years.

Now Ricky is back and, unbelievably, dead. But if he didn't kill himself, who did? And what can I do about it? Murph told me directly to stay out of whatever is going on and I'm not sure if I'm strong enough yet to face whatever that is. What if I get involved and find things about Ricky that I really don't want to know. What if it causes drinking problems again--recovery is, after all, a one-day-at-a-time thing. What I do know is this: first, I need more information and second, I never had the opportunity to say thank to Ricky for saving my life. I roll down the window and with the wind blowing in my face, I shout out "Ricky, I owe you. I will find out what happened to you, even if it kills me." I look toward the heavens. I know he can hear me. But I had no idea that trying to help find Ricky's killer would take more than just shouting in the wind.

And, after thinking it over for a while longer, I pick up the phone and dial a number from the past I have never forgotten.

I'm not sure if the phone number is still in service but after a few rings, a curt voice answers, "Hello, who is this?"

"It's Bobby Paladin," I say. "Look, is there a chance I can talk to you tonight, in person? It's important."

John G. pauses before he answers, "What can I do for you Bobby?"
I tell him about Ricky and he says that we can meet at his house in Laguna Beach at nine this evening. He gives me the address then hangs up the phone.

I met John G. in Hawaii, where he started out dealing drugs to tourists on the North Shore of Oahu. When he became one of the biggest drug dealers in Hawaii, he expanded into Southern California. Over the years he had turned his empire into a multi-million dollar a year business, both legal and illegal. Whether it is weed, coke, heroin or prescription pills, you can bet John G. is getting his cut off the top. If you don't pay John G. his tribute, you end up just disappearing, never to be seen or heard from again. John G. has never been arrested and as far as I know has never been on the wrong end on a business deal. If anybody might know what Ricky was up to, it will be John G.

I hop into the shower, get dressed and head out for a quick bite to eat before driving up the coast to Laguna Beach.

****

DJ sits in his home office, thinking about Ricky. He hadn't seen Ricky in years, but at one time the three of them were really close. Crap, they were blood. He wonders what the owners, will say when they get back from the south of France. Nice way to end a vacation: have someone kill themselves in your brand-new, custom built-home. Custom built by Frasier Construction. Right. That ought to be good for business. Shit. The cops said there would be no access to the job for at least four or five more days. After that, DJ needs to hire that hazardous material team to clean up the jobsite before the city would allow any of the subcontractors back on the job.

He turns to look at the picture on the wall of himself, Ricky, and Bobby at seventeen. There they stood, dripping wet, with their arms wrapped around each other's necks. That was the year San Clemente took the U.S. National Surfing Championship as the top high school in the county. Were they ever really that young and happy?

17

Chapter 5

I cruise up the Coast Highway in my van, trying to figure out why Ricky could have killed himself. Before I left the house, I'd made a few calls, trying to find out what Ricky had been doing all these years. As far as I knew, he was working overseas, at least until a few years ago. After that it seems he just fell off the map. Ricky had been one of the best project managers in the construction of oil refineries. No job was too big for him, too scary or for that matter, too dangerous. He worked hard and, having never married, had partied even harder. But no matter what, Ricky was always there when I really needed him.

****

I pull up at John G.'s house in Laguna Beach. In front of me is a beautiful, stainless steel and etched glass gate. I give a low whistle, roll down my window and reach for the call-button to the house. A female voice crackles over the speaker, "May I help you?" she asks.

"My name is Bobby Paladin. John G. is expecting me." I tell her.

Within seconds, the gate begins to slide open and disappears behind the wall. I pull into the drive and into one of the guest parking spots, off to the side. I get out of the van and start to lock it as it dawns on me how ridiculous that; this place is like a gorgeous fortress, and no one will mess with my sad little surfer's van.

I walk up to the front of the house. The front doors are black walnut, ten feet tall. Before I can even ring the bell, a beautiful woman opens the door and extends her hand. When she smiles, she becomes even more striking. She's tall; about five foot ten, with strawberry blonde hair and eyes the color of emeralds. I must be staring, so I give myself a little shake, stand up taller and shake her hand. "I'm Bobby Paladin," I introduce myself.

19

"Mr. Paladin, I'm Alexis, John G.'s personal assistant," she says. Her voice is sultry yet all business. This woman appears to be the whole package and I wonder what's under that conservative navy sheath dress. Does she shop at Victoria Secret? My mind starts to wander to her wearing VS but I pull myself together and follow her into the house.

I step into the foyer and am speechless. Marble floors extend beyond the rich black walnut doors. I recognize some of the art as the work of local Laguna Beach artists. In the center of the foyer are an original Wayland sculpture of two dolphins swimming upward and a Ruth Meyer painting on one wall. There are also a couple of original paintings from the early days of the California Impressionist Plein Air art movement that made Laguna Beach a haven for artistic creativity. I recognize a Guy Rose and a Granville Redmond. The artwork must have cost John G. a fortune.

As I follow Alexis through the house I can see no expense has been spared. Alexis is watching me, and smiles, "Beautiful isn't it?" She asks, then continues, "John G. designed the house and hand-picked everything from the flooring to the furnishings, the rugs and the art, including the interior and exterior paint colors and all of the plants and trees for landscaping."

Alexis leads me through the back sliding glass door and I step onto the patio. The view is breathtaking. The house sits on a cliff with a view of the surf breaking on the sand. I can see Catalina Island, where the Wrigley family once used the island for their own personal retreat. In front of the island stand a couple of the offshore oil platforms, that helps feed our country's thirst for oil. The lights on them actually make the platforms look pretty in the fading sunlight.

John G. is sitting at the bar, talking on his cell phone. He looks older and has less hair than the last time I saw him, but he still looks sharp and in great shape. I bet he does laps in the ocean or the infinity pool that runs along the patio. The pool looks as though it flows off the end of the patio and into the ocean.

I think back to the last time that I saw John and realize that it was while I was recovering from that horrible wipeout I suffered at the 1995 Pipeline Masters. I spent a lot of time as a guest at his house on the North Shore. He waves me over, still talking on the phone, and I notice that his end of the conversation sounds serious. He snaps his phone closed as I approach. Alexis excuses herself, walking back towards the house, leaving us alone.

"Bobby." He stands to greet me, "Long time no see, bruddah." he says with a slight Hawaiian accent. We greet each other with a handshake that turns into a half hug. "Long way from the North Shore, eh cuz?" he says, speaking a little bit of Hawaiian pidgin. He stands over six feet tall, with dark hair and dark eyes and a smile that never betrays what he is really thinking or feeling.

"This place is insane, John G. Do you know this is the kind of custom home that DJ's company builds?" I ask.

"I remember. I know he does first class work, but I used a company out of San Francisco. I never mix business and friendship," John G. says, and puts his hand on my shoulder and directs me to the bar. "Please, take a seat and we can catch up."

Alexis reappears, carrying a bottle of wine and two glasses. Once we're seated, she pours us each a glass, and then returns to the house. I take a sip. I may not be the most sophisticated guy in the world, but I like good wine, and this is very good wine. It is floral with hints of vanilla and a buttery finish. I read that in a book somewhere.

"This is a very good wine," I say, just to show I know. "Barrel aged chardonnay, correct? It has a great bouquet." I think I read that in the same book.

21

John G. looks into his glass, gives it a little swirl and smiles. "This is a 2005 Brewer-Clifton Chardonnay. Well balanced and quite good," he says.

We talk a little more about wine, but I can tell he's getting a little impatient with the niceties. Finally he says, "Why don't you tell me why you're really here, Bobby?" I can hear a little edge in his voice.

"Have you heard anything about Ricky Weaver being found dead?" I ask and get right to the point.

He nods, but says nothing.

"You guys were very close." I continue. "At least you were at one time. I was wondering if you could tell me anything about Ricky. What he'd been up to lately."

He looks down at his glass for a moment before answering. "I know very little; we weren't that close anymore. I do know that Ricky was living in Cabo San Lucas for the last few years: Surfing, drinking, doing drugs and chasing women. You know Ricky; those were his favorite things to do after he retired. That's all he did, Bobby. That's all I know."

"So he wasn't involved with you or doing any business for you?" I ask.

He looks at me a little ominously. "Bobby, you and I have known each other for a very long time. You must know better than to doubt my word. No, Ricky and I weren't in any sort of business together. My business interests are much different today than they were many years ago. From what I hear, he was still partying and being irresponsible. I am now a legitimate businessman, and am no longer involved in anything illicit. I pay my taxes just like everyone else."

"Okay John," I say, raising both hands, palm forward, but still unconvinced. His look lets me know that this line of questioning is unacceptable.

He studies me for a moment, then smiles and says, "Enough about Ricky and my business." He pulls the bottle from the silver ice bucket and refills my glass. "Tell me all about how you and DJ. How are you both doing?"

We talk for a while longer. I avoid talking about myself too much, focusing on DJ and his family. We finish the bottle of wine, and a second bottle does not appear. I'm starting to get the hint that it's time to leave when Alexis steps out onto the patio and catches John G.'s eye. They must have some sort of telepathy or secret code or something between them.

"Bobby, I must say good night," he says. "It has been fantastic seeing you again and getting caught up. Please give my regards to DJ and let me know if you find out anything more about Ricky." He stands, extends his hand and shakes mine. He turns, "Alexis, will you please show our guest out?" And with that, he disappears into the house.
Alexis walks me to the door. On the way out I try talking to her. Maybe she'll spill a little about John G.'s business dealings. Or, she just might think I'm cute and succumb to the old Paladin charm.

"Alexis, do you enjoy your job here? It must be quite a bit of work keeping up with all of John G.'s business dealings." I say.

"John G. is a very private man. I'm sure you must realize it would be a huge violation of trust if I were to talk to you about anything he has confided in me, Mr. Paladin." she says, a little sternly then softens it with a small smile.

"Please, call me Bobby. John and I go back a long way. Maybe sometime you and I could grab a drink and I can tell you all about it." Go for broke, I always say. All she can do is say no.

"No thank you, Bobby." Crap, she said no. She answers me with what I perceive to be a slight annoyance in her voice. I take the hint and head out the door.

In the van, I can't help thinking John G. isn't telling me the whole truth. After years as a street cop, you know when you're being fed bullshit. As I drive down Pacific Coast Highway I think about our conversation and feel that John G. is hiding something from me, but what? And why?

Chapter 6

Detective Murphy looks up at the line of pelicans in flight as he runs down the beach. He runs every day that he can. The running helps him clear his head, and gives him time to think about his on-going cases. What's bothering him today is the Weaver case. It just doesn't make any sense. Murphy had known Ricky some when they were kids and he just didn't think Ricky fit the personality trait of person who would kill himself. Murphy had called the Coroner's office late yesterday afternoon and asked that a rush be put on the Weaver autopsy. Still thinking about the case, he runs to the bottom of the pier and starts to walk out to the end to catch his breath before heading back. Maybe he'll get lucky and see a pod of dolphins. Walking down the pier, his phone vibrates in his pocket. Shit, he thinks as he recognizes the number.

"Hello."

"Murphy," the curt voice on the other end of the phone says, "What's up with a rush on that body down in San Clemente?" It's his boss, Captain Mark Sprague, a penny pinching bureaucrat. It is way too early for him to be calling; this cannot be good.

"I thought he was just some homeless bum who offed himself," The captain continues.

"Sir, he wasn't a bum and he wasn't homeless," Murphy explains. "My preliminary investigation found that he had a home in Cabo San Lucas, Mexico, and had money in the bank, not a lot, but enough. I knew him a little from when we were in high school. I don't think this is the kind of guy who would kill himself. If he was going to do that, sir, why not just do it in Mexico? Why travel over a thousand miles to kill himself on one of his best friend's jobsites? I have a gut feeling that the suicide is a cover up, but I have nothing concrete." He can almost hear his boss thinking on the other end of the line.

"Okay, Murph." His boss finally says with a sigh. "Try to get a handle on this thing, and do it quickly. You know the County is having all sorts of money problems and they aren't going to be happy about wasting valuable resources, okay?"

"Yes sir. I'll keep you in the loop." He isn't sure Captain Sprague heard his last sentence because the phone is dead before he can say anything else. He turns around and takes off running back up the beach, thinking about where to start looking for the reason that Rick Weaver came back to San Clemente, and why might have he killed himself. Or why someone else might have done it for him.

****

DJ and I had arranged to go surfing the next morning. I wake up early and DJ is knocking at my door at 5:30 a.m.

"Come on in," I call out from the bathroom. "There's a cup of coffee on the table for you."

"Not that instant crap you drink is it?" he calls back.

"No, you ungrateful shit, I brewed it this morning. You're welcome."

After inhaling our coffee, we load the surfboards and wet suits into the back of his truck and make the short drive to the private beach where we're going to surf. It is 6 a.m. when we get to the beach, and the sky is beginning to open to a soft grey blue. We pull up to the guard house at the entrance to Cypress Shores, a private community of multi-million dollar homes. It's a little early to be allowed in to go surfing, but we know the gate guard.

"Good morning, Chris. Bobby and I are going to the Nichols house." DJ says.

"Here's your parking permit, DJ." He says with a nod, "Good morning, Bobby".

Chris has been the gate guard at Cypress Shores since he retired from Boeing when the aerospace industry tanked in the 1990's. He's known both of us from all the work we've done in the ocean front community. He hands us the colored pass required for all guests and service personnel coming in – bright orange for today. The pass color is changed weekly for a quick ID of anyone who is not supposed to be inside these exclusive gates.

DJ remolded the Nichols' house on the bluff a few years ago, and they were so happy with the job that Dr. Nichols told us we could surf at the private beach whenever we wanted. He left our names on a permanent list at the gate. The view is incredible from the bluff. Even though the train tracks run between the bluff-top houses and the ocean, they don't affect the 180 degree ocean view of the Pacific Ocean and Catalina Island.

DJ pulls into the parking lot beside the cliff-top clubhouse and we look down at the ocean.

"Wow, DJ," I say, "It is going off." The surf must be at least six to eight foot, or bigger, and perfect. We look out over the water; it's glassy with the sets breaking out on the second reef.

"Let's get in the water before this place turns into a zoo," says DJ with a grin. He's still as competitive as when we were surfing against each other in contests.

DJ hops out of the truck, grabs a towel and wraps it around his waist. He drops his jeans to the ground, and from under the towel he starts slipping into his wetsuit. Glancing over at me, he says, "The job's going to be down at least until the middle of next week, then the hazardous material clean up team has to get finished at the house, and then the city has to sign off on the cleanup. We will be down for at least another week or more. So, you can do what you have to about Ricky. I'm here if you need any help."

"Thanks DJ There are some things that just don't add up. We both know Ricky was afraid of needles, you know, sharp stuff, so for him to use a knife to kill himself is just out of the question. I'd like to look into how and why Ricky died. Is that cool with you?" I ask.

DJ stops and looks at me and for a moment becomes silent, thinking. Finally he says, "You know it is. Just remember what Murph said. He doesn't want any interference from us."

"I know what he said, but Ricky was our friend. I'll take you up on your offer if I need anything,"

We grab our boards and head down the hill toward the beach, through the gate, through the tunnel under the railroad tracks and onto the beach. We don't say anything more as we start to paddle out.

DJ and I are out of the water by seven thirty a.m., just when it's starting to get crowded. What a great way to start the day. DJ drops me off at my house on his way home. I need to figure out what to do next.

Chapter 7

After a quick shower, DJ heads off to the San Juan Capistrano jobsite. The house is a modernized version of a Spanish Hacienda, high-up on a hill with incredible views of the ocean and Saddleback Valley.

As he pulls on to the jobsite, his phone plays "Little Surfer Girl" by the Beach Boys, letting him know it's his wife, Maria.

"Hi, Babe, what's going on?"

"Hi, Honey. You had a priority envelope delivered this morning with no name and no return address."

DJ loves Maria's voice. She still has a hint of a Spanish accent, even though she's been in California since she was ten years old. Her parents were diplomats and she was raised in Spain before returning to California. DJ always thought her accent was sexy, and he still does.

"Just put it in the office on the boat with the rest of today's paperwork, would you, please?" The beep in his ear indicates that he has another call waiting. "I've got another call, Babe. I've got to go. I'll see you tonight," he tells her as he clicks over to the incoming call.

The other call is the engineer for the T-Street job, demanding to know why DJ is not at their meeting. DJ starts to explain what happened at the jobsite, but the engineer hangs up without letting him finish. What an asshole. Let them have the meeting without him. He has too much else to do. He already knows it's going to be a very long day.

However, the day ends up flying by, with all the crew and sub-contractors asking him what happened at T-Street. After his final meeting, DJ heads down to the harbor to try and catch a few quiet minutes on his boat. Maybe he'll go for a stand-up paddle ride through the harbor. That always helps him relax and think.

As soon as he arrives at the boat, his neighbor jumps down from his Lures 32' Sport Fisher, and heads over.

Shit, DJ thinks, *I can't deal with this nosey bastard today.* The neighbor, Herb, is a retired CEO, a control freak, micro-managing jerk-off, used to telling everyone what to do. Nobody has to do his bidding anymore, but he just doesn't get it.

"Hey, DJ," he says, shaking his head slowly. "I read all about you and your San Clemente job in the paper today. What a mess." DJ suspects that he's fishing for information.

"We've been shut down until the sheriffs complete their investigation. The clients are on vacation and they're going to be very unhappy when they find out someone died in their new home," DJ says as he climbs on board his boat. Before his neighbor can say anything more, DJ looks at him with his best, piercing glare. Maria hates this look. She calls it the Hairy Eyeballs.

"Herb, I've been answering this shit all day. Would you give it a rest, please?" Herb steps back, opening his mouth as if to say something more. He's not used to being spoken to like that.

DJ doesn't give him a chance. He walks down into his floating office, a Yankee 38, one of only seventeen built during the 1970's. He and Bobby spent the better part of four years restoring this boat to near pristine condition. Another month or so and she'd be ready to sail in any type of weather. DJ has been thinking of racing her, the way he and Bobby had when they raced on his dad's boat.

Sitting down, DJ sees that Maria has brought down the mail, and the priority envelope is on top of the pile. Opening it, he looks inside and sees there are two envelopes, one with his name on it and one with Bobby's. He feels a chill when he realizes that it's Ricky's back-handed scrawl. DJ can't do this without fortification so he gets up, walks over to the tiny on-board fridge and grabs a beer. Sitting back down, he twists the beer open, takes a big gulp and begins reading:

DJ
I am in some real trouble and I need you to get the other envelope to Bobby as soon as you can. There are some very dangerous people looking for me and if you are reading this then most likely I have been killed. Tell Bobby I am sorry for bringing him into this shit-storm, but he is the only person that I trust to make this thing right. Thanks, DJ, for everything. Being your friend for all these years has meant more to me than you will ever know. Be cool and cover Bobby's back. He's going
to need it. Stay real.–Ricky

DJ sits for a long time sipping his beer and thinking. He is overcome with sadness and fear as he realizes that Ricky must have been murdered. He finishes the beer before he reaches for his phone to call Bobby.

Chapter 8

Crap. I'm late again. I never used to be late for anything. Yet, here I am, late for my standing weekly appointment with my shrink.

When I got sober and off the drugs, the dreams about the boy got so frequent and so bad that I started thinking about eating my gun. I knew I was in trouble and it was time to get some help. I'd been exonerated by the Department of Internal Affairs and the D.A.'s office. I'd been diagnosed with Post Traumatic Stress Disorder, PTSD, after the shooting. I was still a guilt-ridden mess. I didn't want a police department shrink and a friend had recommended Dr. Kris Summers. It had taken me a long time to make that first appointment, and even longer to trust Dr. Kris, but after a couple of years I was finally starting to feel better. I was 'making progress', as she put it.

I pull into the lot across the street from her office and pay a quarter for every fifteen minutes I'll spend with Dr. Kris. I always wonder what the city does with all of the parking money it raises, because they sure don't spend it on street repair. I cross the road and run up the stairs to her home office, in a condo which overlooks the San Clemente pier.

When we were young DJ, Ricky and I were always playing on the beach near the pier, where we first learned to surf. One day my dad let us use one of his old surfboards. We took turns using the board until our parents thought that it was time for each of us to get our own. We won our first contests there with our parents cheering us on. From then on, we were unstoppable.

"Bobby, please come in," Dr. Kris says as she opens the door, "You're late, again. You need to be on time. I can't give you the whole hour if you're not here."

I look at the ground sheepishly and mumble an apology. At least she's nicer than DJ when she gives me shit.

Her face softens, and she smiles as she says, "Sorry, Bobby. My last client was a hard one. How are you doing today?"

The doc is a looker, standing about 5'8" with a firm body from playing tennis. She has jet black hair, bright blue eyes and a smile that could melt ice. The hair may or may not be natural, and the eyes may or may not be contacts, but who cares? She's beautiful. No wonder people fall in love with their shrinks. She's also very professional, never mixing business with pleasure. I'd often thought about asking her out, but I'm sure she'd say no, at least as long as I'm a client. Right. Like that would be the only reason she'd turn me down. I really do need a shrink.

"I'm all right," I reply wearily as she leads me into her office. I take a seat in one of the two leather chairs that face each other; no couch here. Her office is decorated more like a living room than a shrink's office so you feel at ease when you sit down for your face-to-face session.

She asks me, "You seem a little down today. Are your dreams still occurring with the same frequency?"

"The dream comes and goes. I'll always blame myself for killing that kid. No amount of sleep will ever fix that."

"That young man's name was Travis Lee; he was pointing a gun at you when you shot him. You acted on your training as a police officer." She always tells me to use his name, but I can't bring myself to do it, at least not yet anyway.

"I know." I reply quietly, looking down at my hands. "Being a cop still doesn't prepare you for shooting a twelve-year-old kid."

"Nothing prepares you for shooting anyone, least of all a child." She stops, picks up a pair of reading glasses and glances down at her notes. She decides to take a different tact. "How is everything else going? Are you drinking?"

"I had a couple of glasses of wine the other night while visiting a friend."

"That sounds okay. Please tell me more."

Fasten your seatbelt, I think. "Well, a childhood friend slipped into town and tried to get in touch with me. Apparently he was in some sort of trouble and needed my help. He left a cryptic note in my jeans' pocket; I'd left my work jeans in the back of the truck while I was surfing. Then he turned up dead on a jobsite where I'm working, all in a span of twenty-four hours." I know I'm rambling, but it's the first time I've actually been able to say it all out loud. "I hadn't seen him in a few years and I guess I feel that I wasn't there for him when he really needed me. Yesterday, I called an old friend I knew in Hawaii who lives in Laguna now to see if he knew anything about Ricky being back in town."

When I finally look up, she's staring at me over her glasses. She's trying to process what I've just told her, but resists the urge to push me harder for more information. "And did this friend know anything about Ricky's problems?" she asks, resuming her note taking.

"No, he said he didn't know anything about Ricky being back in town, but my gut is telling me he knows more than he's letting on. His attitude changed toward me when I questioned his answer."

"This friend of yours, how did you two meet?"

I think about that for a moment, wondering how much of this I should share with her. I open and close the clasp on my watch – a nervous habit. I'll break the watch one of these days, and it was my father's watch. Finally, I tell her, "Ricky, DJ and I met John Gomez– that's his name - in Haleiwa, on the North Shore of Oahu in 1991, my first full year on the pro surf tour. DJ and Ricky…" It's such a long story. I don't know if I have the energy to go into it all right now.

She looks up at me again, a question on her face. She's heard me speak of DJ many times before, but I had never really filled her in about Ricky.

"Rick Weaver was the friend who was found dead on DJ's job site, where I've been working. The police think that he cut his own throat. He was found a couple of days ago. Anyway, DJ and Ricky flew over to Hawaii to watch me make a run at the Triple Crown of Surfing."

Another questioning look. I guess the world of pro-surfing is pretty foreign if you're not part of it. "It's the total accumulation of points for surfing the three contests on the North Shore of Oahu. The contests are: the Haleiwa Open at Ali'i Beach, The Sunset Open at Sunset Beach and the Pipeline Masters at Eauki Beach. We talked to John G. for a while and just before he took off, he told us that if there was anything we need, anything, he said, stressing it, you know, he says to call. Then he gave us all cards with his phone number on them – nothing else, just his phone number, and then he left. And a couple of days later, Ricky called him to score some green."

"Green?" she asks.

"Weed, you know, pot. Ricky wanted to see if the Hawaiian pot was as good as everyone said it was. From then on, Ricky and John G. were friends," I explain. "During the rest of our stay, John G. was always around taking us to dinner, you know, hanging out at the contests and getting Ricky stoned."

Dr. Kris and I talk for a while longer and she chides me about smoking pot. I tell her I used to, but I'm too old to do that anymore; although, some days it feels like it might not be a bad idea to take it up again.

We haven't made it back to talking about Ricky when Dr. Kris glances at the wall clock behind me. She smiles as she says, "Our time is up, Bobby. I'll see you next week at the same time. And try to be on time, wont' you?" She uncrosses her legs and unfolds from her chair. I stand up and she walks me to the door, handing me an appointment card.

"You're doing much better," she says, "We're making real progress here. I know this is hard for you. Nobody, especially an ex-cop, wants to admit they need help. It'll take more time, but you will get your life back. You'll be able to go to sleep without having that dream." She smiles as she closes the door to get ready for her next appointment. I like this about her office: you're alone in the waiting room, go into her office, then when your appointment is over and you leave through another door. You never run into another patient. It's very discrete.

While walking to my bus, I turn my phone back on and it chimes. There's a text message from DJ that reads: 'CALL ME ASAP. IT IS IMPORTANT.' Uh oh, all caps. This can't be good. I'll call him back later. I've done enough talking for right now and I just want to go home, pour myself a glass of wine and watch the sunset.

How was I supposed to know that by not calling DJ right back, it would almost be the death of me?

Chapter 9

Detective Murphy was getting ready to call it a day when his phone rings. Looking down at the number he sees that it's the Coroner's Office. Connie Martin is his favorite Medical Examiner. Even though she's young, pretty and new at it, nothing gets by her. Blonde and petite, Murphy often wonders why she chose this career.

"Murphy," he answers.

"Detective, could you come by my office? I found something in the Weaver case that shouldn't be there. You need to see it."

He tells her he can be there in fifteen or twenty minutes.

After turning into the Coroner's office parking lot, he finds a parking space in front of the office, gets out of his car, locks it and heads into the building. At the front desk, he flashes his badge, and tells the deputy on duty that Medical Examiner Martin is expecting him.

"Weapons, please," the deputy asks as he picks up the phone to notify the M.E. she has a visitor.

Murphy signs in and hands over his Glock 9 mm. The deputy puts it in a lock box before asking, "No back-up weapon, Detective?"

"No. I only carry one. I only need one," Murphy says with a smirk.

"Well, go on back. You can pick up your weapon when you're finished," he says, passing him a receipt for his gun.

Murphy heads down the hall and walks into the autopsy room, where the Coroner standing by the autopsy table. She waves him over.

"Thank you for getting here so quickly," Dr. Martin says. "I have something I thought you'd want to see." She's short so she has to step up on a stool in order to reach up and carefully uncover the body. Pointing to the slashed throat, she begins. "On the surface, it does look like your victim cut his own throat. The blood-splatter on his hand where the knife was found and how he bled out all points to a self-inflected wound. But, since you asked me to take a closer look, I noticed something on the back side of the carotid artery. I removed the slashed part of the artery and, under a microscope, found this." She steps down and walks over to a counter at the side of the room. Pointing to the microscope, she says, "Have a look."

Murphy closes one eye and looks down into the microscope and asks. "What am I looking for?"

"Do you see the puncture right behind the slashed part of the artery? That was done with a needle. I think he was murdered when something was injected into the jugular. Then, someone took the time to make it look like suicide. We're running a toxicology screen right now. I'll know more after the test results, but I wanted you to see this. Mr. Weaver most likely did not kill himself. I'm not one hundred percent sure but I'll call your boss and inform him of my findings. When I get tox the screen back, I'll have the answer."

With that, the Coroner steps off the stool, turns on her heel and heads back toward her office, leaving Murphy looking down into the microscope.

Chapter 10

Damn it, DJ thinks to himself, *why hasn't Bobby called me back? His appointment was over two hours ago.* DJ grabs his phone and hits speed dial. The call goes straight to voicemail, again.

"Bobby, it's DJ. Please call me as soon as you get this message. I need to see you right away. I have some news about Ricky. We can meet at my house." His cell beeps in his ear; he has call waiting, but he didn't look to see who was calling. "What the hell took you so long, Bobby!?" DJ yells into the phone.

"No, DJ, it's not Bobby; it's Murphy. Have you been trying to get in touch with him too? I've been trying to reach him for the last couple of hours. I just left the coroner's office and I need to talk to him."

"He hasn't returned any of my calls or texts. His doctor's appointment was over two hours ago."

"What doctor's appointment? Is he sick?" Murphy asks.

"No, no, not like that. It's nothing you need to worry yourself about. He'll tell you about it someday, if he feels like it."
"Just a heads up," Murph says, "Rick Weaver was murdered; he didn't kill himself. Tell Bobby to call me if you talk to him first."

"You're sure he was murdered? I thought you said it was an obvious suicide."

"Just have him call me, and tell him not to go off halfcocked. I'll put his ass in jail and yours too if I catch you guys looking into this on your own. Got that?
"That's heavy. I'll have him call you if he calls me back or I see him first. Thanks, Murph. And you don't have to worry about me." DJ says. But Murphy had hung up already.

Great, DJ thinks, *I need to give this letter to Bobby before Murph finds out about it and arrests both of our asses for withholding evidence.*

****

I pull up to the front of my house and sit for a moment just looking at it. It's a nice house, stucco and tile, built in the late 1950's by a local builder, who paid close attention to detail. It has a large yard, especially for Southern California, where most houses have postage stamp lots. The house is set back from the street. My roses in front of the house are in full bloom; they've been a labor of love.

After a few minutes, I get out of the van. I walk up to the front door and pull out my key as the door swings inward, just slightly. The front door isn't locked. I always lock the door, always. I gradually inch the door open and peak inside. My old cop training kicks in and I'm on full alert. I think about calling out, but if someone is in here, I want to catch the bastard. At first glance everything looks okay and I don't see any intruders or anything out of place. I slowly walk over to the cabinet in my living room where I keep my 9 mm handgun hidden inside a hollowed-out book sitting on the shelf. There's a swipe through the dust. I either have to read more or clean more. I reach in the cabinet, pull out the book and open it. With a sigh of relief, I find the gun is still there. I pull it out and I check the clip.

"Shit," I whisper. Whoever has been in the house has taken the time to empty all the bullets from the clip and the round I kept chambered, but left the gun in the book. The house isn't trashed, but someone had taken their time going through my stuff. They were careful, but I can tell nothing was left untouched. I walk around, opening drawers, and I hear a noise, a kind of hissing sound. This is never a good sound. It's either snakes or gas. When I reached the kitchen, I smell gas. Whoever was in here has disconnected the gas line from the stove. I turn and sprint for the

44

front door as fasts as I can. Then I hear a sound so loud that I know I will always remember it: the ignition of the gas. I feel my feet leave the ground as I sail through the door. The last thing I feel is the piercing thorns as my body hits the rose bushes.

****

Christ, my head hurts. I slowly open my eyes to muted sunlight, white sheets and a bed with a chrome rails. I open, close, and then open my eyes again, trying to focus. Everything is a blur. I must be in the hospital, but I can't remember how I got here. I look around the room and see a shape sitting in a chair next to my bed. I concentrate and realize, as my eyesight starts to clear, that it's a person, Murph. Not my first choice for a hospital visitor. I bet he didn't even bring me flowers.

"How are you feeling?" he says, concern in his voice.

"Not so good, bro. What the hell happened to me? How did I get here?" My throat is dry as I croak the words out. I reach over to the tray on the bedside table for the glass of water that sits there with a bendy straw. Yep, this is the hospital all right. The movement makes me feel like throwing up, but the nausea passes.

Murph says, "The fire department thinks that the gas line to your stove was disconnected on purpose and that the gas was ignited by the water heater pilot. Lucky for you, you entered through the front door and not the back door or you would have induced fresh air into the gas mix and been toasted right on the spot. There was a cruiser right around the corner and they heard the explosion and found you lying on your front lawn, with a gun in your hand. We've impounded the gun for the time being. What were you doing holding an empty gun, Bobby?"

"I don't know, Murph, I really don't. The facts are fuzzy. I remember leaving Dr. Summers' office, but not much after that. I might remember more once my brain settles down. How much damage was done to my house?" I ask. I love that house. I bought it 1992 with my tour winnings and sponsorship money, before the market started to rebound in San Clemente in 1992.

"Just a pile of burnt rubble, I'm afraid. The fire department wasn't able to save anything. The only thing left intact is the garage." Murph reverts to cop-talk to give me the facts with no emotion. He knows how much my house means to me.

"Your bedside manner needs some work, dude. Shit, you mean it's just gone and there's nothing left? That house contained everything that I've worked for my whole life," my voice is starting to get louder.

"Sorry to be so blunt, but something is going on and I need to get to the bottom of it. Tell me anything you remember. Why would someone want to try to kill you?"

"Maybe the gas line came loose. I don't know. I just can't remember anything right now."

I need to stall him while I try to figure out what's going on. I did remember a lot, but I need time to think, and I to decide if I should really trust Murphy. Someone has blown up my house, on purpose, and I need to find out why. If it's the last thing I do, I'll make those assholes pay for destroying my house. But who would want to do this to me, and why?

Murphy focuses his cop eyes directly at me and waits. I can tell I've been thinking too much and he's trying to read my mind, so I close my eyes. I really am tired and my body hurts all over. When I don't say anything more, he says, "Well, if you can think of anything else, give me a call."

He gets up from the chair and starts for the door. He stops and turns around, and gives me that icy stare again. "Rick Weaver was murdered and dumped on the job site, but I think you figured that out already, didn't you? Try and not let that happen to you. Get some rest."

With that he walks out of the door, almost bumping in to DJ.

DJ glances back over his shoulder at Murphy. "What's his problem?"

Before I can reply, he starts up again. Nobody talks nonstop quite like DJ. "Holy shit, dude. You scared the crap out of me! I thought you were dead when I heard about your house. They almost wouldn't let me in to see you – family and police only. Fuck that. I told the nurse I was your brother from another mother. Close enough, right? He said you're a little burned, scratched, bruised and other than a concussion, you were pretty damn lucky. You should be out of here tomorrow or the next day at the latest. I went by your house and it's toast, bro, completely destroyed except for the garage. As soon as the insurance company takes a look at it, I'll arrange to have all the debris cleared away."

"Thanks. Do you know any good contractors?" I laugh with a snort. Damn, that makes my head hurt.

"Good to know we've got another job coming." He says with a little grin. "How come you didn't call me back after your appointment yesterday? I sent you a text and called, but I never heard back from you."

"Sorry, bro. I'm always wiped out after I get done seeing the Doc. I just wanted to go home. I wanted to get some rest, watch the sun set and wasn't up to talking to anyone."

"We received a message from the other side, Bobby. I got a priority envelope from Ricky delivered to me yesterday. Can you believe that? Spooky shit, right? Here, Ricky wrote a note to me saying he wanted me to give you this envelope and that you would know what to do with what's inside it. Now that he's dead maybe this will explain what's been going on."

He hands me the envelope and I stare at it in disbelief. What the hell? I know DJ is dying for me to open it while he's here, but right now it's a little too much for me to deal with. I lay it, unopened, on the bed beside me. He gets the message.

"Okay. I'd better let you get some rest. Before I split, do you need anything?"

"Yes, you asshole, a new house."

"Do you have your set of keys to the boat? You're going to need a place to stay and you're traveling pretty light," he smiles. "Call me if I can get you anything. Later, 'gator," he says as he heads out the door.

Chapter 11

Around 8 a.m. the nurse wakes me up, explaining that the doctor is doing his rounds and will be here soon. Her hands are as cold as ice as she checks my blood pressure and takes my temperature. She's very business-like and efficient, but not unpleasant. Some of the nurses here are so grouchy it makes me wonder why they didn't choose another profession – like executioner – or something more suited to their personalities. This one is nice enough, though, and she looks down at me and says, "You are one lucky guy, Mr. Paladin." She gives my arm a final pat and bustles out of the room.

I don't feel so lucky. That house, besides my van, is all I own. I paid cash for the house in a down-market. Everything I have ever owned, inherited, been given or awarded was now destroyed. I sure have to be grateful to Robert at Three Counties Insurance. It's good to have a relationship with your insurance guy, someone who will look out for you and your interests. He'd advised me to up my replacement value because the house was worth considerably more now than when I'd bought it in 1992. I'll have to buy him a beer when I get out of here.

One lucky guy, the nurse called me. Well, at least she's partly right. As a kid, I'd started traveling the world on the NSSA National Team, then the Junior Pro Surf Tour and finally the World Pro Surf Tour. After a ton of hard work and some luck I had made it as far as ranking number two in the world, after only my third year on the tour, but I could never win that number one ranking that I had worked so hard for. I really felt I was on my way to number one when disaster hit at the 1995 Pipeline Masters. I'll never forget that wave or the wipeout that followed. It was on the third reef at Pipeline, in the finals, with the number one spot in the world up for grabs. I wanted to win that contest so badly that I became reckless. Taking off late on a monster wave, with the drop at least thirty feet, I dug a rail as I started to make my bottom turn. Suddenly, I found myself launched from my board, falling onto the face of the wave and then being sucked back up and thrown over the falls. I remember being slammed into the coral reef, then being spun around on the coral. It was like being in a washing machine. By the time I was spotted in the soup, I had taken on three more twenty-foot plus waves in a row in the impact zone. I was busted up and badly cut by the coral. I don't remember being pulled out of the water or being air-lifted to Queens Hospital in Honolulu. I suffered a fractured skull, four broken ribs and numerous coral cuts. I needed over one hundred and fifty stitches to close all the damage that the coral reef had done to me. The doctors told me the only reason I was still alive was because of the great shape I was in.

After I was released from the hospital, John G. asked me to stay at his guest house at Sunset Beach for a few weeks, until I was well enough to decide what I wanted to do next. Ricky and DJ flew over to hang out for a few days to try and cheer me up, but there wasn't much they could do to help me. That wipeout had really scared me, causing me to doubt my surfing ability, and to doubt myself. In surfing, if you can't take off and make the drop into a wave, any wave, any size, then you shouldn't be in the water, much less on the world tour. So, when a reporter from the Honolulu Advertiser, the local newspaper in Hawaii, came to interview me, I announced my retirement from the World Pro Surf Tour. I was scared but instead of facing my fear, I ran away from it. Less than year later I joined the L.A.P.D. to try to help people. Did I ever screw that up. Yep, one lucky guy, that's me.

I'm just about to reach for the phone to call Dr. Summers when Dr. Augustus Miller walks in the room. I know Doctor Gus from surfing with him at Cotton's Point.

He smiles at me, "What are we going to do with you, Bobby?" He says. He taps a few keys and reads the computer screen in my room.
"So how am I doing, Doc?" I ask.
"You are one lucky guy." He says.

"So I hear."

"No broken bones, a concussion, some cuts and bruising, some singed hair, and that's about it. If you don't have any major medical issues tonight, I'll release you sometime tomorrow, after morning rounds. You should be out of here by noon or maybe a little later. I don't want you to drive for a couple of days and a full recovery will take a while, but you'll soon be as good as new." He pauses, "I'm sorry about your house, Bobby, I know that you loved that place. Did the police..." His pager goes off before he can finish his sentence. He gives me a distracted wave as he leaves the room looking down, frowning.

I spend the rest of the day watching talk shows on the tiny television mounted on the wall across from my bed, getting my blood pressure checked, leafing through old magazines and sleeping when I can. After a surprisingly good dinner of roast chicken, salad – with green Jell-O for dessert, of course – the night nurse comes in and hands me two pain pills in a paper cup. I ask him if he thinks green is a flavor. He gives me a patient half-smile as he watches me wash down the pills. I pray not to have the dream again as I drift off to sleep.

Chapter 12

A nurse wakes me up at two thirty in the morning to check my pulse and take my blood pressure. Her hands are so fucking cold that when she leaves, I'm wide awake. Since there's no chance of falling back to sleep, I decide to open Ricky's letter. I don't know why I couldn't bring myself to open it earlier, but I couldn't. It was dated one week earlier.

Bobby - If you're reading this, I didn't get a chance to talk to you after I dropped this in the mail, which means they finally found me and I have been killed. Sorry that I didn't have a chance to explain to you in person what's been going on or why they have been trying to kill me.

Three or four years ago, while vacationing in Cabo San Lucas, I decided I liked it there and that I'd had enough of the hard and dangerous work that I have been doing all of my life. I was also really sick and tired of all the traveling. So, I decided that I was ready to settle down and that Cabo was the place. I've been working all over the world for all of my adult life with no real place to call home. It was great when I was younger but now that I was older I wanted to put down some roots, you know, a place to call home. The work was getting boring and I wasn't getting rich, but I had saved a lot of money over the years and I was totally vested in the company, so with a little planning I retired to Cabo San Lucas.

A couple of years after settling down here, I was sitting in a bar when an old friend of ours from San Clemente, Sam Conroy, sat down next to me and bought me a drink. I was pretty surprised at the whole 'small world' coincidence. Then after a couple of drinks and catching up on our days growing up surfing and chasing girls, he pulled out a folded-up piece of paper and showed it to me. It was a federal warrant issued for my arrest. Years ago, I'd set up a deal for a friend of mine in Bahrain that went sideways. A couple of undercover DEA agents were killed by the time it was all over. I swear I had nothing to do with the killing. I just introduced two guys so they could work out a deal, I did get some money off the top, chump change really, but that was the extent of my involvement, Bobby, I swear. John G. had me give one of the guys a phone number and that was all I did. Then I flew back out of the country. After the deal went down, the two guys were killed by some Islamic fanatics. John G. swore to me that he had nothing to do with their deaths.

Anyway, Conroy says he can make this whole warrant thing go away if I help him out in the future, if or when he needs me to do something for him. The warrant was for conspiracy and that in itself is pretty vague. He didn't say what he wanted me to do but I agreed because I didn't want to go to prison, especially in some third world shit hole. We shook hands and he left. I was freaking out, but I didn't hear anything for a long time, so after a while I figured that I might be in the clear.

Then about a year and a half ago Conroy shows up again and asks me to set up a meeting with John G. According to Conroy, John G. was really the guy behind the two DEA agents' deaths, and he wanted me to help get the goods on John G. So Conroy told me to tell John G. I was running out of cash and needed a new way to earn some extra income because I had made some bad investments. I don't know how he knew John G. would come and meet with me, but he did. I called John G. and he flew down. He always said he'd be there if we needed him and I guess he still meant it. Doing this made me felt like shit.

John G. offered me a job, running some errands around Cabo for him. Small things at first, I think, to see if he could still trust me. I did that for about a year, updating

Conroy every month or so, but it was all pretty boring stuff, some drug runs, setting up his friends with some hookers and wiring money around. Then one day John G. shows up in town, he picks me up in a rough looking jeep and we drove out of Cabo and up into the mountains. After a couple hours of driving through the mountains and out in the middle of nowhere, we just stopped in front of a sheer cliff that goes straight up, like a wall. From a distance, that's just what it looked like, part of the mountain, but when I looked closer I could see it was a fake, like a movie set or something. He called somebody on his cell phone and after a minute or two a door slides open – like I was with fucking James Bond. We drove into the mountain and the door slides closed behind us. Inside it's brightly lit and there were Mexican troops guarding the entry. Further into the cave, it opened up into this huge, state-of-the art processing plant. John G. said that with the help of the Sinaloa Cartel and a corrupt army general, they'd built the world's largest drug lab – legal or illegal. Production was about twenty thousand hits of Ecstasy a day. At ten dollars a pop wholesale, that's two hundred thousand dollars a day. They were going to ship cocaine from there, too. He told me they were shipping it into Sothern California right now and from there it will be shipped all over the country thru a trucking network that the Cartel controlled.

I told him this was too much for me - that I didn't want anything to do with something this big. As we drove back into town I swore not to say anything to anyone. He said he believed me, but I wasn't sure if he was going to let it go at that. If you're reading this, then he didn't. He told me that someone he called The General was running the show. He wasn't going to tell The General about me, but The General had his ways and now that I had seen the operation, I might not be able to get out so easily. He also said that if I didn't continue to do what I had really been doing for The General up till now, then I would disappear and there was nothing that he could do to help. He said that The General was a cold-blooded killer with no regard for human life. I had come to John G. looking for work and after I had proven myself he had agreed to loan me to The General as a favor. I was going to make a lot more money now that I was working for The General. I strung the D.E.A. along while I decided to gather up as much information as I could to extricate myself from this hole that I had dug for myself. I stole a bunch of paperwork that I knew would free me, but I was found out before I could get it into the right hands.

The details of the location of the lab and shipments are in a box I hid in the old fort we built when we were kids, the one down in the canyon behind my parents' house–you'll find it under some rocks where we used to hide things from our parents. Whatever you do, don't open it without the second clue. I can't put them together–it's too risky–but if you don't open the box the right way, everything inside will be ruined. I'll put the second clue where you'll be sure to find it.

I have got to go, bro. You and DJ are the best friends I ever had. Watch your backs. These fuckers play for keeps, Bobby. Sorry to turn your life to shit but you guys are the only ones I trust to clear my name and get the information into the right hands.

\- *Ricky*

P.S. There is a shipment of over four million hits of Ecstasy and two tons of cocaine coming into Southern California through Dana Point Harbor–soon, Bobby. Be safe and stay away from John G. I still don't know if you can trust him. Get to the fort and find the items that I left behind. I left a couple of clues to help you along the way because The General will stop at nothing to retrieve his information. Aloha, bruddah.

I lay awake for a long time, trying to understand Ricky's letter. So much has been going on that I haven't even taken the time to grieve for my friend and now I find this out? I don't need this – why would he dump this on me? And then go and die on me?

Our fort used to be in the canyon behind his parents' old house. Could it still even be there? I guess it had to be, if Ricky hid something down there. We'd done a pretty good job of building the fort when we were kids. It helped that my dad ran a hardware store –we had all kinds of tools and lumber scraps when we built it, and we camouflaged it really well.

I send DJ a text to let him know that I'll be out of here tomorrow and that I'll let him know when to come and pick me up. I settled down in bed and before drifting off to sleep, I wonder how much I should tell him. I know he's dying to find out what's in Ricky's letter, but he has a wife and kids to think about. My own ass is now on the line, thanks to Ricky. Do I want to put DJ's there beside mine? I did make a promise to find Ricky's killers so I'll tell DJ about the letter and he can make up his own mind if he wants in or not.

****

I must have slept through breakfast and was just starting to come around, when I notice somebody sitting in the chair in the corner of my room. It's Murphy, again. Damn. Does this guy not have any place else to be? He puts his cell phone in his pocket and looks up at me. He doesn't say good morning or ask me how I'm doing. He just starts talking, all cop-like. I don't remember him being this tight-assed in high school.

"The coroner's office won't release Rick's body for a few more days. The Doctor is waiting for the toxicology screen to come back. After that, I think I can get them to release the body to you. No one else has come forward to claim it, and we can't seem to find any other next of kin. His parents have passed away, as you know, and his ex-wife just laughed and hung up on me. She always was such a bitch, even in high school." He pauses for a minute to give me a chance to absorb everything.

"Good effing morning to you, too, Murph. I'm fine, thanks for asking." What an asshole.

He runs his hand through what's left of his hair, and then turns his steely blue cop eyes back on me and says, "Have you found out anything more concerning Rick's death, Bobby? Is there anything that I should be aware of? Are you holding back information from me?"

I guess that's as close as I'll get to good morning from him. He's starting to piss me off.

"No, Murph. How the hell would I find anything out being stuck here in the hospital, flat on my back staring up at the ceiling?" The letter is tucked under my pillow and I can almost feel it throbbing.

"Do you have any idea who – or why – someone would blow up my house? You've had lots of time to do that, or have you spent the last couple of days sitting in that chair, staring at my ugly mug?" As he opens his mouth to answer me, the room lights up just a bit, and in walks Peggy, my insurance agent's wife. Thank God.

"Bobby!" She greets me warmly, leans over and gives me a peck on the cheek and hands me a bouquet of flowers. She could teach Murph a few things. "I'm so glad you're okay," she continues, "You are one lucky guy! You look pretty good, especially considering what happened. Robert and I can't believe it! What a thing to have happen? It's like the movies or something. Honestly! I wanted to just stop by to tell you that we're ready to file the claim as soon as we get the sheriff's and fire department's reports. Aren't you glad you listened to us when we told you it was time to re-assess your coverage? You complained about the extra cost, but look at you now. I know that the money won't replace your personal things, but you'll be able to rebuild the house."

Peggy notices Murphy sitting in the corner of the room. I make a quick introduction. I'm very happy to see her and to have her interrupt any other questions that Murph has in mind for me. She's a doll and super chatty, so I gladly let her take over the conversation. After about twenty minutes, a nurse–one of the grouchy ones – walks in and announces that everyone needs to clear out as the doctor is making his morning rounds. I wonder if having to wear those ugly shoes is what makes them all so crabby. Peggy gives me a finger-wave over her shoulder as she sails out the door. She calls back, "We'll be in touch, Bobby. Get well soon!"

Murphy puts his hands on his knees and pushes himself up out of the chair, looking down at me. I know he has more questions but, after a few seconds of steely eyed stare, he just says, "Get some rest, Bobby. I'll talk to you later." With that he follows Peggy out the door. I'm so glad to see him leave. I was sure he somehow knew that the letter was under my pillow.

"Thanks, I owe you," I say to the nurse and try to thaw her out with, what I hope is my winning smile. "Do you have any idea when I'm going to get out of here?"

"The doctor will be in later to talk to you about that," she snaps, then turns on her crepe heel and squeaks out of the room. I guess I'll have to work on that winning smile.

****

As Murphy walks back to his car, he can't help feeling Bobby is lying to him. After so many years on the force, he can tell pretty quickly when someone is holding out. Rick's murder and Bobby's house blowing up are no coincidence, but he knows he'll have to dig until the connection becomes clear. Bobby knows something, Murphy is sure, but for some stupid reason, he's not talking.

Murphy has investigated Bobby and as far as he can tell, he wasn't involved in anything other than working or surfing. He has a good credit rating, money in the bank–not a lot, but enough. He gets a pension from the L.A.P.D. and he makes okay money from his construction earnings. He also owns his house, free and clear. His classic Volkswagen van is paid for and he doesn't seem to have drug, drinking or gambling problems. Murph can't even find a current girlfriend. As he unlocks the car door, his phone rings.

"Murphy," he answers. He listens for a few minutes. "Yes sir, I'll be in the office as soon as I can get there."

Chapter 13

John G. walks up the beach after having just finished his morning swim, almost a mile out to the buoy and back today. The water is much colder here than in Hawaii or Mexico, but he swims every day. It gives him time to think, and he has plenty to think about. This business with Rick Weaver, working with the DEA, trying to get him busted, is very disturbing. He never saw that coming. What made it even worse was that The General's man had given Weaver too much of the drug they were using to interrogate him. Even with the drug, they hadn't found out anything before he died.

John G. doesn't know the extent of the problem. He doesn't know if Weaver had talked to anyone else, especially Bobby Paladin or DJ Frasier. It was so messy having to dispose of people, especially now that the police were involved. With all that was at stake on this delivery, they could not afford any more screw-ups. His satellite phone rings. Looking down at the screen he sees it's The General.

John G. knows that General Miguel Sandoval spent most of his adult life in the Mexican Military. With hard work and his ruthless, sadistic streak, he'd worked his way up through the ranks until he was the commanding General of Mexico's Special Forces. Then, ten years ago, his troops got drunk one night after a daring raid on one of Mexico's drug cartels and one of his officers had raped the Governor's daughter and the rest of his troops had panicked.

The Governor was the Mexican President's younger brother. The General knew that because of what those under his command had done, his career was over. The rest of the troop would face a firing squad. So he pulled his sorry troops together and explained the situation to them. The men agreed to follow The General into the mountains, where they set up camp in the caves. Since then, the band of ex-military men had earned a fierce reputation as mercenaries: helping the drug cartels, guarding the shipments of drugs and smuggling peasants looking for a better life in the

United States. They even smuggled terrorists, as long as they paid, and pay they did. It was all about the money. The General had built a very lucrative empire: Drugs, smuggling, money laundering, and guns for hire. The General was an evil man and a bully, and John G. knew that; but he still did business with him, and accepted all of the inherent risks. John G. looks around to make sure he was still alone, then answers the phone.

"Yes, General, how may I be of service? No, they weren't able to get anything from Weaver. Your man was careless, and Weaver died before he gave them any information." He pauses to listen, then explains. "I felt obligated to take your man on a one-way fishing trip since he couldn't even manage to get Paladin out of the way." He listens again, "My apologies, sir, but I think we both understand that we can't have anyone that incompetent on our team. Is the shipment on schedule?" John G. waits for the answer, "Yes, General I understand. Thank you."

John G. hangs up the phone, and looks out at the ocean, reminded that The General is a very dangerous man. He believes The General is an idiot in charge of a group of fiercely-loyal, dangerous thugs. He will have to kill The General, too, when all this is over. He's pretty sure The General is thinking the same thing about him. John G. knows he'll have to watch his back, closely.

****

Dr. Gus strolls into my room around 2 p.m., much later than the noon he had promised yesterday. I'm getting a little antsy sitting around here waiting to be released. Again, I try my winning smile. I don't want him to keep me over another night.

"Bobby, how are you feeling today?" he says, looking at the computer screen.
"I'm just a little sore today, Doc." I don't want to tell him how sore I really am or he won't let me out of here, "but other than that,

I think I'll live. Can I go?"

"Well, the paperwork is going through right now so you should be on the curb in about thirty minutes. It's amazing you weren't killed, Bobby. As it stands right now, no work or surfing for at least a week and I want you in my office in a couple of days. Call to schedule an appointment as soon as you get out of here today. Remember, stay out of the water, and nothing strenuous." He clicks off the computer and he's gone.

Crap. No working, no surfing, no house, what else could go wrong in my life? I call DJ and tell him to come and get me.

****

An hour later the nurse wheels me out to DJ's truck and I slowly get in. Shit, everything hurts. Maybe I shouldn't have been in such a rush to get out of the hospital.

"I have to stop by the T-street job for a few minutes," DJ says as he gets in the driver's side door and pulls on his seatbelt. "Then I'll get you down to the boat. Maria stocked it with food, beer and wine. She even found some clothes for you, so you're good to go."

"Thanks, bro. Please thank Maria for me, will you?" I ache; I'm tired and very pissed off. The doctor told me no work or surfing, so what was I going to do for a week? He didn't say I couldn't look into Ricky's death or find out who the hell blew up my house. How strenuous could that be, right?

DJ punches the cigarette lighter, and says, "Can you believe it? It'll cost five grand to clean and sanitize the jobsite before we'll be able to go back to work. The city said they'll remove the red tag when the cleanup company delivers the certificate of completion. What bullshit." The lighter pops and he lights his cigarette. I roll down the window. "What an asshole Ricky was for getting killed on my job," he says as he blows smoke out the window.

"His throat was cut at the jobsite to make it look like a suicide. That letter you gave me points to someone he called The General for his murder. He also said that John G. and this General guy are doing business together, smuggling ecstasy and blow from a lab in Mexico. The dope is worth millions to them. He wrote John G. knew that they were going to kill Ricky. I wonder if he knew that my house was going to be blown up, too? I'll let you read the letter when we get to the boat." I can hear myself starting to get agitated, "Who knows how long this shit has been going on? I can tell you that if it's the last thing I do in this world those assholes are going down for killing our friend and blowing up my house." Now I'm yelling.

"Hey, Bobby, calm down," DJ says. "I saw Dr. Gus in the hall and he told me that you have to take it easy. Leave this investigation to Murphy." We stop for a red light and he turns to look at me. "You best be careful, bro. If you start digging into this mess you could be the next one killed. That was probably what they were trying to do when they blew up your house. It couldn't have been an accident."

"I can look after myself."

DJ lets out a laugh and that brings a smile to my face. "Sure, Bobby", he says, "Especially in the shape you're in right now."

We pull up to the T-Street job. He stops the truck, shuts off the ignition, and unbuckles his seatbelt. "I'll right back. Try not to get into any trouble in the next few minutes, okay? Then I'll get you down to the boat." He gets out of the truck and walks up to the jobsite.

I can't sit anymore. I need to stretch, so I get out of the truck and look down at the ocean. I don't see the next door neighbor, Don, until he's right beside me.

"Hello, Bobby. How you feeling? I heard about your house. I just wanted to tell you how sorry I am."

"Thanks, Don, I appreciate that." Don's a great guy. I know he won't press me for details and for that I'm grateful. "What are you working on today?" I ask him.

"I'm building some cabinets for the Casa. A volunteer's job is never done."

Casa Romantica was the home of San Clemente's original founder, Ole Hanson. It's an historic property now, used for weddings and cultural events, but it requires a ton of maintenance. A dedicated team of volunteers help the staff keep the Casa together. Don's been volunteering there since he retired from the county government. Woodworking is his hobby and he has an amazing shop set-up in his garage.

We catch up on the neighborhood gossip until DJ walks up. He greets Don and puts his hand on my shoulder. "We'd better get going Bobby; you know what the Doc said about too much activity." We say our goodbyes and get back into the truck and set out for the harbor.

We find a parking spot close to the boat, grab a few things from the truck and walk down to the locked gate. DJ pulls out his keys and lets us through the gate to the boat. We climb aboard and I stand there still marveling at how beautiful she is, and remember how hard we both worked to get her looking like this.
"Hey, do you want a beer?" DJ calls out from below.
"Hell, yes." That ought to help the painkillers do their job.

We sit on the deck for a while, not saying anything, just looking out on the harbor. It's so peaceful here in the middle of the week, all the boats swaying gently in the breeze.

"Permission to come aboard," brings DJ and me out of our comfortable silence. We both turn to see Murphy standing on the top of the stairs, shoes in hand, waiting to step onto the boat's deck.

DJ gives me a sideways look before answering. "Permission granted"

"Hey," I say reluctantly and think: Shit, what does he want now? He looks over at me and says "You look like you've been rode hard and put away wet. Feeling any better?"

"Better than what, Murph? Better than being dead?" I manage to force a smile, take a deep breath I hope he doesn't notice and ask, "What can we do for you?"

"Well, I'm pretty sure you already knew Ricky was murdered before I told you." I look down at my beer and he continues, "I've been checking around and it appears that Ricky was retired and living in a nice house in Cabo. He had money in the bank here, approximately ninety thousand in his checking account, more than double that in his brokerage-account, and he had major money in his retirement account. So, don't tell me he was broke or even lonely. With all the tourist women coming into Cabo, I'm pretty sure he could find a babe or two to sleep with. So, what the hell was going on with him? Do either one of you guys want to level with me?"

DJ and I look at each other and shrug.

Finally I say," We don't know shit, Murph. I told you the night he was killed that I hadn't had any contact with Ricky for years. I don't know what he was up to."

"You guys are full of crap. If I catch either of you lying to me or," looking directly at me, "trying to find his killer, I'll put both your asses in jail." He glances down at his watch and smirks. "Aren't you going to offer me a beer, DJ? I'm officially off-duty."

"Sure." DJ gets up, goes down into the cabin and comes back up with three more beers.

I stretch, stand up and say, "I've had a rough couple of days. I'm going to go crash."

Down below in my berth, I lie down and sleep straight through the night. No dreams.

Chapter 14

John G. sits at his bar, watching the sunset and thinking. He had tried to tell The General that killing Bobby was a bad idea. That it would bring undue attention to Ricky Weaver's murder, but The General went ahead and tried to do it anyway. But, the information from his contact inside the sheriff's department had come too late for him to be able to stop the attempt on Bobby's life.

How much had Bobby discovered? Did he know that cocaine and ecstasy were going to be delivered into Dana Point Harbor by the fishing boats the cartel owned? If Bobby knew anything, had he confided in DJ? More importantly, had either Bobby or DJ said anything to Detective Murphy? If Murphy knew, would John G.'s source inside the sheriff's department have that information? There were so many questions, with no real answers. He needs to contain the damage as fast and as soon as possible.

"Alexis," he pushes the button and speaks into the intercom, "would you ask Kawaika to have the Mercedes ready to leave twenty minutes, please?"

He grabs his satellite phone and calls his source at the sheriff's department. "We need to meet. Yes, today. Right now and I don't give a shit what you're doing. Same place as last time, in one hour. Don't be late." He hangs up the phone before getting an answer. He knows the guy will be there because John G. owns him.

He walks into the living room of his home where he finds Alexis talking with Kawaika, who turns to John G. and says, "The car's ready to go, boss." John G. has known Kawaika from their youth. They grew up in the rough and tumble neighborhood of Makaha on the Wai'anae side of Oahu. Kawaika is big, strong and most of all, fiercely loyal. He would do anything John G. asked of him.

"Alexis," John G. says, "would you please make dinner reservations at French 75, for nine p.m. tonight? Have them open a bottle of the 1985 Caymas Cabernet ahead of time." He thinks for a moment, before he continues, "Your company would be greatly appreciated, Alexis."

"Yes, sir. I'll meet you there at nine p.m." She says, turns and walks out of the room toward her office.

John G. and Kawaika get into the car and drive off. They'll meet the informant in the parking lot above Irvine Cove. It was always a risky meeting for both of them, but John G. had to find out what the cops knew and then figure out what he needed to do to keep this operation on track.

They drive in silence through Laguna and arrive a few minutes early. His informant is also early, waiting by his car in the parking lot. This part of the lot is deserted with no place to hide, so John G. feels safe doing business here. Kawaika approaches his informant, running a wand around him, checking for any type of electronic listening devices or weapons. His informant does the same to him. They nod, convinced they are both clean. Kawaika returns to the car as they start walking down to the beach. The informant hands him a manila envelope.

"This is a copy of the Weaver autopsy. Basically, it says he was murdered. It shows there was a puncture wound behind the carotid artery where his throat was slashed. They've assigned Dwayne Murphy from homicide to investigate. He's relentless. If this murder can come back to you in any way, Murphy will find it. We don't have the results from the tox screen yet but the coroner's office has a rush on it. I'll it get to you as soon as possible."

"If Murphy is as good a detective as you say, I guess I'll have to keep an eye on him. I never leave loose ends." He unbuttons his jacket, and his contact tenses before seeing John G. reach into his pocket and pull out an envelope containing five thousand dollars. "Please keep me informed. Call me when you have a copy of the toxicology results."

They walk back toward their cars in silence. Kawaika is in the driver's seat, listening to Hawaiian music. John G. smiles at the memories the music creates.

When Kawaika sees John G. approaching, he gets out of the car and holds the rear door open. "Where to now, boss?"

John G. slides into the back seat and says, "French 75. But, take the toll road back to Laguna. I need some time to read. And could you please turn the music up?" They smile at each other in the rear-view mirror.

The car pulls up in front of the restaurant and John G. gives his driver a pat on the shoulder as he steps out of the car. "Thank you, Kawaika. See you in the morning. Alexis will take me home."

As he enters the restaurant, the hostess greets him. "Good evening, sir. How may I help you?" The girl was tall and pretty, probably an aspiring actress or model.

"I see my dinner partner sitting right over there." John G. nods in the direction of Alexis, already sitting at their table, drinking a martini. She gives a little wave.

"Very good, sir," the hostess replies, but John G. is already halfway to the table. He pulls out his chair and sits down looking over at Alexis, who starts to smile but stops as she notices a look of concern on her employer's face. "Is everything alright, John?"

John G. pauses for a moment, shakes his head then smiles back at her, "Everything's fine."

Alexis is many things to him. She is his personal pilot, bodyguard, companion, but not his confidant. He trusts her with his life but not his personal business.

A waiter in a crisp, white shirt appears at their table with the decanted cabernet and two large round wine glasses. Alexis shakes her head at the waiter.

"No wine for you, Alexis?" John G. asks as he tastes the wine offered and nods his approval to the waiter. The waiter pours John G. a glass and steps away from the table, taking the second wine glass with him.

"I've never acquired a taste for wines. But I did acquire a taste for vodka and I do love my martinis." She smiles.

John G. likes that about Alexis: she tells the truth, no bullshit, no games. She was recommended to him by a client when he made it known that he was looking for a personal assistant. After having her watched for a month and doing an extensive background search, he offered her a full-time job. He paid her extremely well and she was on call 24/7. She had her own home in Laguna and, when they were traveling, he made sure she stayed in first class hotels and dined at the finest restaurants. Despite that, she drank sparingly because she took her job seriously. She worked out five days a week and often went to the firing range. John G. knew she was tough on the inside, even though it didn't show on the outside. She knew how to take care of herself and was able to fit in places where Kawaika would stick out.

They enjoy a leisurely dinner with light conversation about the new art gallery, and of the other cultural events going on during the summer in the small community of Laguna Beach. Alexis only has one martini but John G. wishes she would have shared the wine with him. Maybe he should make a wine tasting course part of her job requirement.

After dinner, Alexis drives him home where he waits in the foyer as she thoroughly checks the house and grounds. Satisfied, she says goodnight and leaves to drive to her own home.

Before going to bed, John G. makes a few notes about Detective Murphy, Bobby Paladin and DJ Frasier. He must talk to Bobby again and try to find out how much Murphy knows. No one can stumble on this business deal. There was too much to protect.

Chapter 15

I wake up early, my body still aching, but force myself to get out of bed and walk up to the deck of the boat. It's quiet and there's no one around, so I start to do some stretches. After about fifteen minutes, I decide that's enough. I grab a towel, soap and shampoo from the stuff Maria left for me and walk over to the showers in the harbor. I have them all to myself. I enjoy a long, hot, shower then head back to the boat and pull on some clothes.

As I get dressed, I realize I have no wheels. I call DJ and my call goes straight to voicemail. Crap. I leave him a message to come get me, so we can pick up my van. I want to take advantage of this time off to find Ricky's box hidden in T-Street canyon. I also need to figure out what John G.'s interest is and what's driving him. Could he have murdered a friend?

Since I'm stuck with no way to leave the harbor, I decide to walk over to Proud Mary's and grab breakfast. I hear a crowd behind me and step aside as a large group of middle-age to elderly people stride past, chattering away and calling out, "Excuse us," and "Good morning." I know this group – mostly retired, they call themselves Fleet Feet and they've been walking the harbor three mornings a week for more than twenty years. I see a few familiar faces and wave hello as they pass. Amazing how this group can lift my spirits this morning. Once they pass, I fall in behind them, walking much more slowly than even the fit eighty year-olds in the group, and make my way to the restaurant. Proud Mary's has been a fixture in the Dana Point Harbor for more than thirty five years and is back up and running after a bad fire a couple of years ago. I know my server, Susie, from high school.

"Bobby!" she hugs me as I walk into the restaurant, "You look like shit."

"I love you, too," I hug her back, turning away slightly to protect my bruises. "Didn't you hear about my house? How did you think

I'd look?"

"I read about it in the Sun Post News. I'm so glad you're okay."
The restaurant is starting to fill up. She glances around, "Grab that
table by the window before anyone else gets it. Let me seat this
bunch and I'll be right over. Coffee?"

I nod and sit where I can watch the Catalina Express taking on
today's group of tourists for their trip across to Catalina Island. I
notice a young couple in their early twenties boarding. They're
obviously on some kind of date. She's wearing short-shorts, very
high heeled sandals and a tank top. He's in jeans, a t-shirt and a
jacket. She might look good but she's going to freeze her ass off
out there. He'll be a gentleman and give her his jacket then freeze
his ass off, hoping that will get him laid. As long as she doesn't
topple off her shoes and fall overboard first.

I finish a leisurely breakfast of huevos rancheros and catch up with
Susie when she has time between customers. When I'm finished, I
stroll back toward the boat. The Fleet Feeters are done with their
walk and have all gathered for coffee on the outside patio of the
Coffee Importers café, laughing and joking as I pass by. They burst
into a round of Happy Birthday, focusing on a very elderly man
sitting on his walker-thingy. He smiles and blows out the single
candle on his cupcake to a round of applause. When I get back to
the boat, DJ is sitting there, drinking a beer.

"Well, what's our plan for today?" He grins.

I shake my head and laugh, "Dude, this is early by even your
standards. I've barely finished a cup of coffee. How come you
aren't at work today?"

"I got your message and decided to play hooky today. I have
everything going at the San Juan job, and we're shut down at T-
Street for at least another week. One of the benefits of being the
boss."

"Damn straight, Skippy. I guess I'll have a beer and explain what I know and you can decide if you want to get involved."
Over the next forty-five minutes and two beers, I explain everything to DJ; about the note Ricky left me, about John G.'s business in Mexico, who was protecting him and all that dope that might already be on its way here. When I'm finished, DJ is looking out toward the harbor, thoughtful. Finally he says, "We have to tell Murph."

"No." I say firmly.

"Well at least we should go find the box and give it all to Murph. He'll know what to do with it. Let's do the right thing, Bobby. They killed Ricky and tried to kill you. Your house blowing up couldn't have been an accident." I can tell he's getting upset.

Did he not even hear what I told him? "Fuck that, bro. I don't know who to trust. Ricky said to trust no one. You're the only one I can trust. I think maybe John G. killed Ricky, or had him killed. If you don't want in, I understand. I can handle it on my own, but you have to keep your mouth shut. Take me to get my van and I'll leave you out of it." I fight to calm down.

He looks down at his empty beer bottle and says, "I have to think of Maria."
"I know that."

"You can't do this by yourself. You're so fucking stubborn, Bobby. You'll get yourself killed."

"So let's go to San Clemente and find Ricky's box."

DJ sighs and pulls himself up out of the deck chair. "I just know I'm going to regret this."
We get into DJ's truck and drive about ten minutes before we pull up to the curb outside Ricky Weaver's parent's first house in San

Clemente. We get out of the truck and slip down into the canyon, which is overgrown with shrubs and trees.

"Remember when we were kids playing down here?" DJ asks with a smile.

"Those were the days, bro. We played with pellet guns, hunted for frogs and snakes and played army with our friends. It looks totally different from the way I remember it."

We find the approximate area where the old fort had been and begin searching for the box. We push away dead leaves and spider webs, startling lizards and a rabbit. After about an hour and a half of looking in the hot, humid canyon, we're scratched, mosquito-bitten and still haven't found anything. We're both frustrated.

I freeze and listen, then say, "Did you hear that? Was that a rattlesnake?"

DJ stops in his tracks, stands silent for a moment, listening. "I don't hear anything. Stop scaring me, you sack of shit. I already saw a Black Widow spider."

After another half an hour of this we discover nothing.

"You know, Bobby, I'm beginning to think it's not here. We've looked everywhere we used to play. There's no sign that Ricky, or anyone, has even been here lately." He reaches into his t-shirt pocket for his cigarettes. I put my hand out to stop him.

"Are you crazy? You can't smoke down here. There's too much dry brush. You could torch the whole canyon." DJ sighs and puts the pack back in his pocket.

We're just about to head back up to the truck, when something catches my eye. Just off the path there's a medium-sized, round rock with no debris around it, like it had been swept clean. I squat down and push the rock away. Underneath it is a small hole. "Hey, DJ, check this out. There was something here, but it looks like someone beat us to it. I wonder if some neighborhood kids found the box and took it. If they did, we're screwed." I sit back on my heels and look up at DJ. I can tell he's unconvinced. DJ leans over, "You're sure this is where Ricky said we would find the box?"

"Sure I'm sure. This doesn't make sense. I wonder if someone found it and doesn't know what they found."

"What if someone found it and *does* know what they've found?"

"So, we might be dealing with kids or bad guys, but we don't know which."

We look around some more, playing detective, but we don't see footprints, or whatever else that those guys on CSI look for. In real life, the crime scene techs look for that stuff, not the cops, so it was never part of my job when I was on the force.

"Bobby, we've looked all over this place and all we've managed to do is get scratched and sweaty, find an empty hole and waste our time. I took today off to help you figure out what's going on and we've found squat. Let's get out of here, take the boat out and go sailing."

"Can't. I have a meeting with an architect in a couple of hours for plans for my house. I need to get some prices together to see if the insurance money is going to cover all the replacement costs. You still want to bid on the project, right?"

He looks over at me with mock distain. "I guess so. Are you sure you can afford me?"

As we make our way out of the canyon and back toward the truck, a flash catches my eye from up on the street. My instincts take over and I push DJ down. We hit the ground at the same time as three or four shots whistle just above us. A couple more shots are fired in our direction and then it's quiet.

"DJ, are you all right?" I whisper.

"Yeah, I think so," he whispers back.

"Did you see who was shooting at us?"

"I didn't see a thing. I was too busy trying to keep from getting hit. Are they gone?"

Just then we hear a car door slam and tires squealing away. I have to make a choice, call the cops or split. I don't feel like explaining what we were doing here, but fuck! People were shooting at us. Somebody was going to get hurt. I roll over on my back, pull out my cell phone and punch in Murph's number.

"Murph – Bobby Paladin. DJ and I were just shot at over by T-Street canyon. No, they missed us. Yes, we'll wait here. I know the drill, Murph." I hang up and look over at DJ, who is pale and obviously shaken. "Murph wants us to stay put 'til the cops get here he said."

DJ nods and we lie there, waiting. After a few minutes, which seems like hours, we hear the sirens coming toward us. We finally feel safe enough to get up off the ground, dust ourselves off and make our way out of the canyon. As we wait for the sheriffs to arrive, I look around for shell casings or any other evidence the shooter might have left behind. I haven't found anything when the sheriff's car pulls up, and right behind him is Murph's car.

"Let me do the talking. That way, if he catches me lying to him, you won't get into trouble. Just sit there on the curb acting as if you're in shock, ok?" I say.

"I am in shock, you asshole. I don't have to act." He sits down on the curb, his face grey.

Murph runs toward us, "Are you guys all right? Do either one of you need an ambulance?"

"No, we're okay, Murph" I say. "Just rattled, that's all."

He looks down at DJ then over at me. "Do you guys mind telling me what you were doing down in that canyon?"

He pulls out his notepad, and for the next forty-five minutes he asks us questions while the two uniformed cops search the area. DJ doesn't say much. He just sits on the curb his elbows on his knees, his head down. I try to explain to Murph the best I can about what we were doing here, without telling him anything about the note or the box that Ricky had hidden. I tell him that because of Ricky's death we'd been feeling nostalgic about playing in the canyon. After I'm done spinning my story, I'm not sure if he's buying it.

"Okay, you guys get the hell out of here but if I call you'd better answer. I might need more information," Murphy finally says. "Bobby, I hope you're telling me the truth. Ex-cop or not, I'll put your ass in jail for obstruction of justice if I find out you're looking into this on your own." He gives me with that steely-eyed cop look of his.

"Yeah, I get it Murph." I reach down and give a hand up to DJ. As we get into his truck, I say, "Can you take me over to the house so I can get my van?"

"Sure," DJ says. And that's the only thing he says as we drive to– what used to be–my house. I know that canyon shit scared him.

81

We pull up in front of what's left of my house, and as we're getting out of the truck, DJ finally says with a forced laugh, "Well, the garage looks good." I'm relieved to hear him finally crack a joke.

"Yeah, thank God." All my tools were in the garage and so were some of my surfboards. Luckily, I had parked my van on the street that day.

I look around the lot but there is nothing really left of my house. The city had red tagged. I open the garage door and look inside to make sure all my stuff is still there and re-lock the door. I still can't believe that everything I had worked for so hard was gone. At least I hadn't ended up dead. Not yet anyway.
I say, "I've got some errands to run and then go to that meeting. Are you going back to the boat?"

"I don't think so. I have a bunch of paperwork to do at home, plus I have to get the kids to practice this afternoon. Call me later. And whatever you do, please don't say anything to Maria about what just happened. She'll freak." He climbs back into his truck, starts it up, waves goodbye and takes off up the street.

I turn and look back from the street. I have had my house blown up, one of my best friends murdered, and someone has tried to kill me, twice. This is really starting to piss me off. I'll find out who did this and get even, if it's the last thing I do.

Chapter 16

DJ is very worried about Bobby, but he has to protect Maria and the kids. He doesn't need this in his life, especially right now with work really starting to take off.

He's preoccupied as he drives down Pacific Coast Highway and doesn't notice the truck coming up fast on his driver's side. He's just reaching for his cigarettes when his truck is hit from the side. Suddenly, he's being spun around and forced off the road. His truck slams into the K-rail so hard his airbag explodes in his face, as parts of his truck fly off into oncoming traffic. He hears a crash, horns and the sound of scraping metal as he losses consciousness. He doesn't register the big black truck with tinted windows pull away from right beside him.

****

"Well, well, well, DJ, what is it with you and Bobby lately?" Dr. Gus says as he walks into DJ's hospital room. "It seems like both you guys are having a streak of really bad luck. What happened?"

DJ is relieved. He can tell by the tone in Dr. Gus's voice that his injuries must not be too serious. "Beats the hell out of me, Doc. One minute I'm driving down coast highway, and the next thing I know, I'm waking up an in ambulance on my way to the hospital. I have to call Maria and let her know I'm okay." He wonders where his cell phone ended up. He looks over to see his clothes, wallet and phone in a neat pile on the rolling tray beside his bed.

"I called her while you were down in X-ray. She'll be here as soon as she can." Dr. Gus puts the chart down and continues. "Your X-rays were negative, but you're pretty banged up. You're going to have some major bruising on your face from hitting the air bag. Your shoulder was strained against the seatbelt and you were bounced around quite a bit, but you're okay to go home."

83

After Dr. Gus leaves, DJ calls Bobby. Fuck, does that guy ever answer his phone? He leaves a message. This is getting serious and DJ has to get Maria and the kids out of town before they get caught in the crossfire.

As he puts the phone aside, he looks up to see Maria frozen in the doorway. He can tell she's been crying. She walks over and gently kisses him.
"Are you alright, honey?" She asks. "Gus called and told me that you had an accident and that you totaled your truck. He said you were just banged up. Nothing was broken, thank God. I was so scared." She starts to cry again. He's so sorry to have upset her like this.

"I'm fine, Babe." He kisses her and holds her away from him a little so he can look into her eyes. "When was the last time you saw your folks? Why don't you to take the kids and go up to your parents' house in Oregon?"

This surprises her and her eyes search his face. "What are you talking about? I am not leaving you. Is it Bobby? Has he got you mixed up in whatever happened to Ricky Weaver? Are you in some kind of trouble? Tell me."

"Maria," DJ says sternly, "You need to grab the kids and fly up to Oregon. Go home, pack and take the kids to your parents' house. I'll call you every day but I want you out of Orange County. I don't know what's going on, but I can't risk you're getting caught up in whatever this is. Stay there until I call and tell you it is safe to come home. Okay?"

****

I walk into DJ's hospital room and see Maria and DJ hugging. She's about to say something to him but turns to glare at me.

"Hi, Maria."

84

"Don't you 'Hi Maria' me, Bobby Paladin. My husband was almost killed today and it's entirely your fault."

"I am so sorry, Maria," I say, attempting to placate her. "I heard what DJ said and I think both of you and the kids should go to Oregon until this is all over. I think that would be best for everyone."

"I'm not going anywhere, Bobby." DJ says. "I'm working on two jobs right now, and I'm not going to quit because of some crazy asshole ran me off the road." He looks at his wife and says, "Maria, please go pick up the kids, call the airline and get the first flight out. Call your parents and let them know you and the kids are coming to visit for a few days. Don't tell them about what happened to me, please. Just tell them you and the kids miss them and you want to come and see them. It's been a while anyway and they'll be glad to see their grandkids."

DJ stops talking as Detective Murphy walks into the room. Maria's eyes go straight for the badge hanging around his neck and pales. "Maria," DJ says softly, "Get going and I'll call you in an hour or two." She nods, her eyes filling again. She kisses DJ goodbye, glares at me and turns to go.

Murph watches as Maria leaves the room, then turns to look at both of us, "Okay, you two, what the hell is going on? I know this is related to Rick Weaver's murder, and before I leave here I need to find out what you are *not* telling me. I'm sick and tired of getting the run-around."

"Bobby," DJ says as he turns to me, pain sliding across his face, "You need to tell Murph what you know. I have a wife and three kids and they can't be part of this."

"Okay," I say and look straight at Murph, "I'll tell you everything I know, but I want in. I want to help you catch the people who killed Ricky. The same ones who've been trying to kill me and my best

85

friend, okay? I still have my gun permit and a license to carry. I can get into places you can't. And I promise to do what you tell me."

Murph glances over at DJ, lying in bed his arm in a sling, then looks back at me and finally says "You're doing a bang-up job so far, Bobby. Okay, I'll let you help out on this case, but unofficially—off the record—okay? I could get into major trouble, maybe even lose my job and pension for letting you in, but if you come clean with me now, I'll share what I can with you."

"Sit down, Murph and let me tell you a story." I say, and can hear the relief in my own voice as I realize I'm actually happy to finally unload this burden on Murphy.

****

For the next hour, Murphy listens to Bobby and DJ tell an incredible story as he tries to figure out what parts are bullshit and what parts are true. He's known Bobby for many years, known the whole Paladin family for that matter, but hasn't spent any real time with him. Hell, he even worked for Bobby's dad at his hardware store, The Nail Apron, before he decided to move to San Francisco. He was pretty sure Bobby would mostly tell him the truth, but there was always the chance he would hold something back, just so he could keep his hand in the investigation. And that could be the single fact that would help him figure out what was going on and who killed Ricky.

Scowling, Murph says, "First thing, I need that letter from Ricky. DJ you're smart for getting your family to safety but not too smart for staying around here yourself. I'll have a patrol car cruise through your neighborhood a few times tonight to keep an eye on your house. I'll also make sure your family gets to the airport safely. Bobby, can you keep an eye on John G.? You'll need a different vehicle. He'll recognize your van. I need you to be upfront with me at all times from now on. Don't ever try to bullshit me again. I know you want to do right by Ricky, but don't get yourself into a situation without any back-up. Call me if you suspect anything. The sheriffs can act on it, and do it legally, so no more of this cowboy horseshit. I'll try to keep everything under the radar, so don't go getting killed on me. I hate the paperwork." He finally gives them a reluctant smile. "I'll talk to both of you guys later. Thanks for coming clean with me." And he walks out of the hospital room.

****

Dr. Gus releases DJ and I take him home. I stick around to make sure he's settled in okay. When his cell phone rings, I know it must be Maria, so I get up to leave, waving goodbye. I head out to the van, get in and check my cell own phone. One missed a call. I know the number, it's John G.'s. I listen to his message and call him back.

"John, it's Bobby Paladin. I saw you called. Yes, DJ was in a car accident but he's fine. Dinner? Sure, I can have dinner at your house tonight." So much for discrete surveillance, I can just sit across the table from him and ask him questions. "I'll be there by eight. See you then." As I hang up, I think, *this ought to be interesting.*

Shit. It dawns on me that I don't have any nice clothes. I drive over to Hobie Surf Shop and pick up some shorts and a couple of nice shirts, so I'll look presentable. You know, in case Alexis is there. I head back to the boat to shower and change. I call Murph and leave a message about my dinner plans tonight.

While I'm driving up to John G.'s house in Laguna, I think about how I'm going to handle this situation. John G. is surely going to ask me about everything that's happened over the last couple of days, so I need to be careful.

I pull up to the front gate of John G.'s house, push the button and the gate opens without a voice coming over the intercom. Before I can ring the doorbell, Alexis opens the door.

"Good Evening, Bobby. How are you?"

"I'm feeling better, thanks for asking."
"I heard about your house being destroyed. That's terrible. I'm so very sorry. You look okay."

"Thank you, Alexis." I try to be smooth, "You are looking quite lovely this evening, yourself." She turns to lead me through the house.

"Why, thank you, Bobby." I see a half smile and I think maybe she's trying not to laugh at me. Nah. "Would you like a glass of wine while you wait?"

I open the door for her as we head toward the outside dining area, trying to remember my manners. "That would be great. Thank you."

"John picked this wine out for you, so help yourself. He'll join you shortly," She indicates a bottle in an ice bucket on the bar, cork pressed half-way into the bottle. As she walks back into the house, I suppress an internal sigh. She's such a babe—more than just a babe. I obviously can't get a date with her and flirting with her is really no fun because she's all business. I guess I'll just have to stick to dreaming about her.
"Bobby," John G. calls, pulling me back to earth. He walks out of the house toward me with his outstretched hand. "How are you doing, bruddah?" he says, a typical Hawaiian greeting. "How's DJ? I heard about his accident. It's awful, just awful."

I shake his hand, "Just a strained shoulder and bruising from the airbag."

"Does he need anything? What can I do to help?"

"Thanks, John. I'll pass that along to DJ."

"Before I forget, I want you to have this. It'll help out with the rebuilding your house." John G. hands me an envelope.

I look at him, confused. I open the envelope and inside there is a check for two hundred thousand dollars. My knees buckle. I have to sit down. I take a big gulp of my wine.

Finally I say, "I can't accept this, John. My house was fully insured and they tell me I should have a check in the next few weeks."

"Take it, please. You, DJ and Ricky always treated me like family. My business is doing well and I would be deeply hurt if you don't accept this gift, from one friend to another."

I look at the check again. I'm not really sure what it all means. If I accept it, what will I owe him in return? Finally I clear my throat and croak out a thank you, then fold the envelope and put it in my shirt pocket. He smiles.

"Good. Now we can get on with our evening. Tell me what's has been happening over the last few days."

Before I can start, John's personal chef walks out carrying a platter.
"I remember how much you like Ahi, Bobby. The fish was caught fresh this morning in Hawaii, and flown here for a special treat tonight."

I don't know what to say except, "Thanks, John. This is amazing." I can't help but be suspicious. I look at the platter of sushi and sashimi and decide to enjoy myself and start back on the detective work tomorrow.

For the next couple of hours we eat fantastic food and drink even better wine. I tell him almost everything, including being shot at in the canyon, but I leave out Ricky's letter and my deal with Murph.

At the end of the evening, he walks me to my car and I finally get up the nerve to ask what I really came here to find out.

"John, do you have any idea who might have tried to kill me or DJ?"

He turns and looks directly into my eyes, "Bobby, I don't know what you're implying, but if I wanted you and DJ dead, you'd be dead. There would be no trace of you. You'd just be gone."

Shit. He looks like he means it. I open my mouth, but before I can say anything, he puts his hand on my shoulder and smiles. "Now, drive safely home and watch your back. Whoever is trying to kill you might succeed if you don't pay attention."

As I drive back to the boat I can't forget the look on John G.'s face. I think he was being truthful about not trying to kill us. I sure as hell hope so.

****

After he watches the gate close behind Bobby's car, John G. walks back into his house and into his office. He presses the button on the intercom. "Alexis, could you come into my office, please?" He sits down in his desk chair and looks out the window.

John G,'s office was built out of Koa wood, imported from Hawaii. Floor to ceiling bookcases, paneling, a coffered ceiling and flooring, all built from this rare and exotic wood. The wood cost hundreds of thousands of dollars and the room pleases him.

"Yes, John?" Alexis says as she walks into the office.

"Alexis, I'd like you to keep an eye on Bobby Paladin and his friend, DJ Frasier, for a few days. Bobby's staying on DJ's boat in the Dana Point Harbor. I want you to try to find out who's behind their recent problems. This should take priority over your regular duties. I'd like updates at least twice a day."

She nods.

He pulls a file across the desk, his reading glasses from the top drawer and begins to flip through the file. When he doesn't say anything, she knows she's dismissed.

As Alexis walks toward the front door and to her car, she wonders how she's going to approach this without being caught by Bobby or DJ. Her boss will not be happy if she screws this up.

Chapter 17

I wake up feeling a little sore but better than yesterday, so I decide to go for a run through the harbor. After an hour of slow jogging, mixed with walking, I arrive back at the boat and see Murph sitting in the cockpit, reading the Sun Post News. He's got two cups of take-out coffee sitting beside him. I step up into the boat's cockpit and sit down opposite him. He sure shows up whenever he feels like it.

"How are you feeling this morning?" He leans over and passes me a cup.

"Pretty good, considering. I just went for a little run. It gave me a chance to think."

"Come up with any answers? Anything you might want to share with me?" he folds the paper.

"Not really," I say.

"How was your meeting with your friend, last night?" he asks, pulling his notebook out of his pocket.

"I straight-up asked him if he knew who was trying to kill us."

"Really. What did he say to that?" He sets the notebook beside him and takes a sip of his coffee.

"He said that if he wanted us dead, we'd be dead. I believe him. I've known John G. for a long time."

"Okay, if you say so."

"So," I ask, "if he isn't trying to kill us, then who is?"

Murph looks at me for a while before answering. "I don't know, Bobby. We haven't found anyone who witnessed anyone around your house or anybody who saw DJ being run off the road."

"He just drove himself into the guardrail in the middle of the day for fun?"

"I don't know. I'm also starting to think the sheriffs' office has a leak. I can't even tell my boss that. I can't figure out who it might be. Keep that close to your chest."

"I wouldn't be surprised if John G. has more than one cop on his payroll. I think it's strange he was so adamant that he didn't have anything to do with my house, the shots fired or DJ's accident. He knows key details that only the cops should know. John G. has always paid people off; that's his way. Check this out bro, he wrote me a check for two hundred grand to go toward the repair of my house." I hand the check to Murphy.

He whistles. "What are you going to do with this? Do you think he's trying to bribe you?"

"I'm going to call my attorney to look into the tax issues. I don't need it, but John G. insisted. I could donate it to the Travis Lee Foundation."

"What's that?"

I take a deep breath. "That kid I shot. His parents took the money they received from the city of Los Angeles to settle the lawsuit and set up the foundation to help at-risk youths with after school tutoring and mentoring."

"I'd heard about the shooting—that's why you quit the force, isn't it? I didn't know what happened to you after that."

"That's a long story. This money feels kind of dirty, but I could also do some real good with it, you know? What do you think?"

"I think you should hang onto the check for now. It might end up being evidence against John G. If John G. isn't behind these attempts on you two, then we might have a real problem trying to figure out who is. He was the obvious suspect. We need to find that box Rick said he left in the canyon. Why don't we start there?"

"Okay. Let me change my clothes and we can go search T-Street Canyon."

I head down below into the boat's cabin and get dressed.

"I need to take my van, Murph. I'm going to swing by and see DJ after. I'll follow you to T-Street canyon,"

****

He's sitting outside the gate, waiting for them. He watches as they get into their cars and pull out of the Harbor parking lot. He doesn't follow them right away. He can't afford to get caught. He's making good money passing along copies of Detective Murphy's reports. He was getting rich and no one was going to stop that, not Murphy or that washed up cop, Bobby Paladin. Big fucking deal, he killed one kid and his life falls apart.

He decides to loosely follow Paladin. Tailing him down PCH, he thinks about Paladin's friend, Frasier, and how he had run him off the road. What's it going to take to get both of these jerks to back off?

As he follows Paladin into town, he quickly figures out where they're going: back to T-Street Canyon. After he'd taken those shots at Frasier and Paladin to scare them away, he'd returned the next morning and searched the canyon, but had come up empty handed. If those guys ever find the information Weaver had hidden, everybody involved would be in deep shit. He has to re-think his plan. Killing a cop and an ex-cop was not ideal but, if they get too close, he'll have to consider it.

He drives through town, down El Camino Real a few blocks past Trafalgar Lane, turns down the street and parks on Ola Vista. He gets out of his car and starts walking toward the canyon. He finds a spot where he can keep an eye on them but still stay out of sight. He'll wait until they came up out of the canyon. If they found the box, he'll have to decide what to do next.

Chapter 18

"Are you sure this is where you guys built your fort?" Murphy asks.

"Yeah, I'm sure." I thought I was sure but I'm really frustrated that we can't find the box. I walk deeper into the canyon and stop. *Am I missing something? Maybe the fort wasn't behind Ricky's parents' house. Maybe it was farther down the canyon.*

"Murph, we need to look deeper in the canyon. I remember now that we had a trail from the back yard down into the canyon. I think we might be looking in the wrong place."

We make our way back through the bushes until we are further down. It's much more overgrown here.

"Hey! What the hell are you doing down there? This is private property and you're trespassing!" We hear a voice holler from above. "I'm calling the cops right now!"

"Hold on, sir. I'm with the sheriff's department." Murph calls up the hill. "My name is Detective Dwayne Murphy. I'm an investigator with the sheriffs' department. Give me a minute to climb up there and I'll show you my ID."
I hear Murph mutter, "Pain in the ass Neighborhood Watch Nazi," as he climbs up the hill to show the homeowner his badge and ID I hope this helpful citizen is unarmed.

The guy says, "Sorry. Thank you, officer. The other day there were some guns shots fired right over there. My wife is a nervous wreck."

I hear Murph placating the guy, which could take forever. Since I'm not here officially, I know he wants to be sure the guy doesn't call the sheriffs' office. I start to move further down into the canyon.

I come to a spot with a fallen eucalyptus tree and remember: when we were older, out of the fort building stage, Ricky, DJ and I, used to sit on this log and talk about girls, surfing and smoke some weed. So I sit on the log and figure I'll just wait for Murph to finish up. I kick at a pile of stones under the log. When I look down between my feet, I notice an indentation in the ground. The dirt has been disturbed and then smoothed out to make it look natural. I kneel down and start to carefully move the dirt with my hands. After a few minutes, I see a square corner. I'm looking at the top of a box.

"Christ," I whisper. There it is. A Japanese puzzle box, just like Ricky said. I hear Murph swearing, crashing back down the canyon. "Murph!" I hiss, "Come here! Quick."

I clear the stones and dirt from around the box, and gently remove it from its hiding place. I sit back down on the log and set it on my lap. The box is totally smooth and it looks seamless. There are no joints showing anywhere on it. Murph works his way over to me. He stops and stares at the box in my hands. I brush more of the dirt away.

"Be careful! Remember what Ricky said about opening the box the right way. We could destroy the contents. Where did you find it?"

"I just sat down to wait for you and found it under a pile of dirt and rocks."

"So how do we get it open? I don't see a lid."

"It's a Japanese puzzle box. Haven't you ever seen one?"

Now that the dirt is cleared off, we can see that the puzzle box is beautiful. It's made of wood that has a black lacquered finish and inlayed with mother of pearl. It's pretty big, too, a little smaller than a shoebox but wider.

"You slide the panels this way and that way and eventually it opens. Sometimes it takes only a few moves, sometimes a lot more. I've never seen one that looks like this. It looks like it might be complicated," I say.

"Well, be careful and don't move anything until we figure out how to open it."

"I know. We're going to have to try to figure this out on our own."

"Shit, the leak. How are we going to open this without the department's help?"

I stand up with the box, look up at the sky and mutter, "Ricky, even dead, you're a pain in the ass."

I'm glad I brought my backpack with me. I take off my jacket and carefully wrap the box in it, then slip the covered box into the backpack. We should feel like we've made a huge accomplishment, but we've just ended up with another problem we can't solve.
"I guess the best thing is for me to take this back to the boat and hide it for now. Then I'll go see DJ."

"Normally, I'd say that the box would be better in the sheriff's hands, but right now, I doubt that."

"Ricky said he left us another clue for opening the puzzle box. It's too important and he wouldn't risk leaving them together. We need to find that next clue and find it fast."

I put the backpack on and we turn to climb back up the canyon.

I stop and turn back to fill in the hole where I found the box. If someone is following us, I don't want them to know we found it.

****

He watches as they come back up from the canyon. Paladin opens the passenger side of his van and gently sets his backpack on the seat. He can't tell for sure if they found something, but the way Paladin is handling that backpack make him pretty sure they had. As Murphy and Paladin drive away, he looks up and down the street before slipping out of his hiding spot. He's just starting back to his car when his phone vibrates in his pocket. He gets into his car before he answers it. He listens intently, finally saying, "Yes, sir. I know, sir. I think Paladin found it, but I can't be one hundred percent sure. Yes, sir. When I find out, sir, you'll be the first to know, sir."

He hangs up, pale and sweating from his conversation. The General is ruthless man. This game of playing both ends against the middle is very dangerous, but very, very profitable. It's all about the money. He checks his watch; he has to get to work or he'll raise suspicion with his boss. If he can pull off his plan, he'll be a very rich man. Then he can retire; lie on the beach, read and drink expensive scotch for the rest his life. Best of all, he'll still collect his pension. He loves the idea of beating the system.

****

I pull into DJ's driveway, lock the van and run inside. DJ's sitting in his recliner, his arm in the black sling from the hospital. "Sorry I'm late, DJ. Are you doing okay?"

"Much better today, but the house seems so empty without Maria and the kids. Get me out of here, will you?"

I help DJ into my van and before I've even come around to the driver's side, he's lit a cigarette. "I could use a beer."

"Aren't you on medication or something?"

"Nothing too serious. Besides, one or two beers won't kill me."

"I'm not going to argue with you. Let's go to the Red Fox Lounge. That way we can get lunch, too. It should be pretty quiet this time of the day."

"Great idea." He turns and blows smoke out the window.

"Well, while you've been relaxing, I've been busy."

He turns to look at me, "Really? Doing what?"

"Murph and I went back down into the canyon and found the box."

"No shit?! That's great!"

"I don't know if it is because now we seem to have a bigger problem. It's a fucking Japanese puzzle box."

"What the hell is that?"

"A Japanese puzzle box. Christ, Murph had never seen one either. Didn't you guys read Hardy Boys mysteries as kids? In Ricky's letter he said not to try to open the box. If we don't open it in the right sequence, whatever is inside will be destroyed. Ricky rigged it somehow. It looks like it's a really complicated one."

"Can I take a look at it?"

"Sorry, bro. I hid it for now. Ricky said that he left us a clue somewhere so we would be able to open the box. He put the box and the instructions in different places for safety.

"If he went to all that trouble to get us those letters, he would have found a way to lead us to the clue that would open the box," DJ says as he crushes his cigarette into my clean ashtray. "So how do we find the clue? It took forever to find that box."

I pull into the Red Fox Lounge parking-lot and find a spot right behind the rear entrance. I help DJ down from the van and we walk into the bar, which is dark, quiet and cool.

"Bobby! DJ! I haven't seen you guys in a long time. You guys look like you went twelve rounds with Mike Tyson." Ray Felix, the longtime bartender, says to us as we sit down. He makes a big deal of checking out both sides of our heads. "At least he left you with your ears. What can I get you to drink?"

DJ says, "Two Coronas, Ray, and a couple of lunch menus, please."

A couple of the regulars come through the front door and shake us by the shoulders as they pass us on the way to the back of the bar. "You guys look like shit. You get hit by a truck and forget to get the license plate number?" One of them says as they sit down at the far end of the bar to play the electronic trivia game.

"That's it." DJ pulls the sling off over his head and puts it on his lap.

Ray says, "I heard about your house, Bobby. I'm so sorry. If I can be of any help, please let me know." He sets our cold beers down in front of us. He moves to the other end of the bar to help the other customers. When he comes back, we order lunch and another beer each.

I say, "Ray, you heard about Ricky Weaver, right?"
He nods. "It's a terrible business, Bobby, just terrible. Ricky was in here the night that he was killed. He was drinking beer and tequila shots and was pretty hammered. He was here by himself and he seemed to be really preoccupied. I tried talking to him, but he just sat there, staring out the window."

102

"Did you tell the police about Ricky?" I ask.

"No. I kept thinking they'd be by to ask me questions, but nobody came. Do you think I should report that he was here?"

"Did he say anything to you, Ray, anything at all?" I lean in and ask him.

"No not really. We talked about you a little, what great pals you were as kids." He pauses, "Now that I think about it, he did say something. It was busy that night so it slipped my mind until now. He was kind of drunk, so I didn't pay all that much attention."

"What did he say, Ray?" I ask impatiently.

"He told me the next time you were in, to tell you that the key was in his head or something like that. I wasn't really listening. It didn't seem important and it didn't make a lot of sense at the time. He left the bar right after that." Ray looks at the door as two new customers come in, calling out for Ray to make them two of his famous Bloody Marys.

DJ and I look at each other, trying to make sense out of what Ray just said. We don't want to talk about it while we're in the bar, so we sit and eat our lunches in silence. We pay our tab and then drive back to the harbor to DJ's boat where we'll be able to talk about what Ray said in privacy. I unlock the boat and head below. I stop short, turn around and come back up.

"DJ, you need to see this."
He walks over to the cabin door and looks down past me. "What the hell?" The interior of the boat had been trashed. The boat has been thoroughly searched, in a way to inflict as much damage as possible. DJ pushes past me into the cabin, royally pissed off. We've worked so hard to get this boat in shape.

"Let's go talk to your nosy neighbor. He probably saw the whole thing."

"No, he's only here on the weekends. Doesn't that just fucking figure? The one time I need him to *not* mind his own fucking business and he's not around."

"Let me call Murph." I dial his number, but it goes straight to voicemail. "He's not answering. I don't think we should wait. You'd better call the sheriffs' office and file a report. Do you think they found the security camera in the bulkhead? We might be able to find out who did this."

DJ is pulling his cell phone out of his pocket as he storms over to the Harbor Master's office.

There's nothing I can do until DJ gets back, so I sit on the dock and wait. I hear a splash beside me as two dolphins surface then slide back under the water. They don't come near the boats very often, but sometimes they get curious and come inside the breakwater. It seems odd to see something so peaceful in the middle of this shit-storm.

After about forty-five minutes, DJ rages back down the dock. "Your house, my truck and now my boat. The insurance company is going to flip out when I call them. There has to be at least twenty thousand dollars' worth of damage done to the interior of the boat. Over a year's worth of hard work ruined."

"At least she'll still sail. It was only the interior."

"We can clean her up and sail her the way she is, but we'll have to redo all of the woodwork and get all of the cushions redone. So much fucking work, down the tube." He's heartbroken, I can tell. Me, too.

"Thank God you sent Maria to her parents."

"She'd freak. We can't tell her."

I nod my agreement. DJ lights a cigarette and we both sit on the dock and wait for the sheriffs to arrive.

Chapter 19

Alexis had followed them to Dana Point Harbor and saw the sheriffs arrive. *This can't be good,* she thinks as she sits down at a table in a restaurant overlooking DJ's boat slip.

She takes in the scene until the cops leave and DJ and Bobby leave to head back to the van. She gets up to follow them, throwing a ten dollar bill on the table to pay for her ice tea when she sees a man glance over at them, trying just a little too hard to look casual. She can't see his face, but as he walks away, she knows she's seen that walk before. She never forgot someone she'd followed, but she just couldn't put a name or a face to this guy.

By the time Alexis gets to the parking lot, the man has disappeared. With all of the cars moving through the parking lot there was no way for her to pin down what he was driving. The face and the name would come back to her, sooner or later. She just needed to remember where and when she had seen that walk.

Alexis assumes that Paladin and Frasier went to DJ's house, since they were running out of places to go, so there was no rush to follow them. She picks up her cell phone and punches in John G.'s number, informing him of her observations. She can't answer all of his questions about why the cops are at the boat, but she tells him there might have been a break-in. He asks her to go to DJ's house and if they are there, to sit on them for a while longer. They schedule a late dinner at the Beach House restaurant in Laguna, where she can give him a more detailed report.

Alexis watches DJ's house until eight thirty and the van never moves. She sees no one suspicious lurking around, so she heads to Laguna Beach to meet her employer for dinner.

She pulls up to the Beach House restaurant at nine p.m. and hands the keys of her Toyota to the valet. The car is perfect for her needs: watching, waiting or just wanting to blend in with the crowd. She sees John G. on the deck, drinking a glass of wine, looking down at Main Beach in Laguna.

"Alexis," he says as he stands up to greet her, "I've taken the liberty of ordering your martini."

"Thank you, John. It's been a long day." She sits across from him and pulls her wrap around her shoulders. It's a beautiful night, but it always gets chilly in Southern California after the sun goes down, even in the summer.

She looks at him and says, "There seems to be another player involved."

He glares at her. "Another player? Who is it?" he snaps.

She's startled by the intensity of his reaction. "I don't know. I spotted someone following DJ and Bobby. I've seen him before, I know it, but I just can't place him. I know that walk, though, and it'll come to me. When it does, I think we'll know who's behind DJ and Bobby's troubles."

"Damn it, you need to find out who this person is, and quickly."

A few patrons on the deck look over at their table nervously.

"Forgive me, Alexis," John says, lowering his voice. "I'm just concerned. I'd like to find the people responsible for the attacks. They need to be stopped."

She looks up as the waiter delivers her martini, and nods her thanks. Once he's gone, she looks John G. directly in the eyes. "I understand how important this is to you. I'll get on it as soon as I get home tonight." She takes a big sip of her drink. When the waiter walks by again, she orders another martini. John G. has never seen her have two before.

The rest of their meal is quiet without further incident. After she finishes, Alexis stands up before John can suggest dessert. "Thank you for dinner, John. I need to get home to do that research. I'll see you at work tomorrow morning at the usual time. Goodnight."

Before he can say anything more, she turns and walks out of the restaurant. She knows better than to let him see her anger, but she's pissed. How dare he question how she did her job? As she waits for her car, she can't get over John's reaction. She's seen that side of him before, but rarely and it worries her. The valet brings her car around and she distractedly tips him twenty dollars. He stares at the bill in his hand, shrugs as she pulls out just a little too fast, but still in control. Alexis is always in control.

****

John G. leaves the restaurant shortly after Alexis, but neither of them notice the tall, heavy set man, sitting quietly in his car. Using the telephoto lens, he'd watched them all through dinner, taking a few pictures, just as The General had instructed.

He had debated about setting up the sound capturing device. It hadn't looked like they'd said much to each other during dinner, but he sure would have liked to hear the first five minutes of their conversation.

Chapter 20

Murphy goes home after a long day at work to relax with his wife and kids. He had promised to take them to a movie, so they load the kids into the car. He debates about taking out a second mortgage on the house to pay for the evening, but decides to put it on his credit card. When did it go from fifty cents for an afternoon at the movies to costing the same as a car payment?

As much as he tries not to, all he can think about during the movie is the puzzle box. He wonders if his kids had ever seen one. Maybe he'll ask them. Maybe he should look them up on the Internet after Debbie and the kids go to bed tonight. The movie is too short to have cost that much. They head home for dinner. He's just started the barbeque when his cell phone rings. He checks the number - his boss. *Shit.*

"Yes, sir, what can I do for you?" Murphy listens as his boss tells him what had happened at DJ's boat. Not one of the neighboring boat owners noticed any strangers or saw anything. So far, the majority of prints found were Frasier's and Paladin's but also his own.

"Do you mind telling me why your prints were found at a crime scene I just found out about?" says Captain Sprague.
Murphy wonders how much he should tell his boss. "I've been down there talking to Bobby and DJ, trying get more information on the Weaver case. We have some history. We all grew up here together, you know, and I thought if I approached them in a casual atmosphere, they'd be more forthcoming. Too many things have happened since Weaver's death to be a coincidence." Whew. That sounded pretty good.

"Good thing none of your prints were found below deck. If you're such pals, how come you didn't know about the boat being broke into and being torn apart?"

"Well," Murphy stalls for a minute, "I was off duty and I took the kids to the movies. I had my phone turned off and just turned it back on." Murphy had seen that Bobby had called, but he hadn't left him a message, so he'd planned to call him back after dinner.

"You're way behind on your paperwork on this, Murphy," the captain snaps. "I want an update on my desk tomorrow morning, first thing." Without saying goodbye, he hangs up.

Debbie comes out to the patio with a platter of hamburgers and looks at her husband staring at his phone. "Is everything all right, honey?"
Murphy turns to look at his beautiful wife, and pulls himself together. He leans over to kiss her, puts his phone in his pocket and takes the platter from her. "Everything's fine, just some paperwork I need to get to the captain tomorrow morning."

"Was that him? Why is he calling when you're off duty?"

"You know how he is," he turns toward the barbecue and starts putting the burgers on the grill. She wraps her arms around his waist and leans into his back. She gives him a squeeze, then lets go to set the patio table for dinner.

When dinner is finished, Debbie asks the kids if they want to go for ice cream.

"Is it okay if you go without me?" Murphy asks his wife. "I should get started on this report right away. The captain is right; I'm really behind on my paperwork."

"We might hit Costco for ice cream, then. I can grab a few things we need while we're there."

He loves his wife so much. She knows how much he hates Costco and with her and the kids there, he'll have a couple of hours.

After they leave, he cleans up the kitchen, loads the dishwasher and turns it on. He walks into his home office and while he waits for his computer to boot up, he wonders how to keep himself from getting fired. The report he'll have to turn in to the captain is going to be less than truthful, but he just doesn't know who he can trust anymore.

His types in a Google search for Japanese Puzzle Boxes. There are so many sites. How come he has never heard of these things before? Over the next hour he learns that the good puzzle boxes are still hand-made, and the really fancy ones can take well over a hundred moves to open them. How could they even determine how many moves I'll take to open this one? None of the pictures online look even close to the puzzle box Bobby found. On the third Google page, Murphy discovers there's a Japanese Exhibition at the Bowers Museum in Santa Ana. Maybe, just maybe, there's someone there who can help them open the damn thing.

Murphy's fingers stop on the keys. Shit. He doesn't even know if Bobby still has the box. Maybe it was stolen by whoever trashed the boat. He picks up his phone to call Bobby just as he hears the garage door open. He puts down his phone, puts the printouts in his briefcase and heads to the kitchen to help put the kids to bed and have a drink with his wife. Talking to Bobby will have to wait until later.

Chapter 21

I take off and look back quickly to see no one is behind me. I drop in, cranking a huge turn off the bottom of the wave. Racing up the face, I smack the lip hard, pushing my surfboard through, floating along the top, dropping back onto the face of the wave. Cranking another quick turn, I see a sweet tube ride opening up. I crouch down, get covered and am about five feet back as the wave keeps throwing out in front of me. I keep tucked down and after being covered up in the tube for about six seconds, I explode out.

"Woo hoo!" I shriek as I kick out of the wave.

I love Salt Creek: the water is a bright sea-foam green and the winds are blowing in from the east, causing an off-shore effect. The water is the only home right now. I can relax and think. And I have some serious thinking to do I have to figure out what Ricky meant when he told Ray the key to the box was in his head. How could it be in his head if he thought he was going to be killed?

I paddle back out into the lineup, still thinking. It might be time to call in some favors. I'd traveled the world surfing, but while the other surfers went to bars to pick up girls and party after the contests, I'd spent my days in museums and antique shops. I loved looking at art and learning about a country's history. While on a surf trip to Japan, I'd spent an afternoon in the National Museum in Tokyo. One of the tour guides caught my eye that day proving there are better places to meet girls than in bars.

The first time we met, I was taken in by her beauty. She spoke perfect English, as well as Japanese. She told me her father was an American naval pilot and her mother was Japanese. She had grown up in Hawaii and had modeled in Japan for a while. She was smart enough to know that modeling is a tough gig, but her parents didn't have the money to send her to University. We spent time together on that trip to Japan and I fell in love with her. She'd come to watch me compete, but after I returned to the States, I didn't see her for a long time. When I found out I'd qualified for the surf contest in Hawaii, we arranged to meet there.

It was while I was in Hawaii recovering from my wipeout at Pipeline that I found out that she and John G. had begun a relationship. Thinking back, it was hard to blame either of them. She was beautiful and he was rich, but dude – nothing like kicking a guy when he's down. She came to visit me and it was then that she told me he had offered to pay for her education. I found out later she earned her degree in Japanese History, specializing in Japanese myth and religion, but now John G. controlled her. She had an obligation toward him. Once I recovered from the wipeout, I knew she couldn't be mine and his at the same time. All I could see in my mind was them that way: having sex. I couldn't stay and she couldn't leave, and that was that. I hadn't spoken with her in years, but if I could find her, I think she might know someone who could help us open the puzzle box. It would have to be an expert because we'd only get one chance at it.

I turn around, paddle hard and drop into another epic wave, pull up into a deep barrel and ride it almost to the beach. I jump off my board, pick it up and start walking out of the water. I get to the van and find a note flapping on the windshield. It doesn't look like a ticket, thank God.

> *Meet me for breakfast at Adele's at 9 a.m.*
> -   *Murphy.*

I look at my watch. I have just enough time to hit the outdoor shower and pull on my clothes to get to Adele's Restaurant on time. I hope he's buying.

I pull into the parking lot at the same time as Murph. Adele's is located in the former San Clemente Inn, where the press would stay when then-President Richard Nixon was living at the Western White House, located not far away from the Inn at the very south end of town. The San Clemente Inn was converted into timeshares a long time ago. Adele was approached by its owners to move her successful restaurant from downtown to the inn a few years ago. The food is fantastic, and Adele greets everyone like they've been friends their whole lives. Murph and I have known Adele for many moons.

He turns to look at me as we wait to be seated. "Why didn't you call me instead of a patrol car yesterday? I had to hear about DJ's boat from my boss while I was cooking dinner last night," He's obviously pissed.

"I tried, Murph, I really did, but it went straight to your voicemail. I didn't think we could wait. How come you didn't call me last night when you got my message?" I say, equally pissed.

"Debbie and I went took the kids to a movie, then came home and made dinner. I forgot to turn my phone back on because I was having fun with my family." He says. "Then the captain called and wanted to know why my fingerprints were all over the boat."

"Oh. Sorry." How the hell was I supposed to know?

"I heard whoever trashed the boat really did a number on it. Was there anything missing?"

"It's hard to tell, but at first glance we didn't think so. DJ has a security camera set up. It comes on automatically when the hatch door is opened. If you know it's there, you can turn the camera switch off. Yesterday, when the hatch was opened, the camera was disabled right away, but not by the switch. All that the camera recorded was a hand placed over the lens, then nothing. DJ's downloading it to a disk right now. He wants to really have a look at it. I'll get the disc to you later on today."

Before I can answer him what he's really asking - if the puzzle box is safe, Adele spies us from across the restaurant. "Bobby! Dwayne! Give me a hug." She says as she gives each of us a one-armed hug, keeping the coffee pot at a distance. She leaves a bright

117

red smooch mark on both of our cheeks. She stops and holds me at arm's length. "I am so sorry about your house, Bobby. Let me know if I can help you out in any way."

"Thanks, Adele; if I think of anything, I'll let you know."

She leads us to our table, waiving away our server, "Back off, girlie, these two are mine."

As we move through the restaurant, I nod at a few people I know. Adele pours coffee and leaves us menus. "You can look at them if you want, but I'll be back in a minute to tell you what you're having." She sails off to the kitchen.

"I was watching you surf from the bluff. You must be feeling better because you looked good out there." Murph says as he sips his coffee.

I stir my coffee and say, "Yeah, it was good to be in the water, no matter what Dr. Gus says. It gave me some time to think."

Adele comes back and tells us we're both having today's special: Hueves Rancheros with hash browns. I can already feel my arteries starting to close. I was going to have oatmeal, but there's just no arguing with Adele.

"Think about what? Murph asks after she leaves. "Do we have a problem? Do we still have a box?"

"Don't worry. I have it hidden where no one will find it. I think it should stay hidden until we can get someone to help us open it." His shoulders drop in relief, as he sits back and relaxes a bit. "Have you thought about how we get it open? The captain is all over me."

"Well, I've been thinking I should call Jeannie Franks, an old girlfriend. She's the only person I know who might be able to help us."

"Who is she? Can she be trusted?"

"Jeannie's a woman I met in Japan," I explain. "She has a degree in Japanese myth and religion. Last I heard she was working for a museum, so she should have connections. She might know of someone who can help us find a way to open it. I'll try to call her when I get home."

Murph looks at me. "Home, Bobby? Where is that exactly these days?"

"Right. I almost forgot for a second. Do you think they'll let me stay on the boat yet?" He shakes his head. "I guess I'll have to hang out at DJ's house."

Murph sets down his cup and continues, "I've been doing some research on my own and there's a Japanese artifacts exhibit at the Bowers Museum in Santa Ana. I was thinking we should meet up there later this afternoon and see if someone there can point us in the right direction."

"That's a great idea. We'll have to tell them we bought a novelty item and we don't have the directions to open it, or something like that."

"First I have to go into the office and fill out a bunch of paperwork that the captain wants on his desk today." Murphy says.

"What are you going to tell your boss?"

"I'm going to try to spin a good story and hope we can figure this out before I get fired for lying to the captain."

We stop talking as Adele comes over with two huge platters of food.

"What are you two troublemakers up to anyway? Sitting over here, being all quiet and secretive?" She sets our plates in front of us. They smell fantastic.

"You know us, Adele, always up to no good." Murphy says, shaking his napkin out onto his lap.

"Well, enjoy being up to no good. I always do." She says with a smile as she sails off to another table. Her feet must ache by the end of the day, but she always seems to be having so much fun.

"What time should we try to meet up?" I ask as I talk around my first bite of food. I close my eyes. There is nothing like an amazing breakfast after a great morning of surfing.

"I'll call you when I'm getting ready to leave the office. Bring the box with you but keep it out of sight. We don't want anyone to know we've found this thing."

I have to out wait Murphy, but he finally reaches for his wallet and pays for our meals. We wave at Adele as we leave the restaurant and she blows us a kiss. Murph gets into his car and rolls down the window. "This is only going to get worse," he warns me. "So make sure you're carrying at all times, okay?"

"Gotcha, Murph. See you later." Crap. I hate carrying my gun.

****

Across the parking lot on the far side of the oleander hedge, sitting in his car, he watches them leave the restaurant. He checks the car's computer monitor to activate the tracking device he placed on Bobby's van while they were inside the restaurant. It's working perfectly. This should make it pretty easy to keep an eye on all of them.

****

After leaving Adele's, I drive to DJ's house and let myself in through the garage door.

DJ yells down, "Bobby, is that you?"

"Yeah, it's me."

"Come on up. I'm in the office."

I set my keys on the kitchen counter and run up the stairs, two at a time, to find DJ sitting at his desk in his home office, going through some paperwork. "How was the surf?" he asks as he leans over and lights a cigarette. You can sure tell Maria is out of town. She's going to kill him for smoking in the house. No matter how much he cleans up, she'll be able to tell. Women can always tell.

"The surf was good, and after that I had breakfast with Murph at Adele's. He found out there's an exhibit of Japanese artifacts opening at the Bowers Museum. We're driving up there later today to see if they have anyone on their staff might be able help us open the box."

"The box! With the boat and all, it just totally slipped my mind. Where was it? Don't tell me it was on the boat."

"No, it's safe," I don't want to worry him anymore than that.

"Have you tried to open it yet?" DJ asks.

"Not yet. I've been tempted, but I keep thinking about what Ricky said, and I don't want to mess up what's inside. I think I'm going to try to call Jeannie Franks. You remember her, don't you?"

121

"You bet I do. Are you sure? You guys didn't part on the best of terms." He blows smoke out the open window.

"I know, but that was years ago."

"She was pretty pissed when you left Hawaii and you didn't even say goodbye."

"I was just thinking she might know somebody in L.A., San Diego or maybe even San Francisco who can help us open it." I'm trying not to think about the last time I saw Jeannie.

"Yeah," he says, "I wonder how much of a bruise the box will leave when she throws it at you."

"If we can't open it or we destroy the evidence inside the box, we're screwed. Once we explain that to her, she'll be cool." I think I've almost convinced myself.

"You're a brave man. Okay, give her a call and let's see if she can help us."

"Uh oh. This may not be as easy as I think, anyway. I had all of her information at my house. I'll have to find another way to contact her."

"Google, dude."

I kiss the top of his head, "My hero!" I jump back as he takes a swipe at me.
"You asshole," he says as he wipes at his hair.

DJ hits a few keys and I we see Jeannie's name pop up as curator of Asian Artifacts at the Honolulu Museum of Art.

I pick up my cell phone and dial her office number. After a few rings, it goes to voicemail. Hearing her voice makes my heart lurch a little. I hesitate and wonder: if I leave a message, will she call me back? Or is she still mad at me for leaving her in Hawaii all those years ago? I decide to leave the message anyway. "Jeannie, this is Bobby Paladin. I hope you're doing well. I know, I know it's been a long time. Would you please call me when you get this message? I really need to talk to you." I leave my number and pause before adding, "Please, it's important Jeannie, Aloha."

DJ snaps me out of my daydream. "I want to go to the Bowers Museum with you."

"Sure. Why not? Murph is going to call me when he's finished at work. He's at the office spinning some story to get his captain off his ass."

****

While DJ and Bobby are inside the house, Alexis keeps an eye on them from a discrete distance. She moves around DJ's neighborhood, not staying in one place too long to avoid being noticed. Prior to leaving Laguna Beach, she placed a small, magnetic realtor sign on each door of her car. The signs have a fake name and a phone number that goes straight to an answering service. She arrives at DJ's house just after Bobby pulled his van into the driveway.
John G. had called her that morning to stress that if she had to make a choice between following Bobby or DJ, she was to stick with Bobby. In a few hours he wanted her back in the office. She knows he wants to know who it was she'd seen following them, but hadn't come to her yet. She's sure it will. She just hopes she remembers before it's too late.

She's been keeping an eye on a cable truck moving around the neighborhood. No one ever gets out of the truck. She tries to get pictures of the truck driver, but it's impossible to do without him noticing her. She wonders if the man was trying to do the same thing to her. She decides to place a call to John G. "I think the

123

person from yesterday is staked out on DJ's street in a cable van. I'll keep you posted. I just wanted you to know."

After she hangs up, she drops that phone on the seat, opens her purse and takes out another cell phone. She presses a pre-programmed number. "Sir, we have a situation. There appears to be another party interested in Bobby Paladin and DJ Frasier. I managed to get a picture of him but not a full frontal shot. He has a beard that may or may not be a fake. I'll upload the photo to you and try to get a better one. Will you see if Intel can come up with a name? I think it's the same guy that I saw down at the harbor, but I'm not sure." She pauses to listen, "Yes sir, I'll update you as soon as I know more."

Alexis hangs up the encrypted satellite phone and uploads the information. She hopes the Facial Recognition software is good enough to pull something out of the bad photo. She has to assume the guy in the cable truck is the same one from the harbor yesterday.

She stays in the neighborhood for a while longer, walking through the streets with papers in her hand, trying to look like she's handing out flyers. She decides that DJ and Bobby look like they're staying put for the day, so she leaves for Laguna. She doesn't want to be late for her meeting with John, especially with the mood he's been in these last couple of days. The cable truck was still there, but, to paraphrase Freud: sometimes a cable truck is just a cable truck. She sure hopes so.

****

The driver of the cable company van notices the realtor's Toyota. There are no houses for sale in this neighborhood that he knows of, so he's suspicious. He'll run the plates as soon as he has a chance. He has to stay too far away to get a good look at her. He watches her putting fliers in doors, so maybe she's just trying to drum up business. He doesn't like that she's hung around for so long, and feels better once she's gone.

He watches as Paladin and Frasier come out of the house and get into the van. With the tracking device on the van, he can follow at a safe distance. A cable truck is great cover; he can go anywhere in it and nobody's curious.

****

After driving for the last forty five minutes listening to DJ talk about work, we exit the freeway in Santa Ana. Another 10 minutes down Main Street and we pull into the parking lot of the Bowers Museum. DJ and I climb out of the van as we watch a cable service truck pull up to the kiosk to pay for parking.

"What's a cable van doing at the Bowers?" I ask as we walk to the front of the museum.
"Maybe the museum has cable problems like everyone else. I wonder if they have to wait the whole day like the rest of us." DJ says.

"Or maybe the cable guy is a culture buff after watching hours of PBS on company time." I open the door for an elderly couple entering the lobby. DJ follows them in and the door closes behind us.

****

He parks the cable truck on the far side of the parking lot. He knows it would have been smarter to have switched vehicles, but there just wasn't time. A cable truck is great for surveillance in a neighborhood, but he hopes it won't draw attention here at the museum. To be on the safe side, he plans to change out of his cable uniform in the bathroom inside the museum. Before getting out of the truck, he puts an Anaheim Angels ball cap, shorts, Rainbow sandals and pair sunglasses into a fake tool bag. He gets out of the

125

truck holding the bag, and a clipboard so he looks the part of a cable guy until he gets into the building. He's worked hard to hide the limp from an old gunshot injury, but it's difficult when he's been sitting for too long. He follows at a distance and watches as they walk up to the Museum box-office.

He follows Bobby and DJ into the museum, noticing Paladin carrying a backpack down at his side. He hangs back a bit as they enter the Japanese Exhibit Room and are swallowed up in the crowd. He walks to the empty men's room, slips into a stall and changes into his new disguise. He lifts the trash bag out of the garbage can and puts the tool bag and clip board in the bottom, before replacing the trash bag.

****

There's really not a lot we can do, other than explore the museum, until Murph gets here. Then we can make some discrete inquiries for assistance in opening the puzzle box. I love this stuff, but it's not DJ's thing and he gets antsy pretty fast. I have to stop him before he tries to hit the gigantic drum hanging on a stand outside one of the rooms. I think I know now why I didn't have children. We enter the Japanese Exhibit. Today's the first day and it's pretty crowded. DJ puts his hand on my arm and stops me.

"Bobby," he says. "Is that who I think it is? Doesn't that look like Jeannie standing over there?" He's pointing toward a group of people.

"Dude, you're hallucinating. There is no way that's Jeannie. She's in Hawaii." I pause and say slowly, "I think."

I stare in the direction DJ is pointing. The woman in the middle of a group of people looks like an elegant tour guide. She seems to be explaining things to the group, first in Japanese and then in English. She turns around slowly, nodding, smiling and answering questions. I don't know if she can feel us staring at her, but eventually she looks across the room and our eyes meet. She stops talking, quickly puts a hand to her mouth and stares back at me. She looks exactly the same as she did in that museum in Japan the first time I saw her all those years ago. She bows and says something to the group, excusing herself, and starts walking hurriedly towards where we are standing.

"Bobby Paladin is that really you?" she asks, her eyes wide.

I can't seem to say or do anything but stare. I'd forgotten how truly beautiful she was. Finally, DJ elbows me and says, "See? I told you that was her! Jeannie, what are you doing here? Bobby and I were just talking about you this morning." He gives her a big hug.

"You mean you didn't know I was the curator of this exhibit? I assumed that was why you were here, to say hello," she says as she stares at us. "The publicity department released my name in conjunction with the exhibit, and here you are."

I'm still confused by the fact that she's standing right here, in front of me, but finally I find my voice. "We didn't know that you were even in California. We went on the Internet to find out some information about a Japanese artifact, and we saw that there was going to be a large exhibit here at the Bowers. We decided we'd drive up here to try to find someone to answer some questions – about what we found – you know, something that was made in Japan." Crap. I'm a blathering idiot.

She smiles, "Look, guys, this is the first day of a major show here. This is the first time many of these artifacts have been seen outside of Japan, and it's the biggest show I've ever put together. I have to finish up with the VIPs from the museum, and deal with the press, but I'll only be about an hour, hour and a half at the most. Then maybe we can grab something to eat and I can look at whatever it is you have. I promise I won't be longer than an hour and a half. Can you wait that long?" She says all this while never taking her eyes from mine.

I finally tear myself away to look at DJ. "Is that okay with you? Murph won't be here much before then, anyway. We can check out the exhibits while Jeannie takes care of business." I turn back to look into her violet eyes.

"Sure," he says, "Maybe you can teach me something new while we wait. Something that'll impress the kids." He turns to Jeannie, "Anything on Ninjas here?"

She laughs and shakes her head as I give her my cell phone number so she can text me when her meeting is finished. She leans into me and kisses me on the cheek. Is it my imagination or did she let her lips linger on my cheek a little long? She hurries away, quickly rejoining her group. I stare after her.

"Earth to Bobby." DJ says.

"I can't believe this just happened," I say.

"Yeah, apparently she's not mad at you anymore. C'mon. Stop staring at her and help me get some culture. How smart can I get in an hour?" He turns me toward a kimono framed behind Plexiglas.

****

He walks around the museum, pausing at different exhibits, blending in with the crowd. Nothing here he'd want in his living room, that's for sure. Just a bunch of dusty old crap somebody should have thrown away years ago. He watches as the beautiful Asian woman crosses the room to greet Paladin and Frasier. She looks like she must work here or something. Is that a coincidence or is she involved in this thing somehow? She sure is a looker.

Maybe this was where the answer would be found. If this works out, he can retire to an island in the sun. Hell, he can buy one, that's how bad The General wants the information Rick Weaver had stolen.

The lady rejoins her group, and Paladin and Frasier turn to look at a ratty old bathrobe behind a glass case.

Chapter 22

Jeannie takes a little more than the hour and a half to complete her business; but finally, just when I think DJ is going to fall asleep on one of the museum benches, she texts us to meet her in her office. As we're about to ask the security guard for directions, Murphy walks in the door.

"Murph! Over here!" DJ yells and is immediately shushed by a matronly patron. She looks as old as some of the museum pieces. We apologize to her for being loud as we head across the lobby to meet Murphy.

"You're never going to believe our luck, Murph!" I tell him, "Jeannie Franks, she's here! She's in charge of this exhibit."

He looks at me, opens his mouth to say something but just stares over my shoulder down the hall. I turn to see what he's looking at. I turn to see Jeannie walking up the hall toward us. She smiles and hugs me. I know this one is real this time. She steps back and turns to Murph. "I don't believe we've met." She looks to me for help.

"Allow me," I say. "Dwayne Murphy, may I introduce you to Jeannie Franks, the Exhibits Director and expert in Japanese myth and religion. Jeannie, this is Detective Dwayne Murphy, a friend of ours from San Clemente."

She shakes his hand, "Detective?"

"Murph is an Orange County Sherriff's homicide detective." I lower my voice. "Is there somewhere we can talk in private? We need some help with something in your area of expertise."

Her eyes search my face and finally she says, "Sure, Bobby. My office is this way." She slips her arm through mine. She leads us to a door marked Staff Only, lifts the key card from around her neck and slides it through the lock. The door releases and she holds it

131

open for us to enter a long hallway. We hear the whirr of the lock as the door closes behind us. Jeannie leads us to her office, located at the very end of the hall.

****

He watches from behind a program as Murphy, Paladin, and Frasier are led into the administrative wing of the museum by the woman. There's nothing he can do now. He can't get in there without a key card. Do they have the puzzle box or not? He must now assume they do.

He'd like to leave, but he knows he should be patient and wait for the group to come back out. He pulls out his Blackberry and accesses the museum building's floor layout. He sees a security door with the access to the staff areas. On the other side of the offices, he sees a door that leads out of the building and directly to the parking lot. A staff entrance he guesses. Even if they leave the building without coming back through the main part of the museum, he'd still be able to track Paladin's van. Should he wait? He'd like to see if they come back out with the backpack. He really wanted to just grab it and run, but there was too much security here. He wanders back into the exhibit room to wait, and to think about his next move. He'll probably wait by the staff entrance and if the opportunity presents itself he's going to go for the backpack.

****

Jeannie leads us into a large office. "Welcome to my home for the next three months." She walks around the far side of the desk and sits in her office chair. "Pull up some chairs and make yourselves comfortable."
We spend a little time catching up, but finally Jeannie asks, "Now, what is all this about? Why all the mystery?"

I don't want to go into too much detail. The less she knows, the safer she'll be. I tell her about Ricky's death and that we have something of we need her help opening. When I'm done, I pull the puzzle box out of my backpack and its water-tight container, and set the box on her desk.

She gasps and carefully picks it up. "Remarkable," she says as she turns it to look at all sides, "A beautiful piece. Japanese, of course, but you knew that. I'm not a true expert on these, but I've seen a few of them." She gets up and opens a box that is sitting on the floor. It's full of heavy-looking books. She lifts one out and after a few minutes of thumbing through it, she finds what she's looking for and sits back in her chair, spreading the book open on her desk. "My guess, from the looks of it, is that it's a Hakone Himitsu-Bako. It appears to be from the Meiji period. As I say, I'm not an expert on these, but they're made by a master puzzle box maker."

"That's a job?" D.J says, "You can be a master at making boxes for people to hide stuff in?"

She looks up from the book, "Not just anybody, DJ, royalty. When you run an empire, you have all kinds of secrets. These boxes were how the Emperor sent out messages or orders, the things they wanted to be kept secret."

"Can you open it, without destroying any of the contents that are inside the box?" I ask.

"No, I can't. That isn't to say that no one can open it, but I can't. These puzzle boxes are unique that way. This one looks like it will take a lot of moves to open," she says while gently turning the box to look at all sides.

"Ricky said that this one might explode," says Murph, grimly. Jeannie sets the box down quickly, but gently. "I've read about that happening in ancient times if they weren't opened correctly, but I doubt that would happen today," she says. "Most likely there are different powders inside that, when mixed together, would destroy the contents of the box. Please tell me that you have the codex to open it."

"The whatex?" asks DJ.

"Codex, it shows you the exact moves you need to make to open the box," she explains.

"No, but we're trying to find it." I say. "That's why we came here, to see if there was an expert at the museum who might know how to open it. I called you in Hawaii too, and left a message on your work phone. It's just a weird coincidence that you happened to be working here."

"Well, there is no way to open this box until you find the codex. Until that time, I suggest keeping it in a safe place."

"So you don't know anyone who can open it?" Murph asks Jeannie.

"No, sorry, I don't. This particular type of box could have over one hundred and sixty-six moves that need to be made in the exact order to safely open it. Do you have any idea what's inside?"

"We think its papers. Important papers" Murph says.

"Pretty important papers, I'd say, if someone went to this much trouble." Jeannie says. "If not done it the exact sequence you will destroy everything inside, and the box itself. In ancient times these were like a modern-day bank vault. Even if you brought me the codex, I might be able to open this box, but it would be iffy at best. Ricky was very smart to put whatever it is that's in there because it's perfectly safe. I'm so sorry I can't help you. I don't know anybody on this side of the Pacific who can."
"What if we tried drilling into it?" DJ asks her. "Do you think that would work?"

"It would trigger the device, mixing the chemicals together, and destroy everything inside. It's a secure system." Jeannie answers, "You just can't tamper with these things without messing up the contents."

Murphy stands up and says, "Bobby, I really have to get back to work. Walk me to my car, okay? Then you can come back and finish up here. It's been nice meeting you, Jeannie," He extends his hand towards her and she stands and shakes it.

As we get to the parking lot, Murph turns to me and says, "You need to get this figured out and quickly, Bobby, before this thing blows up in my face. I just turned in the paperwork that the captain asked for. Withholding major evidence is a crime, and falsifying reports could cost me my badge, and my pension. So get on it. Fast. She has to know someone who can help us figure this thing out. And we need to find the other clue." I nod at him and turn back toward the museum.

"Well," I say to Jeannie and DJ as the guard lets me back into her office. "It looks like we're back to square one."

"Nobody ever solved anything on an empty stomach," DJ says. "Who's hungry?"

"I am," Jeannie says, her eyes bright, "but I still have a little work to do here. I can be done in a half hour."

"Okay, let's go San Clemente and have dinner at Iva Lee's. How's that sound?" DJ says.

"Sounds like fun to me." Jeannie smiles. "Bobby, will you be able to drive with me? I don't know the way."

"Sure," I say, "looking at DJ. "Do you mind driving the van back to San Clemente? That way I can wait for Jeannie to finish, and

135

make sure she doesn't get lost. We'll meet up with you at Iva Lees in a bit, okay?"

"Sounds like a plan." DJ says, and I toss him the keys. He heads out to the parking lot and I walk back into the museum to look around some more while I wait for Jeannie to finish her work. I stand in front of the drum, thinking about how crazy life is.

****

"So, Bobby Paladin, we have a lot of catching up to do." Jeannie says as she turns onto the southbound 5 Freeway on-ramp forty-five minutes later. "Tell me what you've been up to since you ditched me in Hawaii."

"Is it okay if we don't talk about that right now?" I say. "I'm just so happy to see you again. Can we start fresh?" She smiles as she checks her driver-side mirror and merges into traffic. "You're right. I'm sorry. I'm glad to see you, too," She says, keeping her eyes straight ahead. "I don't know how you people over here on da mainland deal with all of dis traffic. I thought da traffic on Oahu was bad," she says tossing in a little pidgin.

I laugh and start to catch her up, not knowing how much detail to go into. I don't want to talk about Ricky anymore, so I tell her a bit about my time on the LAPD. However, I get the distinct feeling that she knows all about my leaving the police department. I don't want to spend too much time on that either, so I tell her that I'm now working for DJ, and about his family. "Sounds pretty dull when I say all this out loud," I say, "but I'm doing fine and I like the work." I'm just about to change the subject over to her when my cell phone rings. It's DJ.
"What's up, bro?" I ask him.

"I'm just calling to let you know I'm going to head home and let you two have a nice, romantic evening together. Who knows? You might even get lucky tonight. You could sure use it. Make up a believable excuse for me," he says with a laugh and hangs up.

I glance over at Jeannie, afraid she may have heard him—he's always been really loud—but she's just looking straight ahead, paying attention to the early evening traffic.

"Oh," I say into the dead phone, "Sure. I understand. You've had a rough couple of days. Go on home and get some rest. We'll catch up with you another time. I'll tell Jeannie. Later." I put my phone in my pocket and turn to Jeannie. "DJ says he's tired and is just going to go home to rest. It looks like it's just you and me for dinner."

"Why are you grinning like you just won the lottery, Bobby Paladin?" she says with a laugh. "This sounds like a setup to me. But, I really am looking forward to having dinner with just you, but don't think I'm that kind of girl."

"You're going to love this restaurant, Jeannie." I say, changing the subject, "The owners are good friends of mine and the food is amazing."

We spend the next half an hour chatting and before we know it, we're in San Clemente.

I direct her into Iva Lee's parking lot and we walk into the restaurant. Lisa is at her usual spot at the hostess station, and her husband, Eric, is behind the bar. They opened this upscale Cajun style restaurant ten years ago, in a town that was desperate for more good places to eat. The original Iva Lee was Lisa's grandmother and pictures of her grace the restaurant. It's become a huge success in San Clemente, mostly because of their hard work and dedication to their customers. Great music and service haven't hurt, either.

"Bobby! It's good to see you. Where have you been keeping yourself?" Lisa gives me a quick hug.

"Lisa, I'd like you to meet a dear friend, Jeannie." Lisa gives Jeannie an approving look.

"Jeannie, it's nice to meet you," Lisa says with a warm smile, and they shake hands.

"I'd stay away from that guy if I were you," Eric calls from behind the bar. "He's been in a lot of trouble lately." I catch his eye over Jeannie's head and give my own head a quick shake. He picks up on my signal. We cross over to the bar. "Jeannie Franks, this is my good friend Eric Wagner." He shakes her hand and then smiles at me.

"It's a pleasure to meet you, Jeannie, how do you two know each other?" he asks. "It's not like Bobby brings many dates in here."

"We go way back, Eric. We actually met in a museum when Bobby was in Japan for a surf contest," she gives me a fond look. Bonus!

"You have a beautiful restaurant. It feels so comfortable and intimate." She looks around, taking in the tin ceiling, copper bar and deep, banquette seating in the back.

"Thank you. We've worked hard." He turns to look at me. "Would you like to eat at the bar, Bobby, or would you like a table?"

"If you could find a table for us, Eric, that would be great." I say.

"Just give me a minute. Grab a seat at the bar and have a drink while I find out what's available." He signals to Lisa and she checks the reservation book and says something to one of the servers.

I find two open stools, and we each order a glass of wine. The musicians are just starting to set up in a corner of the lounge. Suddenly, I can't think of a thing to say to her. I can't believe how nervous I am. I guess when I thought DJ was going to be our buffer I hadn't let myself think about how much I'd missed her. We sit there for a few moments, just smiling and looking away, like two teenagers out on their first date.

"Excuse me, Bobby," says Lisa. Thank God. I was on the verge of making a fool of myself. "I have a table all ready for you out on the patio. We're not super busy tonight so I set you up out there for some privacy." She gives us a knowing smile and turns to lead us through the dining room and out on to the patio. She seats us a table with a view of San Clemente's main street, El Camino Real. There must be a classic car show in town this weekend. We watch as an old woody and a bright red '67 Chevy Corvette drive down the street.

"Thanks, Lisa," I say as we sit down, and she hands us menus. She lights the candle on the table and says, "The first two are on the house." She nods at our wine glasses. "Michelle will be right out to tell you about tonight's specials."

"This place is so beautiful." Jeannie says. I'm relieved she's starting the conversation. I'm trying not to gulp my wine to calm myself. "I was thinking back to when we first met in Japan" she says, "We had a quiet dinner at that little restaurant by the museum. It was so long ago." She sips her wine.

I start to say something but she interrupts me, "I couldn't believe that it was you standing right there in the museum today. I felt like it was just yesterday that I'd last seen you, not nearly ten years. I'm still in shock." She reaches over and lightly strokes my hand.

Suddenly, Michelle is beside our table. Crap. Things were just starting to get interesting. I stand up and give her a quick hug.

"Michelle, this is my friend Jeannie from Hawaii." Michelle is working on her nursing degree, raising a precocious four-year-old, and working at Iva Lee's part-time. I don't know how she does it. Her husband and she make a pretty good team, but they both work really hard. Michelle tells us about the specials and we tell her we need a few more minutes to decide. She offers to bring us wine refills and hurries back into the restaurant.

I pick up our thread of the conversation from where it was before Michelle appeared. "It was a long time ago, Jeannie. So much has changed in my life since the Pipe Masters wipeout." I'm not as nervous now—probably because of the wine—and we settle in to comfortable conversation. Our dinners are brought to the table, along with another glass of wine. As we eat, talk and sip wine, we tell each other the high and low points of our lives.

After a while Eric stops by our table. "How is everything?" We nod our appreciation, mouths full of the bananas foster we're sharing. "Jeannie, I hope you're in town for a few days."

"I'm working at the Bowers Museum for the next three months, Eric, so I hope to get back here again. The food is amazing."

"I hope so, too. Bobby needs to be seen with someone respectable for a change." He smiles and pats my shoulder as a customer waves him over and off he goes.

"Nice guy," she says.

"Yeah, he and Lisa have worked very hard, but it's sure paid off," I say. "What do you say to a nightcap at the Red Fox? We can leave the car here and walk over. It's only a few blocks." Jeannie nods and we get up from the table. I leave a tip for Michelle and we head out the door and into the warm evening. Jeannie takes my arm as we stroll down El Camino Real.

"Bobby, do you ever think about us?" She says playfully. "What might have happened if you had stayed in Hawaii?"

"Sometimes. I guess I feel like I was such an ass that I try to put it out of my mind. I was such a kid back then. I didn't think about how much I could have hurt you." She squeezes my arm and we make the rest of the walk in silence. I open the door for her, and we make our way into the Red Fox and find two seats at the end of the bar.

"Is this your local haunt?" she asks.

"DJ and I usually end up here a couple times a week. It's a real local bar, but they have great lunches."

Ray comes down the bar toward us. I introduce her and order a glass of wine for myself and start to order one for Jeannie when she says, "Just water for me, thanks, I still have to drive back to Santa Ana."

When Ray comes back with my wine and her water, Jeannie excuses herself to use the ladies room. I take this opportunity to ask, "Ray, are you sure that Ricky said the answer to his problem was all in his head?"

"I don't know, Bobby. He was pretty drunk. He was just mumbling, not talking to anyone in particular, but I think he said the answer to his problem was in his head. I think his exact words were something like: 'it's all in the head.' I don't know. He got up and left right after he said it. That's all I remember. Sorry." A couple of young girls in very high heels and very short skirts come in, and Ray heads down the bar to take their drink orders; and hopefully to check their IDs.
When Jeannie comes back I introduce her to a few friends who stop by to say hello. We finish our drinks and I say, "Let's walk down Del Mar before we drive back to the harbor. We can window shop."

141

"That sounds lovely. It's such a beautiful night."

"Great. Let me just use the bathroom."

I keep thinking about what Ray said about Ricky, *it's in his head; it's in the head.* Suddenly, I feel like I've been hit by lightning. How could I have been so stupid? Ricky loved to party. He'd often hide his party goods so that if he was ever searched by the cops, he wouldn't be holding. I remember he once told me he had hollowed out a niche for his stash in a spot behind a tile a men's room. A bathroom is a head to a sailor. I step over to the sink area and check there first. No loose tiles. I start to look around the toilet area, but I don't have much time before someone starts pounding on the door.

"Hurry up, pal. A guy's got to go," I hear through the door.

"Sorry, bro," I mumble, as he pushes past me into the bathroom.

I walk back to the bar and over to Jeannie. "I think that I know where Ricky hid the codex for the box," I take her hand and lead her out of the lounge.

"Where?"

"I'm not sure yet. I'll let you know when I find it," I'm not positive I can trust her yet, and besides, I don't want to get her in too deep.

We walk over to Avenida Del Mar holding hands like teenagers. Jeannie turns to me, stopping us on the sidewalk, leans in and kisses me. "Santa Ana is such a long drive."
It takes me a minute to recover my voice. "Well, ah—I've been staying on DJ's boat in the harbor. That's not nearly as far." I smile and kiss her back. I hope the boat's not too much of a mess.

"The boat sounds romantic," she says, to my great relief. We walk back to the car with our arms around each other. If we were in a cartoon, little hearts would be floating above our heads.

****

He had lost them at the museum and had been hanging around Frasier's house. Frasier came back alone in Paladin's van. What the hell happened to Paladin? He hadn't come back to the house. This should have been so easy. He had better find Paladin and The General's paperwork, but fast. Instead of buying an island, he could find himself buried under one.

Chapter 23

Jeannie and I are suddenly awakened by pounding on the salon door.

"Hey you guys, wake up! C'mon, rise and shine. I have fresh coffee," DJ yells through the closed door.

We get up, throw on last night's clothes, and try to smooth each other's bed head before opening the door. We find DJ sitting with a cardboard tray of paper coffee cups and a pink bakery box set out on the cockpit seats.

"Bobby, you look like shit," he says with a grin, "but Jeannie, you look fantastic."

"Coffee, how nice," Jeannie says, smiling and blushing. "Thank you, DJ."

"Yeah, thanks." Three coffees. Smug bastard. I hope Jeannie doesn't think I planned this with him. I may have to kick his ass later. "What brings you down here so early?"

"You know me. I'm an early riser." He is having way too much fun.
Time to change the subject. "Remember how Ricky never liked to have his stash on him? Well, told me once he'd stuck it behind a tile in the men's room at the Red Fox Lounge. The secret isn't in *his* head; it's in *the* head."

DJ smacks himself on the forehead, "Of course! Why didn't we think of that before?"

"I'll head down there later on when the bar is slow and try to find his hiding spot. Maybe we'll find the answer to opening the box." I help myself to a donut.

Jeannie shakes her head when I offer her one. "I'd like nothing better than to stay here all day, but I have to go home and get changed. I can't very well go into work in the same clothes I had on yesterday." She blushes again. She picks up her purse and kisses me goodbye. DJ helps her off the boat and she heads up the dock.

"Hey, wait! I'll walk you to your car," I say. I vault over the side of the boat and run up the ramp to the gate. "Where are you staying?"

She turns around and smiles at me, "I'm staying at a friend's house in Cameo Shores in Corona Del Mar. Call me if you find the codex. Or, call me even if you don't." She looks over my shoulder to see if DJ can still see us before she gives me a long, passionate kiss.

****

He's sitting on a bench overlooking the sailboat. When the woman gets up to leave, Paladin follows her to her car. They kiss. Interesting. Then she gets into her car alone and drives out of the marina. He has to make a decision. Follow her or stay here? He starts his car and pulls out after the woman. He has the tracking device on Paladin's car, so he can monitor them from his computer. The woman, though, is new. He'd better figure out if she's important or just a one-nighter.

She drives up Coast Highway, through Dana Point, Monarch Beach and into Laguna Beach. He follows, but not too closely, and watches as she pulls into the turn lane and making a U-Turn. Has she spotted him? He can see her in his rear view mirror as she heads up into the hills. He can't make the same maneuver in this early morning traffic without raising suspicion. When he can, he turns around and heads back up the street. He sees her just in time to watch the gate close behind her car. She's pulled into to John Gomez' property. What the hell is going on? He finds a spot across the street from the house and parks his car. In this area of exclusive houses, he won't remain unnoticed for long. The phone next to him starts to beep.

"Yes, General. No, sir. I've been following a female friend of Paladin's. I'm not sure if she's just a girlfriend, but I thought I'd better follow her just in case. Sir, she just pulled into John Gomez' house. Yes, sir. I'm aware of that, sir. Thank you, sir. I will."

He stares at the phone after the call is disconnected. The General just offered him another million dollars to find the container and the papers Weaver had stolen. He knows he has to find it before they're able to open the container. The General had just explained, in great detail, what would happen to him if he failed. Plus now he was supposed to follow and report on this new chick's activities, too? Shit, shit, shit! Every day this money was getting harder to earn.

****

DJ and I head into San Clemente to get breakfast and look for Ricky's hiding spot. Coast highway is deserted this morning. Across the highway, the surf was running about five foot, clean and glassy. It's killing me not to be out there, but we've got more important things to do.

He nods and says. "Then we can stop by the T-Street job and make sure everything's ready to start work again on Monday."

We head into San Clemente along Coast highway which is deserted this morning. Across the highway, the surf is running about five foot, clean and glassy. It's killing me not to be out there.

"So," DJ says, giving me a sideways glance, "You guys looked pretty comfortable this morning."
"I know. It's been so long, but it was like we'd never been apart."

147

"What really happened between you two, Bobby? You never told me why your relationship didn't work out."

"Well," I sigh, "after eating shit at the pipe contest, John G. asked me if I wanted to recuperate at his guest house. He said I could stay as long as I liked. Jeannie had come over from Japan and John G. gave her a job as an aide. She and I just connected. We'd go for long walks, hang out on the beach and talk. She was the one who got me to go back into the water. She helped heal my spirit and I fell in love with her. I thought it was mutual. Then one day after surfing, I headed up to the main house and saw John G. and Jeannie together. I was crushed. They didn't see me and I never told either of them. I went back to the guesthouse, packed my bags, grabbed a bus to the airport and flew into LAX. You know the rest."

"That sucks, dude."

"I don't think I ever really got over her. Spending last night together was magic."

"Are you going to tell her you saw them sleeping together?"

"I don't know," I say, staring out at the ocean as we drive along coast highway.

We pull into the Red Fox parking lot and walk into the bar. It's packed. *Shit.* Word must have gotten out about the food here. The RFL is owned by the same people who own Antoine's next door. The breakfast is amazing and there's almost always a wait. The insiders know you can order the same breakfast at the RFL because both places share the kitchen and chef.

"Grab us a couple of stools at the bar. I'm going to hit the head," I say.

I push open the door the bathroom and it's empty. I lock the door and stand there looking around. Ricky's hiding place would have to be quick and easy to get to. I hear a knocking on the on the door already. Shit. Coffee must be worse than beer. I'll never get this bathroom to myself. I flush the toilet and excuse myself past the guy waiting outside, and walk over to sit next to DJ.

"No luck, yet, but I know it's in there. I'll go and search some more when it opens up."

"Ray's going to think you have a problem. Let's order some food, I'm starving."

We order breakfast. The bar is going off. We're sitting in the middle of a party.

"What's going on, Ray?" I ask.

"It's Sherry's birthday today," he answers. "It's going to be crazy in here all day. You know the day crowd: any reason to eat, drink and be merry."

He sets down two free drink tokens in front of everyone at the bar. "Drinks are on the house, everybody, courtesy of the best owner ever, Antoine!" The bar erupts in cheers. I see the bathroom is empty, so I get up and go back to have another look. Again, after a few minutes, someone is banging on the door to use the bathroom. Shit, at this rate I'll never find the hiding spot.

I sit down next to DJ again and say, "Hey, when we're done with our food let's get out of here. There are too many people. I'll come back tonight, before the night crowd gets going."

"Sure, Bobby."
I wave away the beer Ray offers me. I think I'd better stick with coffee, but DJ thanks him for his. "After we're done with

breakfast, can we stop by my house?" I ask him. "I need to check the garage and pick up my mail."

He nods as he takes a sip of his beer and says. "Then we can stop by the T-Street job and make sure everything's ready to start work again on Monday."

****

The woman's in John G.'s house for about forty five minutes. That gives him time to find out that the car, a Lexis ES5, is leased to Jean Marie Francis of Haleiwa, Hawaii, and is being paid for by The Rigdel Corporation. He's betting the Rigdel Corporation is owned by one John Gomez.

After she comes out of the house and gets into her car, he follows her up the coast into Corona Del Mar. He misses the light and watches her pull into Camino Shores, and out of sight. When the light turns, he drives into the fancy subdivision. He has to cruise up and down a couple of the streets, before he sees her car parked in front of a house that looks like it had been recently remodeled. Landscapers are working on the front yard. Down the street, another house is being reroofed so there are a lot of cars and trucks around. Good. Now he can watch her without being noticed.

He opens his laptop, turns on his Wi-Fi hotspot and locates Paladin's tracking signal. They're at the house that was blown up – Paladin's house. He closes this laptop and starts walking up the street toward the woman's car. A lunch truck pulls up to the first job and a crowd of workers surround it. Perfect. He walks past her car, bends over to tie his shoe and puts the tracking device into the wheel well. He straightens up and walks back to his car.

Ten minutes later, she gets into the car and backs out, obviously in a hurry. He follows her as she turns left at Newport Coast Drive. She's on her way to work at the museum. He's sure of that. He's tagged her car and has her address. If she's going to work, nothing more will happen with her for a while, and Paladin and Frasier haven't moved. He realizes he can go back to his place and crash for a while. He needs to eat and get some sleep. But first he has to call his contact and find out who's behind the Rigdel Corporation.

Chapter 24

"Hey, DJ, let's swing by your house so you can go to T-Street on your own. I'm supposed to meet the architect at my house in an hour or so, and I want to spend some time looking around and maybe even do some clean up before he gets there."

"That's fine. The meeting at the T-Street job could last for a couple of hours and you don't need to sit through all that. Call me when you're done, maybe we can grab a beer."

I pull up in front of my house and walk over to my mailbox. *Crap, it's full.* As I sit down on the curb to sort through it, Murph pulls up in his truck. He parks in front of what's left of my house, and walks over to me. I hear the quick horn of the truck acknowledging it's locked. What is the point of that stupid noise? I never got that.

"What did Jeannie have to say about the puzzle box?"

"She didn't have much more to say about it, but I did figure out where the codex is hidden."

"What? Where?"

"Ricky never carried his stash on him if he could avoid it—he didn't want to get caught carrying drugs, so he had hiding places in his regular drinking spots. He never used the term 'bathroom'; he always used the term 'head.' I tried to find his stash spot at the RFL, but it's was too crowded. I want to try again tonight, around seven thirty or eight o'clock, when it's still slow. You wanna come with?"

"Damn right I do. We need to get this thing open before I get caught lying to my boss. Is the box safe?"

"Nobody will find it. I haven't told anyone, but I guess you should know where it's stashed in case something bad happens to me."

"I'd like to say nothing bad will happen, but I can't the way things have been going. You didn't even tell DJ?"

"No. He's really been an unwilling participant in all of this and with him being so worried about his family, I'm trying not to drag him in too deep. I hid it on the boat. Well, not exactly on the boat. The fender on the port side has a fishing line strung through the bottom of it. The box is wrapped in a waterproof container there. No one could see it, even if they were right on top of it because of the silt at the bottom of the harbor. No matter how well it's hidden, unless we find that codex we're screwed."

"Too true. I'll meet you at the Fox at seven thirty tonight."

Murph waves goodbye as he unlocks his truck – another useless honk - and drives away.

I turn to look at my destroyed house. There was still crime scene tape across the front and a 'Do No Enter' red tag on the front door, issued by the city. My phone beeps and I look down to see a text message from my architect telling me he has to cancel our meeting today and will call to reschedule later next week. Terrific. I came over here just to get depressed for nothing. I spin the combination padlock on the side door of the garage, walk inside and push up the garage door. I find some work gloves and grab the trashcan, drag it over to the yard and start cleaning up the broken glass and other debris on the front lawn. I'll have to order a dumpster, but for now I just pile things up. After an hour or so, my phone beeps but I don't bother to check it. Now that I'm on a roll, I want to get some of this cleared up. Two more hours go by and so do my neighbors. They all say the same thing: how lucky I am to be alive, that I can rebuild and that I'll love the new house even more, yadda, yadda. I know they mean well and I'm grateful to have such good neighbors, but I could really do without the platitudes

It's getting close to the time I'm supposed to meet Murph, so I brush myself off and drive up to El Camino Real to the Red Fox Lounge. I see Murph's truck, but no Murph, so I walk into the bar. The outside deck area is a wreck: beer bottles and glasses everywhere. Cookie, the bouncer, is clearing away all the empties from the afternoon crowd.

"Hey, Bobby." he says. Cookie's big, pierced and tattooed, the way a good bouncer should look.

"Evening, Cookie. It looks like it was a busy afternoon," I say, grabbing a handful of empty bottles.

"Yeah, it was pretty crazy. Then around, five everyone started to drift out and by six it was quiet again. I have to get the place cleaned up before the night crowd gets here and trashes it all over again," he says as I put the empties into the cardboard box beside him. I give him a sympathetic pat on the shoulder as he goes back to cleaning up the mess.

As I walk into the bar, I see Murph sitting at the far end. "Order me a beer," I say, "I'm going to see what I can find while I have the chance."

He nods and I slip into the bathroom and—again—start to search the wall tiles looking for something that sticks out. Nothing catches my eye. I sit down on the toilet trying to think like Ricky. Nothing I ever really wanted to do, but I'm stuck. I lean forward like I might be reading the newspaper on the can and look around from my new angle. As I turn my head to the left, I noticed a tile that is not quite right. It's a little out of square to the pattern that runs through the rest of the bathroom. Can this be it or just a bad tile job? I get up and try to remove the tile, but I can't get my fingers under it. I get out a credit card and try to pop the tile with that, but no luck. I swear under my breath as a corner snaps off of my Visa card.

Damn it, now I have to go back to thinking like Ricky again. If this was his spot, how would he get it open? He'd have made it tough for anyone else to do. Think. Ricky always carried a Swiss army knife. One of the blades was a thin, heavy-duty, flat-head screwdriver. *That's it,* I think. I walk out of the bathroom, go into the area where people order and pick up food. I take a knife out of the silverware container and go to back toward the bathroom. Murph raises one eyebrow and I look down at the butter knife in my hand. He gives me a barely perceptible nod as I slip back into the bathroom. I can't believe my luck. This bathroom hasn't stayed empty for this long in days. I get the knife under the tile and pop it loose. Museum putty. That's why it was so hard to get the tile off the wall. The drywall had been hollowed out and Ricky had inset a small cup into the wall so he could keep his stash hidden inside it. There, sitting in the cup, is a small baggie of coke and a note addressed to me. Someone's knocking on the door. Shit! I grab the note, leaving Ricky's stash—I have no interest in that crap anymore—replace the tile and flush the toilet. I stuff the note in my pocket, walk out of the bathroom and over to sit next to Murph.

"I found a note," I say as I pick up my beer.

"Not in here, Bobby. Let's finish our beers and then head over to the boat."

****

He sits outside on the patio of the Del Agave Café, across the street from the bar, with his computer. He's rented a different car. After resting most of the day, and taking a quick run on the beach, he'd showered and felt human again. He pulls up the GPS tracking program on his computer and sees the woman's car is still at the Bowers Museum. He sees the cop's ride and Paladin's van parked across the street. He orders a couple of tacos and keeps an eye on the bar.

After about twenty minutes, Paladin and the cop walk out of the bar, climb into their vehicles and take off. Shit. He throws money down on the table, grabs his computer and quickly gets into his car to follow them. They look like they're headed back to the harbor. He stays well back.

Chapter 25

Alexis is turning onto John G.'s street when she sees a new BMW pull out of the driveway, cut across coast highway, and head north. She doesn't recognize the car or its female driver. She thought she knew everyone John dealt with, so who's this? She walks into the house to her boss cursing.

"John, are you all right?"

He looks at her, surprised. "Yes. Of course." He takes a moment to gather himself. She rarely sees him lose his cool and this is twice within the last couple of days, "Would you please grab broom, dustpan and a trash bag? I'll be in the office." He's back to being all business.

She walks into the kitchen, opens the pantry door, finds the broom and bag and returns to John's office. The hardwood floor is covered with shards glass.

"What happened? I saw someone leaving as I arrived. Are you all right?"

"Yes, I'm fine. Would you please help clean this up? I was careless and bumped into the Chihuly. It fell to the floor and broke."
"I'm so sorry. That was an expensive vase."

"More than a vase," he says looking at the mess, "A piece of art. Not the end of the world. It's just glass after all."

After they finish picking up all of the pieces, John looks at her "I might need you to keep an eye on someone else, too. Here's a picture of her. Her name is Jeannie Francis. She's an expert in Japanese myth and religion, but is also well versed in most history and artifacts from that part of the world. She's currently in charge of a major exhibit at the Bowers Museum."

"Is she a threat to you?"

"No. She's an old friend. We've had a parting of the ways, so to speak. That's why I want you to keep an eye on her when she's around Bobby and DJ." He scribbles on a piece of paper and hands it to her. "Here's her address in Corona Del Mar and the license plate number of the rental car she's driving. Thank you."

He sits down at his computer and she knows she's been dismissed. She'd much rather be out in the field doing surveillance than stay here when he's in this kind of a mood, but she has some work to finish up. She's completed everything by late afternoon, but her boss hasn't come out of his office. She leaves the house, gets into her car and heads south. She slips on her Bluetooth and taps one number on her phone.

"It's me. I need you to find out all you can about a woman named Jeannie Francis. She lives in Hawaii, but she's currently the curator of an exhibit of Japanese artifacts on display at the Bowers Museum. Call me back when you have something. Thanks." She disconnects without waiting for a reply.

When she arrives at the harbor, she can see DJ working on his boat, but no sign of Bobby. She parks her car and walks into Harpoon Henry's, where she asks the hostess for a window seat. Sitting down, she orders a diet Pepsi and asks her server to give her some time to look at the menu. She has a spectacular view of the harbor, looking right down on DJ's boat. She realizes she's hungry. From the window she watches DJ take out a stand-up paddle board, slide it in the water and paddle out into the main channel of the harbor. She orders and waits for him to come back or for Bobby to show up, hopefully with the woman.

Chapter 26

Murph and I pull into the parking lot in the harbor and walk down to DJ's boat.

"Another beer?" I ask as I head down into the boat. I sure need one. I don't see DJ but his car is here. I look around and notice one of the paddleboards is gone. That sounds so great. I wish I was with him.

"I'll take one more, Bobby, thanks."

Once we're on board Murph says quietly, "Come on, let's open that note."

"Okay," I take a deep breath, pull the note from my pocket, sit down on one of the deck chairs and start reading.

> *Bobby – here's the answer that will open the puzzle box. You only get one chance. If you blow it, all the paperwork inside will be destroyed. I stole these from General Miguel Sandoval - he is a very powerful and merciless man. Good luck. If you're still in touch with Jeannie, she might be able to read the directions and open the puzzle box. Find her if you can, but be careful. You may not be able to be trust her. I just don't know, but she's the only person I can think of that might be able to help you. Thanks for all the fun, Bobby. You were my brother in life, and in death.*
>
> *Aloha, Ricky.*

The rest of the page is in Japanese. I can't make hide nor hair out of it. "What do you think?" I ask Murph, who's been reading over my shoulder.

"We need to get that puzzle box opened right now. My ass and career are on the line. Call Jeannie and get her over here," I grab my phone and punch in Jeannie's number. It goes right to voicemail.

"Jeannie, please call me when you get this message. I need to see you right away." I sit down next to Murph and take a sip off of my beer. I swear I can feel him vibrating beside me.

****

Jeannie's just finished up a meeting with the board of directors of the museum when her phone flashes. She glances at the number and sees it's Bobby. She'll call him back when she's out of her meeting. She's so happy. Meeting Bobby again is such an unexpected bonus and she's not going to blow her second chance with him.

On her way to the museum, she had stopped at John G.'s house and told him it was over. She's going to move into her own home, give up the car, everything. She's done with him. She's in love with Bobby and is not going to lose him again. She picks up her files, bows to this director, says a few words to that director and is finally able to get back to her office. She picks up the office phone and dials Bobby's number.

"Hi, it's me," she's feeling a little shy. Surely she's too old for school-girl stuff, "I saw you called. I'm leaving the museum right now. I should be there in forty-five minutes or so. I have so much to tell you, and Bobby—I love you. See you soon. 'Bye." Oh, shit, maybe she shouldn't have told him she loved him. After all, they had only been together one night. No, she's sure he feels the same way. She can tell.

She's free! Free of John Gomez and the strangle hold he's held over her for years. When she first met him, she'd been entranced. He was good looking, smart, sexy, powerful and connected. At the time, he was running a drug crew on the island of Oahu selling ice, cocaine and weed. She was young and vulnerable. He told her he

162

could protect her and keep her safe. He could send her to the best university so she could make something of herself. Slowly, carefully, he began to manipulate her. She started sleeping with him because she felt she owed him. After that, she was at his beck and call for sex: whenever he wanted it, any time day or night; doing whatever he told her to do, no matter what. He had paid for her college education, cars, and clothes, whatever she needed. When she traveled for work, she would be free of him for a while, but he always called her back, cashing in on her debt. He was the reason she couldn't follow Bobby when he left Hawaii. It had been so many years, she'd forgotten how it felt to be free. Now she was done with John G. and everything he stood for. Now she could stand on her own two feet. She can move forward with her life, free to be with the man she's loved all along.

She opens the bottom drawer of her desk and grabs her purse. She locks her office, waves goodbye to Vince, the security guard, and heads out the employee entrance to her car.

"Free at last," she says aloud as she opens her car door, sits down and tosses her purse on the passenger seat. She can't believe how joyful she feels. She leans forward and turns the key in the ignition.

Her car explodes into a huge ball of flame, killing Jeannie Francis, on the happiest day of her life.

****

As his driver steers the limo away from the museum, The General rolls up his window. He smiles to himself, thinking, *I will clean up this mess myself, once and for all.*

Chapter 27

On the boat, I go below to grab a couple more beers and see my phone blinking a voice message waiting.

"Shit, Murph. Jeannie called and I missed it. I'll call her back right now." I hit redial and it goes to voicemail again, so I leave her another message. "Hey, girl, I saw that you called. I'll check your message. Call me back when you get this. Mahalo, Jeannie." I pull up my voice mail and listen to her message. I feel a stupid smile creep onto my face. I go above deck.

"She says she loves me."

"What?" Murph looks up from Ricky's note. He's been looking at it like it might somehow make sense to him if he stares at it long enough.

"Jeannie's on her way here now and at the end of her message, she said she loves me. Wow." I say, sitting down. I can't seem to take it all in. Murph looks at me skeptically.

"That was pretty quick, don't you think? You guys just reconnected?

I turn to him. I can't seem to stop smiling. I must look like an idiot. "I've never stopped loving her, even after all this time, and now she told me she feels the same way."

Murph shakes his head at me as his phone rings, "Murphy here." He listens for a few minutes and gives me a sideways glance. "I'm leaving right now. I'll get there as quickly as I can." He stands up and puts his phone in his pocket, his voice tense and professional. "I have to go right now. Sorry, I can't tell you any more than that, but right now I have to leave. Trust me; I'll be in touch with you as soon as I have more information."

He hustles up the gangway to the dock gate, runs to his truck, turns on the red light on his dash and races out of the parking lot.
This cannot be good.

****

About ten minutes later, DJ paddles up to the boat, "Dude, that so was great," he says. "I feel like a new man. Hey, what's up, bro? You look - I don't know, scared or something. Did the architect give you his bill?"

"Murph was here. He got a call and told me it was very, very bad, got into his truck and flew out of here. He wouldn't tell me what was up. He drove out with the red light flashing."

"Probably just cop stuff," he says paddling up to the dock and stepping off the board. I come down off the boat and help him pull it out of the water.

"I finally found Ricky's hiding place at the Red Fox and the codex to open the puzzle box."

"Cool. So we're good, right? Puzzle solved?"

"Not so much," I say, "The instructions are in Japanese, and now we're stuck until Jeannie can get here and translate it. Then, maybe, we can open the puzzle box. She's on her way."

"Well, if anyone can open the box, it'll be Jeannie," DJ says as he washes the saltwater off the board and locks it back up in the rack next to the boat.

"Yeah, and guess what? She left me a voicemail telling me she loves me," I can feel the stupid grin come back.

"No shit. That was fast. Are you good with that?"

166

"I really am. I've felt this way ever since we split up in Hawaii. I can't wait until she gets here." I don't want to let him see me get too mushy, so I change the subject. "Have you heard from Maria? Is everything all right with her and the kids?"

"I talked with her today and she said all is good. We worked out a code phrase that will let me know if she and the kids are in any kind of trouble."

"That's a good idea."

"So yeah, for right now, everything is good. But you know, we've stepped in a pile of shit and we need to find a way out of it before it gets deeper."

"Yeah, I can see where this is getting way out of hand. If Jeannie can open the puzzle box, it will get us out from under and maybe even turn it around in our favor. We can give all the paperwork to Murph, and he can hand it over to his superiors. Then we can walk away safely and maybe not get killed ourselves." I say as I pull a beer out of the cooler. "Want one?

"Sure, but first I need to clean up." He picks up his towel and shorts, and heads off to the showers.

While he's gone, I pick up my phone and punch in Jeannie's phone number. It goes straight to voicemail again.

"Call me, Babe. I can't wait to see you." And before I hang up, "I love you too, Jeannie."

I must have been daydreaming about Jeannie because suddenly DJ appears before me, wet from the shower, with his hair slicked back.
"Let's go get some something to eat. I'm starving. When Jeannie gets here, she can join us."

"Yeah, I guess so." I hesitate. I pick up my phone and wallet. I'd really rather wait until she gets here. "Where do you feel like eating?"

"How about Harpoon Henry's? We'll ask Gina if she can get us a window seat. That way we can keep an eye out for Jeannie."

"Sounds good. I'll leave her a quick text to let her know where we'll be."

"Hi Gina." DJ says to his favorite server.

"Hi guys. DJ, I saw you paddle out of here a couple of hours ago. How was it?"

"Great. I even got pretty close to a pod of dolphins."
"That must have been amazing!" She says.

"It was, but I was a little afraid one of the big ones was going to bump my board. Do you think you could wrangle us a window seat for dinner? We're waiting for one more."

"Anything for you," Gina says with wink and a sweet smile, showing her perfect teeth. "Give me about twenty minutes. We have a couple of tables opening up shortly, and I'll jump you to the head of the line."

"Thanks. We'll be sitting at the bar," We walk into the bar, find two empty seats and sit down where we can watch golf on the TV.

"Hey, guys, long time, no see," says Vicky, the bartender. "What's your pleasure? The bartender?" she gives DJ a sultry smile. Why do they all flirt with him when I'm the single one? Well, maybe not for long.

"If I only wasn't married, Vicky. But since I am, I'll settle for a cold Pacifico with lime, please"

"And what can I get for you?" she asks me. I sure don't get the kind of charm he's getting from her. I wonder if we've ever had a bad date I don't remember.

"I'll take a glass of the Nickel Nickel Chardonnay, Vicky, thank you."

As she walks away to get our drinks DJ says, "She sure has a great ass."

"Indeed. She doesn't care if you're married or not. You know that, right?"

He sighs, "Yeah, I know, but my heart belongs to Maria. Besides, if I stepped out on Maria, she'd cut my balls off and hand them to me on a plate for dinner. It's nice to look though." We both watch Vicky walk down to the end of the bar.

My phone rings. It's got to be Jeannie, letting us know she's here. Unbelievably, it's not. It's Murph. Shit. I'd forgotten all about him splitting in such a hurry earlier.

"Hey, what's up?" I say. I mouth 'Murph' to DJ as I point to my phone and step outside to take the call.

"Bobby, where are you? Are you alone?"
"No, I'm at Harpoon's with DJ. Jeannie'll be here in a minute and we're going to get a table by the window and watch the sunset. Why?"

"So DJ is there with you?"

"Yes, he's sitting at the bar." He's starting to piss me off, "What the hell is the matter?"

"I don't know how to say this. There's no easy way, so here goes. Jeannie has been killed."

169

"What? What are you talking about? She's on her way here." He can't be telling me what he's telling me.

"I'm so sorry. You need to get up to the Bowers as fast and safely as you can. How much has DJ had to drink? Can he drive you up here?"

"Yes, he's fine. He just ordered a beer. What do you mean she's been killed? Like a car accident? How do you know? Is that why you took off?" I feel my head start to spin and I have to put my hand on the wall to steady myself.

"Look, Bobby. I'm so sorry. You're not next of kin or anything, so I can't tell you much more right now. I'm only calling you because I didn't want you to see it on the news. Just get up here, okay? When you get here I'll explain everything but there isn't much we know at this time. Have DJ drive you. I've got to go." The phone goes dead in my hand.

Lean against the wall for a few minutes before I can walk back into the bar. On the TV is a breaking news story of a car bombing in Santa Ana. Oh my God. Can that be Jeannie?

DJ looks away from the TV, "Jesus, Bobby! You're white. What the hell happened?"

"She's dead. Jeannie's dead. Murph just called me. I think that might be her." We both look back toward the TV as we see The Bowers Museum printed at the bottom of the screen.

"Oh my God, DJ, someone killed her! I need to get to Bowers Museum now. Right now. Can you drive me?"

"Let's roll," he says, throwing a twenty on the counter.

Chapter 28

"I am so sorry, Bobby. I know Jeannie meant a lot to you." DJ says as we drive up onto the North Bound 5 freeway. "I just can't fucking believe this has happened."

I nod my thanks. I don't trust myself to speak as tears run silently down my face. I turn to face the window. I want to wipe the tears away, but I don't want to draw attention to the fact that I'm sitting here crying like a baby.

We make the drive in record time and thirty-five minutes later arrive at the Bowers. There are sheriff's cars, fire trucks, crime scene trucks and news vans scattered all around the perimeter. I can hear news helicopters overhead. Vultures. DJ and I get out of the car and stand looking at the scene. I don't think we'll be able to get close. I see Murph talking with a group of people. He notices us when DJ waves at him. Murph signals a uniformed cop to escort us over to him. He introduces us to his boss, Captain Michael Sprague.

"I am very sorry for your loss, Mr. Paladin. I understand you and the victim were close."

Victim? Shit. "Bobby," I interject, still not sounding like myself. "Call me Bobby."

"Bobby. There wasn't anything we could do. She died instantly. We want you to know that she didn't suffer. Do you know if she had any family? We'll need to contact them as soon as possible."

I swallow and say, "Her parents live in Gaviota. Her father was the police chief up there. Is it okay if I call them? Or does it have to be somebody official? I'd rather they heard it from me."

Captain Sprague looks at Murph. "Stay with him when he makes the call in case they have any questions."

Murphy nods. "How long do you think it would take them to get here?" he asks.

"I guess we could expect them late tonight or at the latest tomorrow afternoon. Her mother and father are going to be devastated."

DJ pipes in, "I'll reserve a room for them over at the Hilton."

"Thanks, DJ."

"Bobby, do you know anyone who would want to do this to Miss Francis?" Sprague asks.

"No. I mean, we just reconnected, so I don't know anyone she was hanging around with recently," I say. "Maybe someone at the Bowers knows something?"

"We're checking with them now. If you can think of anything, call me. Here's my cell number," he hands me a business card, turns away from me and walks over to the crime scene. Crime scene. Victim. Christ.

"Bobby." Murph brings my attention back – away from where it's headed. "We're going to have to tell the Captain about the puzzle box. We're withholding evidence that's a key part of this murder investigation. We've already waited too long. The sooner we tell the Captain about the puzzle box the better my chances of keeping my job."

"I know, Murph, I know. Let me call her parents first. Can we deal with it tomorrow?"

"Okay, tomorrow, Bobby. Sorry, dude."

Murph takes me to a quiet spot where I can make this dreaded phone call. I get my phone out, call 411 and have them patch me through. I had met Jeannie's parents after I quit the pro tour. Her dad had been the police chief in Gaviota, a small California beach town, after he retired from the service. His wife was born and raised in Japan, and he had grown up on a Native American reservation in Florida. They had met after the Korean War while he was with the military police and she was a diplomat's daughter. They were going to flip out when they heard the news that Jeannie was dead. My only consolation was that at least they were going to hear it from someone who cared about her and not a stranger. After five rings I hear Mrs. Francis answer the phone.

"Hello?"

"Hello, Mrs. Francis? This is Bobby Paladin. Do you remember me?"

"Bobby! What a nice surprise. Jeannie just told me she saw you at the museum. How are you?"

"I'm fine, thank you," I pause, not quite sure how to do this. "Umm, is Mr. Francis home? I'd like to speak to him."

I hear her hesitate, "Yes, of course. Let me get him for you. Ron! You'll never guess who's on the phone."

"Hello!" Ronald Francis bellows into the phone.

"Mr. Francis? This is Bobby Paladin."

"Bobby! Yes, Jeannie told us she saw you. How are you? Are you taking care of my little girl?

I squeeze my eyes shut to stop the tears, "Not exactly." I swallow, "I have some bad news, sir. I didn't want you to hear it from the police or see it on the news."

173

"What are you talking about? Explain yourself, son." I don't blame him snapping at me.

"Your daughter, Jeannie. She's been killed."

"I don't understand."

"She was leaving work at the Bowers Museum. Her car exploded."

"I can't believe you're telling me this. How did it happen?"
"I don't know, sir," I say. "The police don't know why."

After a long silence I say, "I'm so sorry, sir." I can't stop my voice from breaking. "You need to get here as soon as you can. My friend made reservations at the South Coast Hilton for you and your wife. Are you still there?"

Finally he answers, his voice cracking, "Thank you, Bobby. Chako and I will be there in five or six hours. Would you please arrange to have a detective there to brief me when we arrive?"

"Yes sir, of course. I'm so very sorry to be calling with such horrible news." Tears are running down my cheeks. There is no way I was going to tell him over the phone about how his only daughter and I had rekindled our relationship, how we both found out we still loved each other.

"Thank you, Bobby, for taking the time to call us personally. For not passing it off to someone who doesn't know us. It must have been very difficult. I'll contact you when we get there." He hangs up the phone.

I stand there staring down at the silent phone in my hand, not quite believing this. It's surreal. I fell in love with Jeannie the very first time I saw her in Japan. So many memories come rushing back. Now it's all gone. Just like that. Gone.
DJ walks over to me and puts his arm on my shoulder.

"Hey, Bobby, let's get out of here," he says gently. "There isn't anything more we can do here. Murph says he'd call us later and fill us in when they know something."

"Sure, DJ, let's go."

****

He's sitting in his car, watching, waiting. He knew something had happened when the woman's car stopped sending a GPS signal, but he had not anticipated this. Whoever did this made sure she was dead. He felt a shiver run up his spine. The stakes were higher. Live or die. Those were the choices. If he wants to live, he has to find that box or end up just like her. He can't even figure out who would do this or why. Was she important or were they trying a different way to get at Paladin? The only person who could have arranged this so quickly was The General. And he was playing for keeps. The General had struck a blow to the opposition, swiftly and brutally.

Chapter 29

Captain Sprague finally walks over to Detective Murphy. He's pretty sure the asshole isn't telling him everything he knows. "Murph, keep me posted on what you find," he says. "There is some shit going on here and you and I both know it's connected. I want reports on my desk the minute you find out what happened here. Got it?"

"Yes sir," Murphy answers. He's not sure the Captain even hears his reply before he storms over to his car and drives off.

A voice from the crowd calls, "Detective Murphy."

He turns. With relief he sees it's one of the older guys, Don Dunn, not one of the snot-nosed kids who grew up watching CSI, where everything is solved in sixty minutes or less. This guy has experience and his results can be trusted.

"What is it, Don?"

"I found something you need to see."

Murph walks over and squats down on the ground near the tech.

"I found a piece of the detonation device. Military grade, but not our military," he holds up a chard piece for Murphy to see. "This is not something you can buy at a garage sale. It comes from some very high-tech equipment. I'll run tests when I get back to the lab and see if I can figure out what the explosive was. I'll call you when I know more. The Captain told me to make this case a priority."

Murphy stands up. "Thanks. Great work everyone," he tells the techs, even the young ones.

"I think we're going to have to bring the Feds in on this one," Don says. "It's either black market or we have foreign military on US soil. I'll let the Captain know when I get a chance."

"Let me know first, will you?" Murphy says. "I'll pass it along to the Captain." Having the Feds around is not going to be fun.

****

DJ drops me off at the boat. I get out and tell him, "I'm going to crash for a few hours and wait for Jeannie's parents to call me. I'll talk to you tomorrow."

"You're sure you'll be okay? Why don't you stay at my house?"

"No thanks. I think I just need to be alone right now. It's a lot to process."

"Okay, if you're sure. If you need me, just call and I'll be here in a flash," DJ says. I nod my thanks as he drives away, headed for home.

Home. I have no home. I have no girlfriend, nothing. In the course of one week, my life has turned to shit. It's late and I decide to bring up the box tonight and turn it over to Murph in the morning. I look around and don't see anybody. There's a blind-spot created by DJ's paddle board rack. I should be able to bring up the box and unpack it from its water-tight container without anybody seeing me. I move over to the rack, pull the fender up and pull up the fishing line attached to the water-proof container. I look around again, relieved to see I'm still alone. I bring the container onto the boat, open the hatch and go down into the salon. I dry it off, open it and pull out the box. It is so beautiful. All this death and destruction for a box with stolen paperwork locked inside. I'll be so happy to turn this over to Murph tomorrow and let the sheriffs figure it out.

"Sorry, amigo, I just don't think I'm the one to solve this puzzle," I say quietly, hoping Ricky can hear me, wherever he is. I tuck the box into my backpack and put it at my feet in the bed. I crash and it seems like I've only been asleep a minute or so when my cell phone rings.

"Bobby, this is John G. I just heard about Jeannie. Terrible. She was a wonderful person. She cared for you very much."

I mumble a reply and he continues, "Do you think you could drop by my house tomorrow sometime? Just call me when you are on your way, okay? Goodnight." I don't even get a chance to reply before the phone goes dead in my hand. I'm too tired to think about what was just said to me and go back to sleep.

****

John G. hangs up the phone and looks out his office window. There's only one person who could have done this: General Miguel Sandoval. He's a very dangerous man. He must be here himself to make sure there were no loose ends; to ensure the deal was completed as planned. This was by far the biggest deal John knew about. Between the ecstasy and the two thousand keys of pure coke, this deal will net over forty million in cash. John knows he'll do the deal, take his cut and then, when the time was right, he'll kill The General. An eye for an eye, even if it turns out to be his last act on earth.

****

He sits in the shadows outside John Gomez' house, waiting, watching.

Chapter 30

"Hello?" I answer groggily. The phone wakes me -again, but this time the sun is shining.

"Bobby. Ron Francis, Jeannie's father." He says in his gruff voice.

Jeannie's dead. Not a nightmare after all. It really happened.

"Good morning, sir." I sit up in the bunk. "Are you here in Orange County?"

"Yes we are. Could you meet with Chako and me this morning? We'd like to see you. We have some questions about – well, you'd seen her recently."

"Of course. I can be at your hotel in an hour or so, Mr. Francis. Do you want me to try to reach Captain Sprague to see when he can meet with you and your wife?"

"Yes. Thank you. To explain what happened. Yes." I can hear him take a deep breath on the other end of the line. "We'd like to get Jeannie's remains released, as soon as possible, so we can have a ceremony to honor her life. Chako and I will have to fly to Hawaii to pack up her house." He clears his throat. I can tell he's trying to hide his emotions. Having been a police chief, he knows what's involved, and I can tell he's just trying to get through it the best he can.

"I'll get to you as soon as I can." I say.

"Thank you, Bobby," He hesitates, "I look forward to seeing you again, even under these circumstances." He pauses for a minute as if he has something he wants to say to me then hangs up without saying anything more.

I stand up and pull on some clothes. My mind is reeling. I grab my backpack with the puzzle box and head out to my van. I put the backpack in the rear of the van and jump in the driver's seat. On my way out of town, I hit the drive-through coffee place, get a bear claw and a large black coffee and head out to the Hilton.

****

He's parked in the harbor parking lot with Paladin's van in plain sight. The van pulls out of the lot – he'll follow this guy wherever he goes. He needs that box or he's a dead man.

He doesn't notice a car pull out of the lot behind him. A lapse of observation he'll soon regret.

****

I pull up to the front of the hotel and a red-vested valet opens my door. I hand him five dollars. "Park it close and keep an eye on it for me. There's another five dollars in it for you when I pick it up." I hand him my keys. I have to give this kid credit. He doesn't bat an eye at my 12 year-old van. He treats it like any Lexis or Mercedes he's asked to handle. I watch as he parks the van next to a brand new Ferrari, right up front.

I walk into the lobby and the young woman at the front desk smiles at me.

"I'm here to see Mr. and Mrs. Ronald Francis in room 1030. They're expecting me."

She asks my name, calls up and confirms before saying, "The elevators are to the right, sir. At the tenth floor, make a left. There room is located in the middle of the hallway."

182

I thank her and walk to the elevator. I ride up to the tenth floor, and find the room. I stand there, and before I can get up the nerve to knock, the door opens.

"Bobby. I am so glad you are here." Chako says as she hugs me. "Thank you for getting here so quickly. Please come in. Ron is out on the balcony talking with Captain Sprague on the telephone."

Looking through the sliding glass doors I see Jeannie's father, leaning on the railing with a cell phone to his ear.

"Bobby, while we have a moment, I'd like to tell you some things that you may not know," Chako says, putting her hand on my arm. "Jeannie and I spoke the day she died." She stops to gather herself before continuing, "She was very happy and excited to have seen you. She was in love with you, you know. She always was and when you left Hawaii, it broke her heart. My daughter was very stubborn, like her father, but she always knew what she wanted out of life. What she wanted was to be with you and to raise a family." Chako looks at me and I see a single tear running down her face. She wipes it away.

"Thank you, Mrs. Francis, for telling me." I look down at the floor. "I loved Jeannie and spending the rest of my life with her would have made me the happiest man in the world."

"Bobby." Ron Francis says, coming in from the balcony. "Thank you for coming. Captain Sprague has been very helpful. Thank you for putting us in touch." Ron leads me over to a small sofa.

"Please, sit down."

I find a seat on the couch and Ron sits down in the armchair across from me. "Now why don't you tell me what really happened to my daughter?" His voice has a hard edge to it and for the next forty-five minutes, I explain all that I know.

183

When I'm done, he says, "Thank you, Bobby, your story sheds some light." His cell phone rings. He answers it, waves an apology and walks out onto the balcony, closing the sliding glass door.

"Bobby," Chako says, sitting beside me. "Jeannie told me about your problem with the puzzle box. I think I may be able to help you. I don't think she knew I was born in that part of Japan where many of the puzzle boxes were made. My family knew Mr. Nueriuma's family. We were often allowed to play with some of the simpler boxes as children. It is possible that I might be able to help you open your puzzle box."

I'm dumbfounded. "She didn't mention anything about that. She said she didn't know of anyone who could help us get it open. We never talked again after she left the boat." Another wave of sadness washes over me.

"I don't speak of my childhood much, so I'm sure she didn't know. We were so poor, there weren't many pleasant stories to share."

Mr. Francis walks back into the room, "Bobby, I have a meeting with a Detective Murphy. Thank you again for stopping by and explaining the situation. Chako, would you show Bobby out?" He stalks into the bedroom, leaving Chako to walk me to the door.

"I'm very sorry for Ron's behavior, Bobby. As you can imagine, he is taking Jeannie's death very hard."

"Understandable. We're all pretty shaken up."

"May I have your cell phone number?" She asks me. "I will call you later today. Maybe we can meet and I will see if I can help you open your puzzle box. Ron usually takes a nap around five p.m. I will call you and meet you downstairs in the bar. I like to have a glass of wine before dinner." She says with a little smile. Then she wraps her arms around me and hugs me tightly. I hold on to her to keep from losing it completely. She releases me from her hug and turns around to step back into the room. She looks up at me with tears running down her face.

"Thank you" I say. She nods and gently closes the door.

I hurry to the elevator and ride down to the lobby where I find a place to sit down and think about what Chako told me about Jeannie from their last conversation. It was very comforting. And slowly, it registers what Chako said about the possibility of opening the puzzle box. I grab my cell phone and call Murphy.

"Murph, it's me, Bobby." I rush on without even giving him a chance to say hello. "Jeannie's mom, Mrs. Francis – Chako – she thinks she can open the puzzle box. She's going to call me around five p.m. and meet me in the hotel bar to give it a shot. Do you think you can make it here by then?"

It takes him a few seconds to process what I've just told him. "That's incredible. I'm meeting her husband this afternoon. Can she try then?"
"I don't think she wants her husband to know. She said he takes a nap at five, so she wants to try then. Hey, I never mentioned anything about the puzzle box or the drug deal, to him, okay? I just thought it would be too much."

"Yeah, you're right. He doesn't need any more to worry about. I'll see you at round five in the hotel bar." I disconnect. I've got a few hours and I need to get some fresh air, so I decide to go for a drive to clear my head.

I walk out of the Hilton, and the van is right where we left it. I spot the valet and hand him my ticket and another five dollars.

"There was some guy checking out your van, but I told him to get lost. I just thought you should know." The valet starts to walk over to the van.

"Wait a second. Could you just give me my keys? I need to check something out." I grab the keys, walk over to the van, open the back hatch and take out the backpack. I bent over to check the undercarriage of the van and noticed something attached there. I get up slowly and back toward the valet.

"Stay right here," I say and dial Murphy's cell phone.

"Murph, I think there's something attached to my van. I'm afraid it might be a bomb. It could be on a timer or set off by remote control or the ignition."

"I'd better call the bomb squad. Where's the puzzle box?" Murph asks me, "Do you have it or is it in the van?"

"It's safe," I tell him.

"I can be there in twenty minutes, but the bomb squad will be there sooner. Don't leave that spot. Keep everyone away. Is there someone who can alert hotel security?"

"I'll send the valet."

I tell the valet to inform the front desk of my suspicions and that the sheriff's office has been informed. He turns a little grey, nods and runs into the hotel. I hear the sirens off in the distance.

The first unit to arrive is from the Costa Mesa police. A uniformed officer strides into the lobby, I assume to tell the manager they need to set up a perimeter to keep people safe.

The Sheriff's Department is the next to arrive, sirens blaring. They seal off all the entries and exits to the hotel. Murph pulls up, the car still rocking as he gets out and I follow him into the lobby.

Ron Francis walks up before we get very far, "What the hell is going on here, Bobby? I'm supposed to meet with Detective Murphy. He's bringing release papers for my signature."

"Mr. Francis, this is Detective Murphy."

They shake hands and Murph says, "I'm so sorry for your loss, sir." He turns to look at me, "I think the local police and the bomb squad have everything under control."

"Bomb squad?!" barks Ron, "Does this have anything to do with my daughter's death?"

"Mr. Francis, can we go up to your room to talk, sir? It will be much quieter," Murph says. "All of this," he waves his hand toward the front doors where police are swarming, "is purely precautionary, I assure you." Wow. Was I ever this calm when I was a cop? "I have the papers for you and I can explain what's happening there.

Murph leads Jeannie's father back toward the elevators. I call DJ and explain the situation and tell him I'll call him back later today. I hope my van stays in one piece, but the way my luck's running, that's asking a lot.

Chapter 31

Alexis has noticed the man who followed Paladin to the hotel and parks where she can keep an eye on him. She calls her handler and explains that Bobby Paladin has someone tailing him. She wants to know what her options are. Her handler tells her to sit tight, observe his actions and wait for further instructions. She positions herself in a coffee shop across the street and settles in to watch and wait. Paladin comes out and looks like he's going to leave, so she stands up to go. She sits down again when he returns to the valet. She's startled when she sees police and sheriffs pull into the hotel parking lot, sirens blaring, followed by a bomb squad van. They effectively shut down the hotel. No one was going to be able to enter or leave. This was definitely out of the ordinary.

She decides to go on the offensive and try to catch Paladin's shadow. She sees Detective Murphy arrive and he and Paladin walk into the hotel. Through the glass lobby doors, she can see Bobby walk to meet them. If the bomb squad is there and Paladin is talking to Detective Murphy, it must somehow concern Bobby. She notices the tail getting out of his car and heading toward the hotel. She clicks three quick pictures of him with the special zoom on her phone and quickly sends the picture to her handler, just as the media vans start to arrive. Bobby Paladin looks like a ringmaster in this particular circus.

****

Four hours later the bomb squad has finally safely disarmed and removed the bomb from my van. A black Lincoln SUV pulls up and a short, stocky bald man with glasses gets out of the passenger side while the driver gets out and stands by, apparently waiting for orders. They look like suits. They must be ATF, FBI or some other government agency.

I can hear the deputies and cops quietly talking to each other. It looks like the feds are taking command after the local guys did all the heavy lifting, and they're pissed. The bald guy walks over to the Site Commander and presents him with some paperwork. After some arm waving, finger pointing and yelling, the other agent walks up, confiscates the evidence from the bomb squad and puts it in the rear of the SUV.

Murphy walks out of the hotel with the Costa Mesa police chief, looks at me and says, "What the hell is going on now?"

Before I can answer the short, bald suit walks up to Murphy and asks, "Are you Detective Dwayne Murphy?"
 "Yes. And you are?"

"Agent Art Peterson with the ATF. I have a federal warrant requiring your men to surrender any and all evidence in the Jeannie Francis murder investigation. We've taken your computer files from your office and I want the rest of your notes. Now." He hands Murphy the warrant.

Murphy reads it through and looks disgustedly at Peterson, before he says. "You guys can't just walk into my office, take whatever the hell you want, then come to my crime scene and demand I give you my notes. I don't give a fuck about any warrant. This is my case and this murder happened in my jurisdiction. I'm calling the Captain right now."

"Suit yourself, Detective. Your Captain was the one who allowed us to remove the items from your office."

Glaring at Peterson, Murph gets out his phone and calls the Captain. I can hear Sprague yelling from where I'm standing, telling Murphy to surrender every bit of evidence he has or he'll suspend him until hell freezes over. Murphy disconnects as the color rises to his cheeks. He reaches into his inside jacket pocket, opens his black notebook and rips out a bunch of pages.

"That's all that I have, Peterson. You have everything else." His voice sounds calm but I can see that that the muscles in his jaw tightening.

"Thank you, Detective Murphy," says Peterson, smugly. "Stay out of my way on this or you'll find yourself suspended. Understand?"

As Peterson turns back to his partner, I see Murph extend the middle finger of the hand at his side. Peterson and his partner talk for a few more minutes before stepping into the black Lincoln and speeding off up the street. Murphy turns around and is about to say something when we hear a huge explosion. Everyone hits the ground and we cover our heads. When we look up, we see that the Feds, and their car, with all the evidence they had confiscated, have been blown to bits. Murphy's computer with all of his files from all the cases he was working on, including this one, his written notes and the bomb evidence, are all gone.

"Holy shit!" Murphy finally manages.

"I thought the bomb squad disarmed the bomb that was under my van."

"They did. Maybe it had a second kind of trigger. I don't know what the hell is going on but this has turned into a real shit storm. I'd better call Debbie. We're going to be stuck here for quite a while."

When he's finished talking to his wife, Murphy walks over to the bomb squad guys. "Could you guys have missed anything in the bomb you removed from the van?"

"No way." replies the taller of the two. "We double-checked it all and it was completely disabled. We don't fuck with that stuff, you know that. We don't want to end up like those guys." He nods towards burning Lincoln. "It had to be a second bomb."

191

"Okay," says Murphy. "You guys do your job and search the area surrounding the crime scene and see if you can find any traces of another bomb." He turns to the remaining officers. "The rest of you help out with the search of the hotel grounds. Remember, no one in or out of the hotel. Check all IDs. If you find or see anything suspicious —and I mean anything—you let me know right away. Let's get going." The group scrambles into action. He turns to me and says, "It's like a mine field here, for shit sake."

"Murph," I say, "The hotel must have video."
"Right. I need your help, but do your best to keep it low key. Check out all the public areas and see if anyone might have been hanging around. You know, acting funny or nervous."

"Okay." Uh oh. I'm starting to think and feel like a cop again. I was a good street cop but now I'm just a carpenter. Playing detective is not my thing anymore, but Murph needs all the help he can get before the Feds step in and take it all away again. "It's a bitch they got all your evidence."

He looks at me and grins. "You should know me better than that. I always back up my current cases and keep them with me." He holds up his keys and I see a flash drive hanging from his key ring.

"What about your notebook?"

"Oh that. I gave them Debbie's shopping list. That's why I had to call her."

****

General Sandoval stands in the hotel lobby and watches the police scurry around like rats. He goes totally unnoticed, hiding in plain sight. In a polo shirt, shorts and deck shoes, he's in the same outfit as almost every other man in the lobby who wasn't in uniform. Paladin had walked right by him.

192

He turns toward the elevators to return to his room. No one would stop him from completing this deal, no one! As the doors slide open, he steps aside to make room for a frantic family with their luggage, trying to get out of the hotel. He'll check out tomorrow. He knows there's no way to leave the hotel tonight. His fake documents will hold up to Homeland Security's scrutiny. He'll be long gone by the time the Americans find that he's a phony – if they ever do. He'll only be here for a few more days, tying up loose ends, like John Gomez and Bobby Paladin. He has already made arrangements to move to a country with no extradition treaty with the Mexican or the United States governments. He knows if he can pull off this deal and safely escape the United States, he will never be caught. A few more days and a few more bodies is all it will take.

Chapter 32

Detective Murphy stands at the front desk and identifies himself. There is panic all around him with guests trying to check out. He catches the attention of the hotel manager who comes over after Murphy flashes his badge.

"I need to see all the video tape from every camera you have on the hotel site," he says.

"Don't you need a warrant for that?" asks the Manager.

Murphy finally loses it. He shouts, "Don't you understand what's happened here?" "We've found two bombs in the immediate area. I've requested a warrant, but I need to see those tapes right away! We're running out of time."

The lobby goes quiet as everyone turns to face him. What the hell. Murphy steps up on a coffee table, holds up his badge and says, "Thank you for your attention. I need all of you to return to your rooms. No one is checking in or out for a least a few hours. We're in the middle of an investigation and we require your full cooperation."

He jumps down from the table as the questions start. Over the roar of voices he leans in close and says to the manager, "Would you like to stay here in the lobby or would you like to show me those surveillance tapes?"

"Follow me."

The front desk manager returns with the hotel's Executive Director, who introduces himself as Ian Mackenzie. He's tall and slender, almost to the point of being cadaverous. Even his skin and hair are ashen. He has a slight accent, but Murphy can't place it.

"My desk manager says you're demanding the surveillance videos from every monitor on the premises. Is that correct?"

Using what he hopes is not the last of his patience, Murphy says, "Listen, Mr. Mackenzie, there were two federal agents killed right down the street a few moments ago, so yes, I need that video."

"I don't think I can do that without..." Mackenzie stutters.

Murphy holds up a hand to cut him off, just before he explodes, "You're costing us valuable time! I need to see that fucking video!"

Murphy watches with some satisfaction as Mackenzie turns in a huff and snaps, "There's no need to use that kind of language, sir." He heads down the hall, the desk manager scurrying behind. Murphy follows them to the security office.

"Detective Murphy," Mackenzie hands the tapes to Murphy. "Here are all the security tapes for the last eight hours."

"You use VHS tapes? It's not digital?"

Mackenzie sniffs, "The system is old but still works perfectly well. We record over the tapes every 30 days."

Murphy takes the tapes. They have the date, time and location written in pencil on the label. Talk about old school. He distractedly nods his thanks as Mackenzie steps back to the reception desk, where he has a big job ahead of him.

Murphy has to figure out a way to copy the tapes before the Feds get here. Who the hell has VHS anymore? If they can't be copied in time, maybe he can hold some back. Surely the Feds won't know how many tapes there should be. "Bobby," he says into the phone. "I'll meet you in the lobby. We have to figure out how to copy some VHS tapes and fast."

****

I'm sure the two Feds were killed by the same people who killed Jeannie. I'm looking around the crowded lobby when I hear yet another argument break out at the front desk, this one louder than the others. A group of Canadian tourists is trying to check out. There's a shouting match between the desk clerk and a very large man wearing very short shorts, sandals and a Montreal Canadians jersey. On the floor beside the group I see a huge video camera bag. The bag's outside pocket is slightly open and I can see a couple of extra tapes showing. *Could I be this lucky?* The man is switching from French to English, swearing in both languages.

"Merde! Our plane leaves Orange County airport in three hours and if we can't check out right now, we will be stuck here for a least another day. Shit! Bombs and plastic women. This is such a fucked up country. I just want to take my family home!"

"Sir, the sheriff's department has closed the hotel to anyone checking in or out until further notice," the desk clerk says with remarkable patience, considering.
I walk up to the group, pull out my wallet and quickly flash my Costco card, covering most of it with my hand and put it back in my pocket before anyone can look at it too closely.

"May I be of assistance here?" I ask. "I'm with the sheriff's department." Not a complete lie.

The clerk looks at me with relief, hoping I can help her get this group to calm down. "These people want to leave to catch an evening flight home and we have strict instructions. No one is to check in or out. I've been trying to explain this to them, but they insist on leaving."
I put my hand on the big guy's shoulder. "I might be able to help you out, sir. Let me make a quick call." I step away from the group and turn my back to them as I punch in Murphy's number.

"Murph, I found some video tapes that we can swap out with a couple of the security tapes and give those to the Feds instead."

"Brilliant! Grab them and get over here."

"It won't be quite that easy. The tapes belong to a group of French Canadian tourists trying to leave the hotel. Can I interview these people and let them go if I think they had nothing to do with the bombing? It's a husband, wife, two kids and a grandmother. I don't think anyone in this group is our killer."

"OK, just be damn sure they are who they say they are before you let them go. And hurry up."

"Great. I'll find you when I'm done"

I turn and walk back to the reception desk and look at the manager, who is standing behind the desk clerk, "Sir, would you prepare the paperwork to check this group out? I'll interview these people over in the cafe and, if everything is in order, they'll be free to leave."

"But Detective Murphy said no one was to leave," says the manager.

"It's on his authority I'm interviewing these people so they don't miss their flight," I look toward the grandmother, and flash my most charming smile. "He'll be here momentarily."

I turn back to the rather large husband. "I need a few minutes of your time to ask you and your family members a few questions. It won't take long, and then we can let you check out and be on your way home."
"Merci," he says, grateful. I reach over to help with their luggage, picking up the camera bag.

"This way, please," I lead them into the café.

I let my jacket slide off of my arm and onto the camera bag. We find a table in the café and I put the camera bag at my feet. I scoop both of the video tapes from the side pocket and roll them into my jacket, which I set with the backpack on the bench beside me. I pull a pad of hotel scratch paper and a pen out of my pocket, hoping this guy won't wonder why I don't have a black police notebook. Maybe Canadian cops don't have those. I spend the next fifteen minutes getting the group's information—names, ages, passport numbers, addresses, home and work phone numbers. They're from a small town backwater Quebec and scared. The grandmother doesn't even speak English. They just want to get home. After a while, Murphy comes over—I must be taking too long, but I don't want the Canadians to get suspicious. Murphy looks at my notes and their passports and asks the man a few more questions. Finally, we escort them through the front doors and Murphy tells the deputies to allow the Canadian family to leave. With my jacket and the tapes under my arm, I hand them their video camera case.

Murphy turns to me and whispers, "That took way too fucking long. Where are the tapes? We need to switch them out right now. The Feds will be here any minute."

I pass my jacket to him and we walk to a quiet part of the café, behind a big potted plant. Murphy works his magic, switching around labels. I feel a little pang of guilt when I see the hand-written "Marguerite's Wedding" label transferred to the security tape. Murphy has just finished when a group of suits walks into the hotel lobby. I slide the video tapes into the back waistband of my jeans and pull on my jacket. Murphy picks up the remainder of the tapes, stands and walks up to the group of agents.

"I'm Detective Dwayne Murphy, Homicide, Orange County Sherriff's Department. Who's the Special Agent in Charge of finding out who's in charge here?" He asks. I notice the suits are not amused.

The tallest agent pulls out his wallet, shows his ID to Murphy and says, "Detective Murphy, we're taking charge of this investigation. I'm hoping we can work together."

Murphy reads the agent's name as SAC Findley. Murphy takes his time looking at Findley's badge and finally says, "Yes. Yes, we can."

Findlay puts his badge back in his inside jacket pocket. "Great. Thanks for your cooperation. We can use your help keeping the perimeter secure and getting all the guest information for us. We also need help from your forensics team gathering evidence on the bomb that killed those agents. Can we depend on you and your people?"

Findlay looks at me, but Murphy doesn't bother to introduce me.

"Absolutely. Let me start by giving you the security tapes from the hotel."

"Have you had a chance to look at them?"

"Not yet. I was just handed them a few minutes ago," says Murphy. "I'll inform all the OC Sheriff's Department personnel to stay on site until you tell us otherwise."

Findlay nods and takes the tapes. Murphy turns and starts walking outside and I fall in behind him. Once we're outside and out of earshot, I say, "Are you pissed? This guy seems to be less of a jerk than the guy who was blown up. I mean, I didn't want to see him blown up but that last guy was such an asshole."

"This guy's better than most of them, but the Feds aren't our biggest problem right now. Opening that puzzle box is. With this place crawling with Feds, we won't be able to meet with Chako this evening. Can you call her and see if you can get her to meet with us tomorrow?"

"Sure, Murph," I say. "Can I split? You don't need my help anymore today."

"You've done enough. Get some rest, but stay close to your phone and keep me in the loop, okay?" He walks over to one of the deputies, talks to him, points at me and walks back over.

"I cleared you and your van, so you're good to go. Get out of here before the Feds get a different idea."

"Thanks, Murph. I'll call you if I hear anything."

I waste no time getting to my van. I don't want anybody changing their mind.

Chapter 33

From her vantage point across the street, Alexis watches the Feds get in their car. Once she recovered from the shock of the explosion, she realized it was time for her to get into the game.

She calls her boss. "Sir, two agents from the ATF have just been killed in an explosion here at the hotel. We can't sit around anymore. We need to get out in front of this. I believe General Sandoval is behind all the killings." She listens for a minute before continuing, "I want to bring Murphy and Paladin in. I know Paladin has the puzzle box. We need him and that information." She pauses again. "Thank you, sir. I think it's a good decision. I'll keep you apprised."

She disconnects and thinks, *but how do I to get them to play ball?* She decides to be straight with them and convince them to help her and the agency for which she works. Then, she'll get Paladin to bring Murphy on board. Paladin has to have a source to open the puzzle box or he would have turned it over to the Sherriff's Department by now and she knows for a fact the sheriff's department doesn't have it. She gets into her car and puts in her AC/DC cd. As Highway to Hell starts playing, she turns up volume and merges onto the 5 Freeway heading south.

She arrives at Dana Point Harbor and spots Bobby's van. She parks and makes her way to the gate at the dock. She pushes down and pulls back on the dock gate and it pops open. Top of the line security. She walks over to DJ's boat.

****

"Ahoy! Permission to come aboard!" A voice calls from the dock.

"Alexis," I say, surprised and confused. "Yeah, sure, come aboard."

I lean over to give her a hand up. "DJ, this is Alexis. She works for John G. Alexis, DJ Frasier."

"Is there somewhere we can talk in private?" she asks. "I need to speak with both of you."

"Sure." I'm confused. Why is she here? "We can go below. On a boat, it's about as private as you can get." I lead her down into the salon.

"Wow! This is beautiful."

"Thanks," says DJ "Bobby and I busted our asses on this thing. Then somebody trashed the boat's interior. Luckily, they didn't damage the wood. I just picked up the new couch and table cushions this morning."

"You did all this restoration work yourselves? It's amazing."

DJ and I sit down on one of the benches and Alexis sits across from us. "What I'm going to tell you is a matter of national security. You both need to swear that whatever I say here will not be told to anyone else. That includes your wife, DJ. Are we clear on this?"

We look at each other. "Is this a joke?" I ask, "I didn't think John G had a sense of humor."

"No joke. I'm deathly serious. And so should you be. Can I have your assurance what I'm about to discuss with you will go no further."

She's pretty hot when she's all badass like this so we both say, "Yes," almost at the same time.

Alexis unzips her purse and pulls out a small leather case. She opens it to display an ID card that identifies her as a federal operative with an agency I've never heard of.

"I work for a government agency that goes after the worst of the worst," she begins. "We have virtually unlimited funding and resources. We only answer to the current sitting president, but even he has no real authority over our agency. The agency was set up during the first Bush administration and we carry out work inside the United States as well as internationally. Right now we're focused on General Miguel Sandoval, one of the most vicious criminals in the world. He's been over-seeing the passage of drugs, arms, money and possibly terrorists into the United States. He doesn't think twice about killing anyone who gets in his way. Weaver had agreed to help us. General Sandoval killed Weaver's girlfriend and her family in Cabo. Apparently word got back to The General that Weaver wanted out. The General felt the need to impress upon him what happens to people who cross him. Weaver was privy to some very sensitive paperwork; information so damaging that it could bring down General Sandoval and his entire empire."

She pauses to give us time to process what she's just told us.

"Ricky." I say quietly.

"I'm sorry?"

"His first name was Ricky."

"Of course. I apologize. I know you were close."

DJ finally says, "Is that what's in that puzzle box?"

I elbow him to shut him up.

205

"He's not telling me anything I don't already know, Bobby."
Alexis says. "We know you have the puzzle box that Weav – sorry
– Ricky hid for you to find. If you still have it, we need your help.
Have you found a way to open it?" She pulls a pack of cigarettes
out of her purse and asks, "Is it okay? It's a bad habit, but I can't
seem to shake it."

DJ nods, pulls out his lighter and lights her cigarette before pulling
out his own. He blows the smoke out slowly.

"Holy, shit," I say, running my hand through my hair. I open and
close the clasp on my watch. I stand and climb up the stairs to sit
on the top step, get some fresh air, and collect my thoughts.

"We didn't know anything about Ricky having a girlfriend," I say,
"let alone that she and her family had been murdered. We have
some communication from Ricky explaining what was in the
puzzle box was important and telling us to be careful. He said not
to trust anyone. He stressed that, Alexis. Would it be okay if DJ
and I had a minute alone to talk about this?"

"Understandable. I'll finish my cigarette up on the deck." She
stands up as I come back down into the salon. She walks past me,
up the stairs and steps out on to the deck. She sits down, takes out
her cell phone and makes a call. I reach up and close the hatch.

"What do you want to do?" I ask him. "Do we help her? You've
already had to move your family and your boat has been trashed. I
think you have the most to lose."

"Your house was blown up and Jeannie was killed."

I can't seem to speak after he's said that, so I just nod.

"I don't think we can get out of it at this stage; we're both in too
deep." He crushes his cigarette into the ashtray and lights another
one. "We both could lose everything, but this asshole General

killed our best friend and killed his girlfriend's family. He's ruthless and apparently won't stop there. I think we need to do anything we can to help."

I clear my throat, "Ricky would have done the same thing for either of us. He would have put his life on the line, just like we're about to."

"So we're in?"

"Looks like."

I open the hatch and ask Alexis to come back down. She sits, crosses her legs and looks over at us.

"The answer to your question is," DJ pauses for a moment, as the severity of what we're about to agree to sinks in, "Yes. Yes, we'll help you."

I say, "The answer to your other question, is yes, we think we have a way to open the puzzle box. Tomorrow afternoon we hope to meet with a person who has agreed to help us."

She stands up, "Really? That's good news."

She looks around, "Is there anything to drink on this boat?" DJ glances at me and we both burst out laughing.

I grab three beers, open them, hand one to DJ and one to Alexis. She takes a swig straight out of the bottle. My kind of gal. She continues. "Do you think you could call your cop buddy and get him over here before we go any further? He needs to be on-board with what we're trying to achieve as a team."

"That might be tough," I tell her. "Murph hasn't been exactly forthcoming with his bosses. He thinks there's a leak in his department and he doesn't trust anyone right now. When he can

207

get away from the Hilton, he's going home to watch the security tapes from the hotel."

"I thought the Feds took all that stuff."

How does she know that? "Well, we sort of switched a couple of tapes out when we handed everything over to the Feds. It'll only be a matter of time before all this becomes known and Murph's out of a job. He might even be looking at charges from the DA or even the US Attorney's office."

"I can handle his bosses," Alexis says. "Call him and try to get him here so I can talk to him. It's important. I'm the only person who can identify General Miguel Sandoval if he's on that tape. If The General is in the US, and we can get him, we can put him away for life, shutting down one of the biggest, most violent criminal organizations in Mexico."

I nod my understanding, pick up my cell phone and push Murph's number. He answers and I say "We need to meet up as soon as you're free. We've had an interesting development that might make your life a little easier."

He starts to ask me a bunch of questions, but I stop him. "I don't want to talk about it over the phone. There's too much to explain."

Finally he says, "Sure. Come to my house in an hour. I've got the equipment to look at the tapes and I want to do it ASAP. The Feds have taken control of the Hilton crime scene. My wife and kids went to Disneyland, so we'll be alone for a while. They always stay until the bitter end to see the parade and fireworks."

I hang up. "We can meet at his house in an hour. We can explain everything to him then."

"Perfect. Let's go grab a bite while we can. I'm starving," she says, setting her beer on the table and grabbing her purse. She turns to inspect DJ who's sitting with his head down, cigarette ash about to fall to the floor.

"Hey DJ," I ask gently. "Are you coming with us?"

DJ lifts his head and looks at us. The pressure of the last few days shows clearly on his face. "No, not right now. I'm not hungry and this is all way too crazy for me. I just want to surf and have my quiet life back." He sighs. "But, if you really need me, I'll come with you and help out any way I can. I'm in this thing to deep to quit."

"Go surf, DJ." Alexis says sympathetically. "We're going to need your help soon enough, so jump in the water and clear your head. Not a word to anyone, do you understand?"

I nod my agreement and head up into the cockpit. Alexis puts one foot on the stairs to follow me and turns back to my friend. "DJ, we might need your boat at some point. How ready is it to sail?"

"She's always ready." DJ says.

Alexis and I head up the dock toward the parking lot. She pulls out a key ring and hits a couple of buttons, disabling her car alarm and starting the car while we're still about twenty five feet away.

"This comes in handy at times like this, when people are routinely being blown up in their cars." It dawns on her what she's just said and she stops and turns to me. "I'm so sorry, Bobby. That was stupid of me. I know Jeannie meant a lot to you."

How does she seem to know everything? I shake my head. "It's okay." I look over at her car, an older dark blue Toyota. "I thought you secret agents had fancy, souped up sports cars," I say, changing the subject, "Is it safe?"

"Of course. It doesn't draw any attention, which I need in my work. Hop in and I'll run a diagnostic on the car systems before I put it into drive. The engineers at our agency install cameras and surveillance systems on all our cars. We know right away if anyone's been trying to tamper with them."

She punches up a screen on the dashboard. After a minute she says, "All clear. So, where would you like to eat? I'm buying. This job is comes with a killer expense account." She smiles, puts the car in gear and pulls out of the Harbor.

"I know a great sushi place on Coast Highway, not too far from here."

When we arrive at the restaurant, she finds a parking spot in the rear lot and we walk inside, where it's cool and dark. We opt for the sushi bar because we don't want to be late for our meeting with Murphy.

Back in the car she asks me, "What's your take on Detective Murphy?"

I have to think about my answer for a minute. "Well, I just reconnected with Murph since Ricky was murdered. That first day, he struck me as a bit of an asshole, but from what I've seen since, he's hardworking; willing to take chances to catch the bad guys. Right now, he doesn't trust many people because of the leak in his department, especially the Feds. Any Fed, if you get my meaning. I'm not sure he'll be receptive to all this."

I give her Murphy's address and she punches it into her GPS.

"He worked for my dad, you know." I say.

"Who worked for your dad? Detective Murphy?"

"Yeah, my dad owned a hardware store called The Nail Apron and Murph worked there before he figured out he wanted to become a cop. My dad really liked him. By the time he left for San Francisco's police academy, I was already on the pro surf tour. We hadn't seen each other until this all happened."

It takes us ten minutes to drive to Murphy's house and we finish the ride in silence. When we knock on the front door, we hear him shout, "The door's open. Come on in. I'm in the office in the back."

We head toward the back of the house. It's a two-story affair with beautiful grounds that Murphy and his wife Debbie have landscaped themselves and maintained over the years. The office is wood paneled and nicely appointed; very manly.

I say, "Murph, this is Alexis. She'd like to talk to you."

Murph stands up, "Sorry, Bobby, I thought you were coming alone." He reaches out to shake Alexis's hand. "Dwayne Murphy."

"Nice office." Alexis says with a smile as she shakes his hand, looking around. "Pretty fancy on a cop's salary."

Murph says, "When we sold the house in the Bay area, we did pretty well. I bought all the materials and did it myself. I learned a lot working for Bobby's dad. I spend more time in here than anywhere else, so I wanted it to be done right. Debbie and the kids aren't allowed in here without an invitation."

He gestures to a couple of chairs, "Have a seat. How do you know Bobby? I don't think he's mentioned you before." He sits back down behind his desk.

"I could tell you the false pretenses under which Bobby and I first met, but I know you to be a no-nonsense guy," says Alexis, "and we don't have a lot of time. I need to explain what and who I am,

211

so it's essential you to just listen for a few minutes. I'll answer all your questions when I'm done. Are you okay with that?"
Murph glances over at me, leans back in his chair and says, "Shoot."

Alexis explains everything to him. Since I've heard it all before, I get up, head into the kitchen and help myself to a beer. I sit down in the back yard waiting for them to finish. About thirty minutes later, I hear Murph call me back into the office.

"That's a lot of fucking information you just dropped on us," he says to Alexis. "Bobby, how okay are you with all this? Does DJ know?"

"It's taken me a bit of time, but I know for Ricky's sake we have to help nail this Sandoval guy. DJ doesn't love it, but he's willing to help."

He shakes his head, "Okay. If you guys are on board." He turns to his computer, "We'd better start with the hotel tapes. I downloaded the security video from the Hilton to disk."
I get up to look over his shoulder but my phone rings. I look down at the screen. It's Chako. "I need to take this. I'll be right back. We might get some answers soon." I step out into the backyard again.

I come back in to the office and say, "That was Jeannie's mom. She's going to the house where Jeannie was staying in Corona del Mar tomorrow. She's going to pack up her things."
Alexis says, "That house belongs to John. He and Jeannie got into a huge fight on the day she was killed. Someone, I don't know which one of them, broke a very expensive Chihuly vase during their argument. John wouldn't talk about what happened or why, but I feel that it was very personal between those two. He was upset for the rest of the day."

"It was personal, all right," I say. "The reason I left the islands was because I saw Jeannie and John in bed together. I don't think either

212

of them knew I saw them. I packed up my shit and caught the first plane out of Hawaii. The other day was the first time I've seen her since that awful day."

"So that's what happened," says Murph. "I always wondered why you never went back to the tour. I followed your career pretty closely. You were as good as Slater. You could have been the world champ if you hadn't left the tour."

"Guys, we're getting off track here," Alexis interrupts. "We need to look at the video and see if we can spot anyone who is on my list of people who are persona non grata in the United States."

For the next two hours we watch the hotel video. It's so boring I almost nod off a couple of times. Suddenly, Alexis jumps up. "Stop the tape!"

Murphy backs it up for about a minute and then starts running it forward, a frame at a time, focusing in on a man walking toward the bank of elevators.

"Stop there. Do you see that image there?" Alexis says, pointing at the computer screen. "See the guy standing in the corner, by the elevator. Can you adjust that image and make it clearer?"

Murphy plays with the image and cleans it up as best as he can with his home equipment. He brings the face into focus, crops the image and prints it out.

"That's him, that's General Sandoval!" Alexis cries. "That's the son of a bitch. He's had more plastic surgery, but I never forget a walk. That's what your friend Weaver was trying to let us know. He must have current pictures; maybe he even knew his new ID. That must be part of the information that's inside the puzzle box."

Murphy picks up his phone, "I have to tell the Captain."

213

He glances at Alexis to see if she's going to stop him. She nods and he punches in the number.

"Cap, Murphy. Paladin accidentally ended up with one of the security videos, so we thought we'd check it out before turning it in. What?" Murph glances at me, "He says he found it on the lobby floor. One of the Feds must have dropped it. That's not important right now, sir. The guy who killed the Feds and the Francis woman was hiding right under our noses. He was a guest at the hotel and we walked right by him. We need to go back and search the hotel and see if he's still there."

He listens for a minute, his jaw tightening. "What?!" Murphy shouts into the phone. "Captain, that isn't right. Fuck the Feds. This guy has killed at least three people here that we know of and we're expected to just stand by while the Feds trip over their own dicks?"

He listens a minute longer. We can hear the Captain yelling through the phone. "Yes sir," Murphy says finally and hangs up, his face reddening. He takes a deep breath before he turns to look at us.

"The Captain's getting heat from the Feds about their missing tape. They've frozen us out of the case. The Captain wants all the evidence on his desk today. Alexis, can you call your boss and get the Feds to let us back into the game?"

"I'm sorry, Detective, that's not how we operate. We run our own ops. We don't share or let anyone know we're in the game." She pulls out her phone, "However, I do know some people at Homeland Security. They might be able to buy us some time and get your Captain off your back. After that, you're on your own." She looks over at me. "I owe that much to your friend, Ricky. He was really helping us out."

She puts her phone to her ear and walks out of Murphy's office.

I turn to Murph, "What do you think?"

"Shit, Bobby, I don't know what to think. But, if she can make this happen, I'll be impressed. In my experience none of these agencies play nice with each other. They're glory grabbers. They'd rather see their name in headlines than do the right thing."

Alexis walks back into the room. "The clock's ticking," she says. "We have five days to get this case wrapped up before the shit hits the fan. Let's get to work."

We continue to review the tape to see if Alexis can spot any of The General's henchmen, while I look over Murphy's notes to see if that might shed some light on Jeannie's and Ricky's deaths.

Murphy finally says, "You guys better get out of here. Debbie and the kids'll be home soon."

"Right," Alexis looks at her watch. "I have to go, anyway. I need to bring my boss up to speed on what we've found here today." She picks up the printouts. "I'll catch up with you in the morning, Detective, and thank you for your help. Let's go, Bobby."

Chapter 34

John G. is pacing in his office. He's been watching the news all day and the deaths of those two Federal agents have galvanized him into action. He had called General Sandoval and, as expected, The General had not answered his phone. With the deal a little less than ten days away, he should be answering his fucking phone.

"Shit, shit, shit!" John yells in his office. That murderous son of a bitch is here, in California, killing anybody who could put the kibosh on this deal. Including, he suspects, Jeannie.

He needs to come up with a plan, quickly. Where the hell was Alexis? He needs her – now!

****

Alexis wakes to her cell phone beeping. It takes her a few seconds to get her bearings. She and Bobby had crashed at DJ's house last night. She knows John G. will be looking for her and until she has a plan, she'll have to stay away from him. She reaches in her purse and shuts off her phone. There's a gentle knock on her door.

"Come in," she says. "It's open."

Bobby and DJ open the door and stand, a little shyly, at the threshold.

"Morning, guys. What's up?"

"We're going to catch a few waves and wanted to let you know we'll be back in a couple of hours," says DJ.

"Have fun. I think I'll sleep a little longer. Thanks for letting me know."
"We'll lock up on our way out."

217

"Is there any food in the house?" she asks.

"Yeah, Maria left me pretty well stocked."

"Then don't eat when you guys get out of the water, okay? I'll make us breakfast."

"Great! We'll only be gone a couple of hours," says DJ.

John G. has her at work early. It's been a long time since she's slept in. She closes her eyes and drifts back to sleep.

****

DJ and I load our boards into his truck and start to back out of the driveway. "Where to, bud?" I ask.

DJ thinks for a second. "Let's check out T-Street. That way we can look at the clean-up to make sure we can go back to work tomorrow."

He pops in the cigarette lighter and I roll down my window. Ten minutes later, we pull up in front of the T-Street job.

"Well," says DJ. "The crime scene tape is gone. Let's hope we can get this job going again."

We walk up on the view deck and look down at the pier. We see a set roll in that had to have at least six, maybe eight foot faces.

"Check that out, DJ, it's going off, bro."

When he doesn't answer me, I look over and see he's preoccupied as he walks across the deck to read the paperwork taped to the window. It's from the clean-up company allowing us to resume building.

218

"We're good to go," he calls, then turns to look at the ocean and sees a big set hitting the pier.

"Holy shit, look at that," he says, "This swell looks like it's going to get a lot bigger."
It's hollow and clean, with only a handful of guys out in the water. "Let's go get wet."

We head back to the truck, grab our boards, rash guards and wax and walk down to the beach. As we sit waxing our boards, I look up at the ocean. I tap DJ on the shoulder.

"Check this out," I say, pointing.

We look out at the set coming in and a lone guy is taking off. Instead of standing up, he gets to his knees, drops into a monster left and cranks a turn so hard that all we can see is the bottom of his board. He pulls into a big tube and disappears for about ten seconds. Then he comes blowing out, cranking a turn up to the top of the wave, punching through the lip before free-falling back down the face of the wave and heading to the shore. He picks up his board and starts walking toward us. He's not a young guy and has been riding kneeboards as long as we can remember.

"Hey, guys. What's going on? It's pretty insane out there," he says to us.

"Nice tube ride, Dougie. When are you going to learn to really surf?" DJ says with a grin.

"Why would I want to be a nondescript surfer like you guys when I can be a first class knee-boarder?" Dougie says as he shakes water out of his hair, getting us wet. "I still get deeper in the tube than you ever will. Watch it out there, guys. It's getting hairy. Later." He gives us a back-handed wave over his shoulder and walks up the beach.

219

"Hey, Dougie, give me a call next week. I need a painting and finishing bid on the house across the street, ok?" DJ calls after him.

Dougie's company's slogan is 'I paint San Clemente.' It makes him sound like one of the many plein air artists around town, but he's been painting homes in town for thirty years.

"Will do. Thanks."

"Let's go ride some waves, bro," DJ says to me. He gets to his feet and picks up his board. We hit the water and paddle out in between sets.

"Outside!" I shout and we keep paddling hard. I paddle over the first-set wave and the second one, but turn around and start paddling hard for the third one. I catch the wave. I jump to my feet and glide down the face of the wave. At the base of the wave, I make a drawn out bottom turn and set my line. Just then, the wave wraps around me. The next thing I know I come flying out of the wave. I feel exhilarated. I wish I could feel this good all day, every day. I paddle out to try and catch that feeling as many times as I can, before I get too tired.

Chapter 35

Something awakens her. Has she heard a noise downstairs? Alexis sits up in bed and listens. She reaches under her pillow and pulls out her Glock 228. It's her favorite gun. It has the stopping power of a 45 caliber handgun, with less weight and more accuracy. Quietly, she chambers a round and slides the safety off. Barefoot, wearing only the long t-shirt DJ lent her as a nightgown, she slowly swings her legs over the side of the bed and creeps to the bedroom door. Carefully, she eases the door open. Someone else is in the house. Bobby and DJ haven't been gone long enough. She pulls the bedroom door almost closed behind her. With her back to the wall, she slowly slides down the carpeted hall into DJ's office. Crossing the office, she moves into the Jack and Jill bathroom and through the door into the adjoining kids' bedroom, where Bobby slept last night.

She hears a noise outside Bobby's door, but whoever's in the house keeps walking toward the bedroom where she had been sleeping. She eases the kids' room door open a crack, just enough to see the back of a very large man facing her bedroom door, holding a gun in his hand. She pushes the door fully open and steps into the hall, gun raised, bare feet planted firmly on the floor. The hammer makes an audible click as she pulls it back. The man starts to make a half-turn toward her.

"Stop right where you are," she says. "Put the gun down on the floor very slowly and turn around. I want to see your hands."

Lifting his left hand into the air, he bents his knees and carefully puts his gun on the floor. He stands and raises both hands.

"You're making a big mistake," he says over his shoulder.

Alexis can see he's a big guy with no neck and short cropped blonde hair, like her dad's old crew cuts.

"I don't think so," she replies.

221

"I'm DEA. My badge is in my pocket," he says, his hands still in the air, "I'm going to turn around slowly and show it to you, okay?"

"If you make a move—any move at all—that I feel is threatening, I will shoot you right where you stand. Understand?"

He slowly turns toward her and reaches with his right hand to the left side of his belt. Not to his breast pocket where his ID should be. This realization dawns on her as he pulls a gun from under his jacket. She quickly lowers her weapon and shoots a bullet into his upper thigh.

He screams and drops the second gun to grab for his leg. "You fucking bitch! You shot me!"

"If you make a move toward either gun, I'll aim higher next time. Now, down on the ground, face to the floor with your hands behind your head."

"I'm bleeding. I need a doctor right now!"

"Down on the ground asshole or I'll shoot you again! Now!" She yells.

He slowly turns and leans against the wall. In that instant she recognizes her assailant. He makes an odd movement with his right hand and she sees a small pistol slide from his sleeve into his hand. She doesn't hesitate, raises her gun and fires three shots into his chest. The force pushes him back against the wall and. He hits his head and slides to the floor, eyes closed. She rushes over to him and kicks the guns out of the way. There's no blood from the chest wound. This asshole is wearing a vest. He's not dead, as she hoped but knocked out from the impact of the bullets and his head hitting the wall. She picks up the guns and takes them into DJ's office. She puts them on his desk and grabs the roll of duct tape she had seen in there yesterday. She snatches a towel from the bathroom and walks back out into the hall. He's still out cold. She tapes his hands together and then tapes the towel around the wound in his thigh. She reaches into his jacket pocket and pulls out his wallet and cell phone. Opening his wallet she curses under her breath. She steps over him, goes back into her bedroom, turns on her phone and calls her boss.

"We have a major problem, sir," she opens the wallet again to confirm her nightmare. "I just shot Bill Conners. He used to work for DEA and his last assignment was in Mexico. He was the one who got Weaver involved with John Gomez and The General. He just tried to kill me." She listened for a moment. "No, he's not dead, but I got him pretty good. What do you want me to do?"

She listens for a while longer and finally says, "Yes, sir," and disconnects.

Alexis allows herself a big sigh before getting up off the bed and heading back into the hall. She can see Conners is starting to come around. She checks the leg wound and see the bleeding is under control. She had just grazed him, really, the big baby. Her boss is sending a 'clean-up-team' to remove Conner and any evidence left behind. She reaches into his side pocket and removes his car keys. She backs away from him and into the bedroom to pull on her clothes and leave the house.

She walks purposefully up the street, pushing the trunk release on the keys until, about halfway up the block, the trunk of a brand new Black Lexis sedan pops open. *Bad guys don't deserve nice cars,* she thinks. This one will be confiscated. She might even add it to the collection of cars she drives. Inside the trunk she finds a laptop and a briefcase, which she picks up, carries into the house and sets on the kitchen table. The briefcase has a combination lock. So much for opening that up. It'll take too much time to try and figure out the combination herself. She turns on the laptop and sees the DEA logo appear on the screen. When the clean-up crew shows up to haul this clown away, she'll have them deliver the computer and briefcase to the tech guys at the agency.

A couple of minutes later, Alexis hears the garage door open and Bobby and DJ walk into the kitchen, hair still wet from surfing.

"Hey, what's up, girl? You look upset." DJ says.

"Yeah, I've had a rough morning. Somebody broke in while you two were surfing and tried to kill me. Not my favorite way to start the day. I haven't even had my coffee yet."

"What?!" DJ shouts, "Who? What happened? Are you okay?"

She holds up her hand to stop him. "I'm fine, but it's definitely not cool. It's a rogue DEA agent—we've had dealings in the past. He's upstairs, bleeding away on your hall floor. Relax. He's not dead, but I did wound him. I duct taped him up and even patched his wound—not that he deserved it—but until my boss and extraction guys show up to haul his ass out of here, he stays where he is, okay?"

****

DJ and I stare at Alexis then we both look up toward the second floor of DJ's house. We look at each other and I see DJ's mouth open to say something, when my phone rings. What else could possibly happen?

"Hello? Oh, hello, Chako," I say into the phone. "Ah, yes. Sure. I've kind of had some stuff going on, too. We can meet you later today. What time? Okay, see you then, and thanks."

I disconnect and look at DJ and Alexis. "Jeannie's mom wants to meet with us at the hotel restaurant. Murph, too." I dial Murphy's cell number. When he answers, I tell him that Chako wants him to be at the meeting when she tries to open the box. "We can meet

224

you in the restaurant of the Hilton at five-thirty; that's the time that Chako is available. Okay, see you soon." I say and hang up.

I look at Alexis. "What's going to happen when your team gets here?"

"They'll arrest Conners and confiscate all of his gear, including his car. Then they'll take him to be interrogated by the people at our agency who specialize in this sort of thing. They'll also need to debrief me, but probably at our offices, not here. They may want to grab you guys, too, for questioning. My advice is to get out of here before they arrive. I'll meet up with you later at the hotel, okay? Five-thirty, right? I'll make sure that the house is locked up when we leave."

DJ says, "Let's get down to the boat, Bobby. We can hang out there for a while." He turns toward Alexis. "Will everything be cleaned up? Will Maria be able to tell any of this shit happened here? What about the neighbors? Is your team going to come in here with sirens blaring?"

Alexis shakes her head as she gets up to walk us out to the garage. "These guys are pros. They'll come in a van marked for carpet cleaning or something like that and I'll get them to pull into the garage. The neighbors won't know a thing. My gun has a silencer and he didn't get a shot off. The house will be so clean Maria will think her mother's been here. Now you guys get out of here. They'll be here any minute."

I open the passenger door to the truck and get in.

"Bobby, I have to be there at the opening of the puzzle box," Alexis says, closing the truck door. "If I'm late don't open it without me, understand? DJ, don't look so worried. I'll look after everything."

DJ presses the button on his visor, opens the garage door and backs out of the driveway. As we drive down the street, a cleaning company's van passes us. I look into the side mirror to see the van pulling up in front of DJ's house.

"We got out of there just in time, bro." I say.

DJ's jaw is set in a firm line. "I am just not cut out for this cloak and dagger shit, Bobby. My wife and kids are stashed in Oregon at her parent's house, and I have a guy bleeding on the carpet in my upstairs hallway—this sucks on so many different levels. A few weeks ago I had nothing more to worry about than drywall shipments. Now I have to get out of my own house while some mystery clean-up crew removes blood and a bad guy." He presses the cigarette lighter.

"We've got Murph and now Alexis on our side." I say. "We'll get through this— hopefully in one piece." The lighter pops and he shakes a cigarette out of a pack he has on the dashboard. He fires it up and inhales deeply.

We pull into the harbor parking lot and notice a crowd around the boat, then see Harbor Patrol and Orange County Sherriff's uniforms.

"Shit," says DJ under his breath. "Now what?"

"Should we just turn around and get the hell out of here, too?" I ask.

"No. No point in that. Let's see what's going on. Shit."

He unlocks the gate and we walk down the dock to the boat. DJ walks up to one of the sheriffs. "Excuse me. I'm the owner of this boat. Is there some sort of problem?"

The sheriff lifts her sunglasses and gives DJ the once-over. She says, "May I see some ID, please?"

"Sure." DJ pulls out his wallet and opens it to his driver's license. "Here you go."

"Mr. Frasier, would you step over here, please?"

She motions me to stand back and takes DJ closer to the boat. Two of the harbor patrol deputies are escorting a hand-cuffed man down from the deck of the boat. He's about five foot eight, maybe mid-forties, scrawny with too-long, thinning hair.

"Do you know this person, Mr. Frasier?" she asks.

"No. I've never seen him before in my life."

"Your neighbor noticed him trying to break into your boat and called us. He has no ID on him and won't say anything to us."

"What the hell was he doing on my boat?"

"We don't know. We'll know more once we get him to the station and run his prints. For now we can charge him with breaking and entering."
She turns to the other sheriff, "Let's get ICE involved and see if they can find out who this loser is, okay?"

He leads the man up the dock and toward one of the squad cars.

She turns back to DJ. "We found no damage to your boat, Mr. Frasier, but would you please take a closer look and see if anything is missing?"

DJ boards the boat and after about ten minutes comes back onto the dock.

227

"It looks like everything is here," he says.

"Do you need any further assistance from us, sir?" she asks.

"No. I don't think so. Thank you for your quick response."

She pulls apart the paperwork she's been writing up and gives him a copy. She fishes a business card out of her top pocket and hands it to him.

"If you notice anything missing, please give me a call. We'll be in touch. It's a good thing your neighbor was paying attention."

She turns and follows her colleagues up the dock. DJ looks at the card in his hand. He looks over at his nosy neighbor, who's been watching the whole drama play out from his own boat. As much as he hates to, DJ says, "Thanks for keeping an eye on my boat, Herb."

"No problem, DJ. We neighbors have to stick together, right?"

This guy is such a jerk, but I know DJ is very grateful that he called the cops. DJ nods at his neighbor as we board the boat, open the cabin door and step down into the salon.

"You told her everything was okay DJ, but it's not. That guy obviously has searched the boat."

The searching had been done very professionally. It wouldn't have been apparent to anyone who didn't know the inside of the boat as well as DJ and I do.

"That guy wasn't trying to get into the boat. He was locking it up when Herb called the Harbor Patrol. He was trying to get out. Luckily they were nearby or he would have just taken off and no one would have stopped him." DJ says, "Where did you stash the puzzle box, Bobby? Do you think he got it?"

"Not a chance, bro," I say with a grin, "I put it in a waterproof container, weighted the whole thing down and tied it to one of the fenders. It's buried in the silt down there. You could be right on top of it and never see it."

DJ sits down. "That's a relief. I'd hate to be going through all this shit for nothing. You'd better get that thing up to the surface before someone else comes after it. You'll need to have it with you when we meet Chako this afternoon. You might as well get it up off the bottom and we'll keep it safe until the meeting."

"Good idea. I don't think that anyone else is going to try to take it away from us today. If Chako can open the puzzle box, and we turn over the information to Alexis, we should be done. Then we'll get our lives back."

"Yeah, right. I'll believe that when it happens. You get the box, then we'd better call Alexis and tell her what just happened."

"Don't bother," says a voice from the dock. "Permission to come aboard?"

"Come on down, Alexis," DJ yells up. He turns to me and says under his breath, "Jesus, she's like a blood hound, Bobby, always sniffing around."

"I hear that a lot, DJ." she says smiling. "The clean-up crew will be finished with your house within the hour. You'll never know they were there. I'm so sorry I had to shoot that guy in your house, but he pulled a gun on me. Hell, he pulled three guns on me. If he hadn't been wearing body armor, it would have been a lot worse. Now tell me, what happened here?"

"Thank you for that, Alexis," DJ says sarcastically. "I'm so stoked that you didn't blow that guy away in my house. Bobby, go get that box and I'll explain what was happening when we pulled up to the dock."

"Is this about someone found on the boat again?" She asks as she steps aside to let me pass.

DJ fills her in as I pull the fishline that brings the box up out of the water, still safe in its waterproof container.

"I took his picture with my cell phone," I say, coming around. "Have a look and see if you know him, Alexis."

I call up the picture on my phone and hand it to Alexis. "Uh, oh, I know this guy. His name is Captain Julio Castillo. He's one of the top operators in the Mexican Navy. He can fly anything: jets, planes, helicopters, ultra-lights. He went through the Navy SEAL program. He's never been linked to General Sandoval - until now." She says, studying the picture. "I'm surprised he didn't put up some kind of a fight. He's a real bad ass. Send that picture to my phone, will you? I need to let my boss know right away. This could be the breakthrough we've been looking for."

She hands me back my phone and reaches into her purse for her own. While she's at it, she grabs her pack of cigarettes and lights up. She takes a deep drag and dials her boss while she exhales the smoke from her lungs.

As Alexis makes her call, I walk back down into the salon with the waterproof bag that holds a clear watertight box. I set the bag in the sink and carefully unzip it, open the container and gently remove the puzzle box. Alexis comes back below. I set it on the table, between the three of us. We all look at it in silence for a while as DJ and Alexis finish their cigarettes.

Finally I say, "We have to get going."

"I don't think that I'm going to go Bobby," DJ says. He looks tired. "I want to stay here on the boat, if you guys don't mind." Alexis looks at her watch, "That's fine. If there's traffic it'll take us longer to get there and we don't want to keep Mrs. Francis waiting. DJ, let me know if you find anything left behind by the good Captain, okay? Listening devices or maybe a wireless camera?"

"Sure, Alexis," says DJ. "I'll take a good look."

I pick up the box, wrap it in a clean, dry towel and put it in my backpack. I motion Alexis to go up the stairs ahead of me.

"I'll call Detective Murphy to tell him about Castillo, too," she says, "I have to let Murphy know what a risk Castillo is to the sheriff's department."

I look back at DJ as we start up the stairs. He sits with his hands on his knees, looking around his beautiful boat. Then he sighs, stands up and starts to carefully search. I hope he'll know a listening device if he sees one.

Chapter 36

Murphy's rushing to get to the Hilton on time when he sees the bulletin for Julio Castillo's intake. He calls Captain Sprague to relay what Alexis has told him, without telling the Captain how he knows. The deputies transporting Castillo have to take every precaution when handling him.

Murphy thinks maybe that Castillo is the asshole responsible for killing the ATF agents at the hotel. He has to get to the jail quickly. He needs to question Castillo before the Feds show up and take him away.

He can't stop thinking how close they had come to catching General Sandoval yesterday. By the time The General's image was found on the tape, the bastard had already disappeared, leaving nothing behind in the hotel room. It had been wiped clean better than any housekeeping staff could do. Right now there was no direct evidence linking The General to any of the murders. Sooner or later he would fuck up and Murphy would be there to arrest him.

He reaches for his phone to call Bobby just as a call 911 flashes on the phone display. He calls the Captain, who fills him in. It just gets worse and worse. He calls Bobby. "I can't meet you and Mrs. Francis," he says. "The guy they arrested at DJ's boat has escaped. Somehow Castillo unlocked his cuffs and beat the shit out of the deputy; took his radio, his gun, cuffed him and stuffed him into the trunk of the cruiser. By the time anyone realized what had happened, Castillo was long gone. I'll catch up with you later. Call me when you get the puzzle box open. I don't care what time."

Without waiting for a reply, Murphy ends the call, lights up the car, pulls a U-turn, and speeds back south.

****

I hang up from my call with Murph just as we pull into the Hilton parking structure. When I tell Alexis what's just happened, she slams the heel of her hand on the steering wheel. "Shit! I knew it! My agency should have assisted the Sherriff's Department when they were transporting Castillo."

As we pull into a parking space on the second floor Alexis removes a cigarette from her bag. It takes her a couple of tries to light it. We get out of the car and start to walk toward the hotel lobby.

"It's not your fault, Alexis," I say, "You did your job. You called your boss and we called Murphy. They didn't take this guy as seriously as they should have and now we're all in trouble."

Alexis stops in front of the lobby doors and finishes her cigarette.

"Those things are going to kill you, you know."

"Castillo being on the loose scares me more the than a few cigarettes," she replies, putting the cigarette in the sand-filled bowl outside the revolving doors. "If he does kill us, it'll save me the trouble of quitting."

We walk into the hotel lobby. I glance over at the lounge, and see Chako. Then I notice she's not alone. I take Alexis by the elbow and lead her to where Chako is sitting. What the hell is John G. doing here?

"Good afternoon, Chako," I say. "I would like to introduce you to my friend Alexis, Alexis this is Jeannie's mother, Mrs. Chako Francis."

"So pleased to meet you, Alexis," Chako stands and bows slightly. Alexis returns the bow, but hesitates when she turns toward John. I can see she's as confused about his presence here as I am.

"Bobby, Alexis, thank you so much for joining us," John G. says. "They're holding a quiet table for us. Follow me. We have a lot to discuss, so please bear with me."

He speaks to the hostess, who leads us into the hotel lounge, to a dark banquet at the back. A server comes to take drink orders and Chako orders tea, John G. a Pellegrino and Alexis just shakes her head. I'd like nothing more than a beer right now, but I don't trust myself. I have the feeling I'd better stay clear-headed, so I just ask for a glass of water. Once she's gone, John G. gets right down to business.

"I need whatever is in that puzzle box and I know you have it, Bobby," he says. "Chako and I have talked about it and she's relatively certain she can open it. Hopefully the contents inside are complete and undamaged. If what I think is in it, I plan to use those documents to stop a terrorist attack."

"But, I don't understand," Alexis finally finds her voice.

He smiles at her, "I know you just thought I was your rich, eccentric boss." He slides a small leather case towards her and she opens it. It's some sort of ID I don't recognize.
"I'm with the National Security Agency," he continues. "I've been under deep cover as a drug dealer for the past twelve years. That's all I can tell you right now. You'll just have to be patient." He turns to me, "Bobby, would you please give Chako the puzzle box and let's see if she can open it?"

"Wait just a minute," I say. "I thought you were one of the bad guys."

He laughs, "If I were, you wouldn't be sitting here and I wouldn't be politely asking for the box. Please. We don't have much time. You have to trust me, Bobby. Alexis, help me out here."

"He's right, Bobby," she says. "I'm not one hundred percent sure what's going on, but I've worked for John G. long enough to know if he wants something he just takes it. I think we have to trust him."

I'm not sure. I wish I could call Murphy before I do anything, but he's still tied up. I look between Alexis, John G. and Chako. Our server comes back with our drinks and gives me another minute to try to clear my head. Alexis has still not revealed her true identity to John G. It's very surreal sitting here in the middle of all this. When our server leaves again, Chako says, "It will be alright, Bobby, I promise you. Please, our time is very limited. Let me see if I might be able to open your puzzle box."

I look over at Alexis and she nods. Reluctantly, I pull the puzzle box from my back pack and hand it across the table to Chako. She turns it over in her hands.

"It is very beautiful. Mr. Nueriuma built these between the late eighteen and early nineteen hundreds. These boxes took many hours of intense labor to make, each one was different. This one is exquisite. Each piece was hand crafted and fitted. Mr. Nueriuma had a specific number of moves to open each box he designed. The puzzle boxes ranged from very small to quite large and they were opened using as few as four moves to as many as one hundred and twenty-two. I estimate that this puzzle box will take sixty-nine separate moves to open."

"How do you know that?" Alexis asks her.

"I grew up opening these as a child. Bobby, do you have your friend's letter? There may be a clue in the letter that my Jeannie might have missed." Her eyes mist over at her daughter's name. She takes a napkin and wipes away a tear.

I reach into my backpack again, this time into one of the interior pockets and pull out Ricky's letter. I open the zip lock bag I've

236

been keeping it in and pass it over to Chako. Then we sit quietly for the next fifteen minutes or so as she studies the letter, picks up the box, turns it around and sets it back down again.

Finally she says, "I do think I will be able to open it. However, if I do make a mistake—just one wrong move—we may forever lose the contents inside. Are you prepared to suffer the consequences if something goes wrong?"

We look at each other, waiting for someone to make the decision. After what seems like forever, John G. speaks, "Chako, please do your best. You're the only hope we have. We all understand the consequences if you fail. "

She nods, "This is going to take some time. The letter does contain many answers, but it also leaves us with many questions."

As Chako starts to work, Alexis looks at John G. "John, I can't go into detail right now, but you and I have a great deal in common. I work for a shadow government agency that has been trying to take down General Sandoval for the last few years. We're on the same side. I'll explain everything to you later, but right now I need to call my boss and apprise him of the situation. Am I to assume that you won't want your identity to become known just yet?"

If he's surprised, he's hiding it well. "Yes. Thank you. It's important that I keep my cover. My agency also wants to take down General Sandoval, but it's much larger than that. What's inside this puzzle box may allow us to shut down a major drug and terrorist organization."
"Okay." She pauses and takes a deep breath, "I'll leave your name out of it for the time being, but if we are unable open the puzzle box, then we'll have to re-evaluate our positions in this matter. I can't keep my boss in the dark for long."

"Fair enough."

237

"Wait, I need to notify Detective Murphy," I say. "He wants to know if and when we open the box."

"I'm going to ask you to hold off on that for the moment," John G. stops me. "You can inform him once we know the outcome."

Alexis gets up and walks out of the lounge to make her call. During our conversation, Chako has opened the first six locks of the puzzle box. This is going to take some time.

"I think I could use a beer," I say to John.

"Amen to that," he says and signals for our server. Alexis returns to the table and sits down.

"We all needed something to calm our nerves, so I took the liberty of ordering you a martini," John G. says to her.

She sinks into the banquet and nods her head gratefully as we all turn our eyes toward Chako to watch her make the many intricate moves it will take to open the box.

Chapter 37

Murphy had been at the crime scene for the last hour and a half, when Captain Sprague finally shows up. *What the hell took him so long?*

"Bring me up to speed," he barks.

Murph checks his frustration before answering, "Well, what we've figured out so far is that Castillo had a universal key or a lock-pick hidden on his person and was able to unlock his cuffs. It was probably missed when he was searched at the boat, since the arresting officers just thought he was some petty burglar. Somewhere en route to the jail, he convinced Officer Baker to pull over for some reason. He must have overpowered Baker when he opened the back door. Castillo took Baker's service revolver, cuffed him, put him in the trunk, and moved the patrol car to a spot where it would take time to be found."

"Who assigned a rookie like Baker to transport this guy anyway?"

"The deputies thought he was just pulling a daytime B and E. We didn't find out his true identity until later."

"Is Baker alright?"

"Yes, sir. He's showing no sign of damage, except maybe to his pride. He was taken to the hospital, as a precaution."

Captain Sprague shakes his head. "What's damaging is that Office Baker failed to follow the proper procedures."

Murphy can tell the Captain is just warming up to one of his rants. Over Sprague's shoulder he sees a man say something to one of the uniforms, who points toward them. The man walks up behind the Captain and puts his hand on the Captain's shoulder. Thank God, rantus interuptus.

239

"Excuse me, gentlemen. Let me introduce myself. I'm Special Agent William Delaney with the NSA," he says holding up his ID. "I need to speak with both of you. Come with me right now, no questions asked, please. This is a matter of national security."

Captain Sprague takes Delany's proffered ID and inspects it carefully before handing it back. "What's this about, Delaney? As you can see we're very busy. One of my officers has been attacked."

"I'll bring you up to speed as soon as I can, Captain, but right now, you need to come with me." Delany looks at the Captain then at Murphy. "Please, gentlemen, this way."

Sprague takes a moment to speak to the sergeant, who is interviewing the couple who had found the deputy's squad car. Delany turns and walks toward a very large, very black Cadillac Escalade. Murphy looks at the Captain who shrugs and follows the NSA agent toward the waiting vehicle. The windows are tinted dark black; no surprise there. Delaney opens the front passenger door for the Captain, as Murphy gets into the back seat. Delaney walks around, gets into the driver's seat, starts the engine and pulls smoothly into traffic.

"Wait a minute. Where are we going?" barks the Captain.

"The information I'm about to divulge is classified, top secret, eyes only and all that other bullshit they say in the movies. Only this time, it's for real. Understand?" Delaney waits until they agree, then says, "I've had both of you checked out and I hope I can trust you. This case really isn't about dope; it's about terrorism. We have it on good Intel that the Richard Weaver case is linked to our case, the investigation on General Miguel Sandoval. John Gomez - you may have heard his name around Laguna Beach as John G., - has been working deep undercover for our agency for the past twelve years. It was he who helped place your murder victim in The General's employment. Over the years, Mr. Weaver helped gather sensitive information for this agency in the countries where he worked. He was a paid asset. We believe Weaver got photos of The General after his plastic surgery, and that's what he hid in your friend's puzzle box, Detective Murphy. That and information concerning the drop points of drugs, and other materials important to the security of the United States."

The Captain shoots Murphy a look which he avoids by turning to look out the window.

Delany goes on, "We're on our way to the Hilton Hotel where Chako Francis, Jeannie Francis's mother, is attempting to open the puzzle box. From what I've been told, it's slow going. She's gradually making her way through the moves to open it."

Captain Sprague looks at Murphy, "What puzzle box?! Murphy did you know about this?"

Delaney stops him, "Don't be too hard on the detective, Captain Sprague," he says. "Detective Murphy has had a feeling for a while that there is a leak in your department. He was following his survival instinct—wisely as it turns out."
"His survival instinct may just have cost him his job. We'll talk about this later. In private, Detective," Captain Sprague says tersely.

The rest of the trip is made in silence. The Escalade pulls into the Hilton parking structure and the men get out of the car and head into the hotel. Murphy drops back a little, to avoid being too close to the Captain, at least until he cools down enough for Murphy to explain his actions. As they walk into the lounge, the hostess offers to seat them, but Delany waves her away and points to the table where Chako, Bobby, John G. and Alexis sit.
John G. stands up. "Bill," he says, putting his hand out to Delaney, "It's been a while. Bobby Paladin, Chako Francis, Alexis Clayton, this is Special Agent William Delany, my boss and handler with the agency."

241

Introductions are made all around, but Chako just nods, keeping her head down and her focus on the box.

"How is it going?" Delaney asks quietly.

John G. waves them to sit. "Slow, Bill. If Chako makes a wrong move, it could destroy anything stored inside. Luckily, Mrs. Francis is familiar with the maker of this particular type of puzzle box. She's thirty moves into opening it, but thinks she still has another thirty plus to go."

Chako finally looks up at Delany, "This particular box is meant to be used to hide important documents or valuables. Mr. Nueriuma and his disciples handmade each one and they all open differently. There is a chamber inside which holds a powder. If the box is opened incorrectly, the powder will release and destroy the contents of the puzzle box."

"Is there any chance the powder was released by all the juggling it's taken?" asks Murphy.

"The box itself is made to withstand some abuse. The compartment that holds the powder will open only if there is a wrong move made in opening the puzzle box," she replies. "Whatever is inside will still be safe."

"Will it explode?" asks Captain Sprague, pushing his chair back a little. "Is it like gunpowder or something? Aren't the Japanese big on fireworks?"

"No," she says with a slight smile. "It will not explode. I think that it is some sort of corrosive powder."
"Thank you, Mrs. Francis, for helping us. I know this is a difficult time for you," says Delany.

Chako nods and bites her lip, fighting back tears, "If this helps to find my daughter's murderer, I will do anything."

The table is silent as they watch her move three more locks of the puzzle box.

Finally Delaney says, "Captain Sprague, and John, I need a moment of your time."

John G. looks at Delaney, "Sir, Alexis needs to join us in this conversation; she represents another government agency that has a vested interest in outcome."

"Ms. Clayton, I need to see some sort of identification if you're going to join our little party," Delaney says.

Alexis pulls out her cell phone and dials a number. "Let me just make a call to set that up."

The three men get up and start to walk out of the hotel lounge, leaving Bobby, Murphy and Chako at the table. Alexis follows the men and holds out her phone, "For you, Agent Delaney." Delaney takes her phone tentatively. "This is Special Agent William Delaney, to whom am I speaking?" The next moment Delaney is answering, "Yes? Yes, ma'am, we will ma'am. Thank you, ma'am." He closes the phone, white as a ghost and hands it back to Alexis. "That was the Vice President of the United States. She just vouched for Alexis's identity. How do you happen to have the Vice President's personal cell phone number, Alexis?"

Alexis just smiles and says, "That, is classified, Agent Delaney. Shall we go?"

As soon as his boss is out of sight, Murphy signals our server and orders a beer.

"Aren't you still on duty?" I ask.

"Fuck it. The Captain is going to jump all over me as soon as he gets back. One beer on duty is the least of my problems."

I glance at Chako.

"Oh, sorry, please excuse my French," he tells her. "It's just that the Captain now knows I knew about the puzzle box's existence all this time and didn't tell him about it. I'll be fired for cause if this whole thing turns out to be a bust."

"Wow, Murph, that's brutal. You were just trying to protect the integrity of the investigation," I say.

"Yeah, but Delany also told the Captain there is a major leak in our department. That news will probably keep me off the hot seat, at least until we find the leak. The Captain's got a pretty good memory, though, so I won't be able to dodge him for long."

Our server comes back with Murphy's beer and another for me.

"If this all goes south do you think that DJ will give me a job?" Murphy says half smiling.

Chako is looking at me, "Bobby, I may have caused a problem."

Murphy has the beer halfway to his mouth and stops. "What kind of problem?"

I hold up my hand to stop him. "Let her explain. What do you mean, Chako?"

"These boxes were made very precisely," she replies. "If you push a piece too far, you may cause the powder to be released. I fear I may have pushed one of the pieces too far. I will still open the box, but we are unable to know until I finish opening the box if what I have done has destroyed the contents inside. I am so very sorry. It is the best I can do." She carefully sets the box on the table and puts her hands in her lap. She's trembling.

"We asked for your help, Chako," says Murph gently. "There was no way we could have opened the box without you. If the evidence is destroyed, it's not your fault. No matter what, at least we kept it from falling into the wrong hands."

"Besides," I say. "It could all still be okay, right? You're not sure you did anything wrong."

"We knew the odds were against us from the start," says Murph. "We'd still like you to finish opening the box. Please?"

She nods.

"How close are you?" I ask.

"Very close. However, this is where a puzzle box gets very hard to open. The last few steps are the most challenging." Chako's voice is strained and I can tell this is taking its toll on her.

I see Delany and his group walk back through the lobby and toward the lounge. I get up to meet them and block their view of Murphy as he finishes his beer and sets the empty bottle on the floor under the table. I take them to the side and quietly explain what's happened and that Chako almost has it open. We all turn to watch her as she takes both hands and ceremoniously sets the box in the middle of the table.

"Bobby, will you please do the honor of removing the lid? You were the one who found the clues to locate your friend's final gift," she says with a slight bow of her head.

I look at Agent Delaney who nods then at Captain Sprague, who shrugs his okay. I sit down across from Chako and the puzzle box. I reach for the top. My hands are shaking a little, so I pull them back and wipe my palms on my jeans and try again. I place my thumbs and forefingers on the corners of the lid.

"Do I have to do anything special to open it, Chako?" I ask.

She shakes her head, "Just lift the lid straight up, it will need to be wiggled a little as the top is released.

"Oh for criminy sakes, Paladin," says Captain Sprague. "Just open the damn thing. There might not be anything inside but dust."

I slowly lift the lid and, after it comes free, I set it on the table beside the box. We lean in as one to look inside. Inside the box is not black powder or ashes, but a large, white, letter size envelope, folded in half. There is a collective exhale. The envelope simply reads, "Bobby" on the outside in Ricky's unmistakable backhand.

"What do I do?" I look around the table.

"Well, it's addressed to you," says Delany. "But it's still evidence in this investigation. Pick it up carefully by the edges and let's see what's inside. Mrs. Francis, is it safe now? Can he release the powder if he takes it out of the box?"

I look at her and notice she's been crying. She wipes her eyes with her napkin. "No, no damage can be done now. The contents are safe."

I carefully reach into the box and take the envelope by the edges, as instructed. Our server comes to the table and Delany flashes his badge without looking at her. She backs away. Two strips of photo negatives slide out of the envelope and onto the table. Delaney carefully picks them up by the edges.

"Are there any more of these in there, Bobby?" he asks.

"No, sir. Just a letter." I open the letter and start to read to myself, with everyone anxiously looking over my shoulder.

Bobby,

These pictures are of General Sandoval after his plastic surgery and of a guy that I only heard addressed as Aziz. Aziz is carrying a chemical bomb that he plans to set off in downtown LA during the President's visit, at the end of July. The drugs and weapons are a smoke screen to get this guy into the United States. There is an agent named Bill Delaney. Get these pictures to him. He'll know what to do with them. You can reach him at 202-555-1745.

The submarine that's transporting the drugs, guns and this Aziz clown was built by the Russians and will be almost impossible to detect by any of our current technology. The sub will be arriving between July 25th and the 27th, around eleven p.m., off of Abalone Point. If Delany hasn't found you yet, get this information to him.

Bobby, I knew you'd figure out how to get the puzzle box open. I'm so sorry for any problems I may have caused you or DJ. You guys are the best. Paddle my ashes out at Pipeline.

Stay low, go slow, be safe my Brother. - Ricky

I stand and hand the letter over. "Mr. Delany, here's the information my friend died for. If I can be of any further assistance, you know how to find me." I nod to Chako and turn to walk out of the restaurant. Alexis is right behind me.

"Bobby! Wait!" says Murphy. "I need a ride back to my car."

Before Captain Sprague can say anything, Murphy runs to follow us out the door.

Chapter 38

DJ and I are paddling out on our boards at San Clemente State Park. It's nuts; eight foot plus waves with top to bottom barrels. There are only three other guys out.

"It all just keeps getting weirder and weirder, but it was cool that Chako opened up the puzzle box without wrecking anything." DJ says.

"It was something, watching her open it. It was full of the pictures and information that Ricky had stolen from General Sandoval."

As I look at the horizon, I see a large set of waves building. We push harder to try to catch one. I start to paddle after a killer wave that's just starting to hit the roof. I come into it just a second late, and as I stand up, I can really feel the bottom start to fall out from underneath me. I push my right foot back on the tail. I feel the board start to stabilize and lean into the bottom, carving a big bottom turn and pulling up into the pocket. The waves at State Park are crazy when it's this big. This wave sets up and I feel it getting hollow. I keep getting further and further back in the tube. I come blowing out with a gush of air and spit following me. It takes my breath away.
"Great wave, bro," another surfer calls to me as he paddles by, his too-long, blonde hair matted from the water.

I wave my acknowledgment, turn and watch DJ pull up into a monster barrel. He gets an incredible ride. I could never figure out why DJ didn't make the tour. He was way better in contests than I ever was and won more than I did.

We surf for a couple more hours, catching wave after wave, but it starts to get crowded, so we decide to pack it in and let the amateurs have a go at it. We grab our boards out of the water and walk up the beach toward my van. I unlock the back and notice my cell phone blinking on the floor where I had left it. Shit. What now? I hit the message button and listen as we towel off.

"Bobby. This is Special Agent Delaney. It's important I see you as soon as you get this message. I need help from both of you and your friend, DJ Frasier." He left his phone number before he'd hung up.

I look at DJ. "Shit. The Feds want to talk to us. I thought we were finished with all this. What do you think? Delaney said he needs both of us. Should I call him or blow him off?"

"Good luck blowing off a Fed," he says with a sigh as he peels his wetsuit to his waist. "If this lets me bring my family home then I'll help. I'm so tired of my wife and kids being away, but I don't feel like it's safe for them yet. Call him back and see what he wants."

"Alright. I'll call him as soon as we get cleaned up." We put the boards and wetsuits in the back of my van. We get in, I start the engine and we head for DJ's house. I cross over the freeway, wait for the light to change and turn left onto El Camino Real. As we're driving through town, quiet at this time of day, I notice a pair motorcycles in my rear view mirror. They were following us when we left the parking lot at the beach. I look ahead just as a car pulls out in front of me and I slam on my breaks.

DJ looks up from his texting, "What the hell, Bobby?"

Suddenly, one of the motorcycles is pulling alongside of the van and I see a gun in the rider's hand. I swerve, trying to force the motorcycle off balance. He dodges two cars in the oncoming traffic, pulls up again and fires a couple of shots at us, blowing out the windshield, showering us with glass. The other motorcycle is coming up fast on DJ's side of the van. I swerve to keep him at bay. I notice that he also has a gun.

"Fuck, Bobby! Get us the hell out of here!" DJ shouts.

"I'm trying, but these guys are working together. My gun is in the glove box. Grab it, rack the slide, flip the safety off and hand it to me."

"What the f– it's in the van?! You drive around with a loaded gun!?" He yells, head down, rummaging through the glove box.

"Just give it to me!" I'm looking for a place to pull off onto a side street. There's not much traffic, but I don't want to hurt anybody who's not trying to hurt me first.

"You can't drive and fire a gun at the same time, you asshole!"

"Shit! Where's a damn sheriff when you need one? See if you can get a clear shot at the motorcycle. Aim low. Try not to hit anybody."

"Jesus, Bobby, I don't know."

"Just release the safety, aim for the tires and pull the fucking trigger!"

The guys on the motorcycles are trying to pull up next to us and I'm doing my best to make sure they don't. I keep swerving from side to side but they speed off ahead of us. Then out of nowhere a car suddenly pulls up behind us and I notice in the rearview mirror that the passenger has a gun sticking out his window. I was paying too close attention to the motorcyclists and not paying attention to what was happening behind us. My mistake.

"DJ, if you can get a clean shot at the car behind us, take it. The guys on the motorcycles have disappeared."

DJ leans out of the van window, closes his eyes and shoots off three rounds in rapid succession, blowing out their windshield. I look for the motorcycles but I don't see them anywhere. The tires on the car squeal as the driver tries to pull up on DJ's side of the van. DJ fires three more shots at the car and again it falls back. The passenger leans out of the window and fires a half a dozen shots at us, blowing out the rear and side windows.

"Crap. Where did they go? Keep a sharp lookout for the motorcycles. I'm going to take a right at Pico and see if we can catch the sheriff's attention at the city yard."

"Bobby, the car's not following us anymore and neither are the motorcycles."

"Just keep your eyes open."

I make a right on Pico and pass the new outlet mall built on what used to be tomato fields when we were kids. Just then, one of the motorcycles appears in front of us, coming right at us, his gun firing. His aim is off because he's trying to steer the bike, but he still manages to get a shot over our heads that buries itself in the roof of the van.

"DJ!" I shout, "Shoot that asshole before he kills us!"

DJ holds the gun straight out through the broken windshield, both hands gripping the handle. He closes his eyes, turns his head slightly, takes aim and fires off the rest of the clip. Unbelievably, about fifty feet in front of the van, the gunman is blown backwards off the motorcycle. The bike skids to the side and I crank the wheel to the left, hoping to miss the bike, now sliding to the right of the van. I jump the curb, blowing out one of the front tires. We come to a stop as the motorcycle slides to a stop beside the van.

"Drop your weapons!"

We turn to see – finally – a sheriff's car with its doors open and a lone sheriff yelling into a microphone, crouched behind the open driver's side door. "Now!" he repeats. "Drop your weapons, turn around and walk slowly toward me. I want to see your hands!"

"You know, Bobby" says DJ quietly, as we get out of the van and he sets the gun on the ground. "Some days, it's not easy being your friend."

We walk toward the cruiser, hands up and the officer points down.

"On the ground. Now," he shouts. "Put your hands behind your head."

"Shit," I say under my breath as I do what I'm told.

Chapter 39

"Damn it, you two! No one, I repeat no one drives through San Clemente and shoots up my town! Have you got that?!" roars Captain Sprague. "You are so lucky no one was hurt. There was no major damage to any of the businesses on El Camino Real, other than Roger Merrill's art gallery."

"Have you identified the guy on the bike?" I ask.

"His name is Thomas Whitman. He's a trained mercenary who works for the highest bidder. Currently we are assuming he was hired by General Sandoval." says Sprague. "Why didn't you cowboys just wait for us instead of starting a gunfight?"

DJ has his head down. I never should have asked him to fire the gun. I'm trying to figure out how to explain this, when Agent Delaney walks into the room.

"Captain Sprague, these men are under the protection of the Justice Department and are to be released into my custody right now," he says as he hands the Captain a court order.

Sprague puts the papers down on his desk without looking at them. "Agent Delaney, these men may have just shot an agent working for General Sandoval and I, for one, would like some answers. My office has cooperated with the Feds throughout this entire matter and all I want is for them to answer a few questions, then they can go. Is that alright with you, Agent Delany?"

If Delany hears the contempt in Sprague's voice, he doesn't show it. "Captain Sprague, in the spirit of cooperation between our two departments, you may ask your questions, but please make it as brief as possible. I have my own questions for these men."

Crap. I thought Delany was going to get us out of here before we had to deal with Murphy's boss, whose face is an epic shade of crimson right now.

After another half-hour of questioning, Captain Sprague seems to be satisfied that any actions we took were in self-defense. I do most of the talking, since DJ still isn't saying much.

Sprague looks at Delaney and says, "These two knuckleheads are all yours. Good luck with them." He gets up and walks out of the interrogation room, slamming the door behind him.

"Let's go you two," says Delaney and we follow him out of the San Clemente Police Services Building.

****

"Murphy," says Captain Sprague from the other side of the one-way glass, watching as Delany escorts Paladin and Frasier out of the room. "Keep an eye on those clowns. I want to know what Delaney wants with them.

"Any sign of the car or the other motorcycle that were chasing them?" Murphy asks.

"No. For right now I believe their story, but just watch them."

"You got it, Captain. I think I can catch up with them at the boat in a couple of hours. I don't think I'll have any problems."

"Make sure of that. Keep me in the loop, Detective. I mean it this time. You're lucky I'm so busy with all this shit right now, but I haven't forgotten that we'll need to have a little chat, soon detective, very soon" Sprague says, giving Murphy a very direct stare before walking out of the room.

As Murphy leaves the building, he pulls out his phone and calls Debbie to tell her he's working late again and not to hold dinner. He reaches in his pocket for his keys and looks up to see Alexis leaning on his car.

"Murphy, we need to talk," she says before he can greet her. She walks around to her Toyota parked beside Murphy's car and opens the passenger side door. "Get in," she says.

Not a question, but an order. Murphy notices as he gets into the car. She closes the door behind him then walks around to the driver's side and gets behind the wheel. She starts the car and drives out of the police parking lot and onto the I-5 Freeway, heading south.

"Where are we going?" Murphy asks.

"I just want to talk to you alone and get some feedback on what your thoughts about these latest turn of events. I need answers. Too many things have happened that need an explanation," she says as she the merges car into traffic.

"Good idea. I think it's time we shared. Maybe between the two of us, we can figure a few things out."

As they drive down I-5, through Camp Pendleton and its twenty-six miles of almost untouched California real estate, towards Oceanside, Alexis recounts the facts of the case as she sees them playing out, from Ricky's quirky note in the beginning to DJ and Bobby being assaulted in San Clemente just today; Murphy fills in gaps for her.

"It just feels like there is someone who is feeding Sandoval inside information," she says finally. "It seems to me we're always two steps behind."

They drive in silence for a while, the ocean on Murphy's side of the car, and he watches two Blackhawk helicopters fly back towards the Marine Base. After a few minutes, Murphy says quietly, "Do you think the leak could be on your side of things, Alexis?"

She looks at him, shocked, as if she had never considered that possibility. "It seems to me that all of us have been one step behind from the beginning. Bobby and DJ don't even know this, but DJ didn't shoot the attacker on the motorcycle. He was hit by a high-powered rifle. I feel like someone is cleaning up with deadly force. They kill them before we even have a chance to take them into custody. I don't know what to think. I will say this: there's a leak somewhere and it's high up in the chain of command. It could be on either side, but I think it's on yours."

"Just a minute," Murphy bristles. Is she accusing him of being the leak? Is that what this is about?

"Relax, Murph." she says knowing what he's thinking. "We know it's not you.

He looks over at her and says, "I hate to admit it, Alexis, but I think you're right." He turns back toward the window, wondering if he should confide his all of his suspicions. They continue in silence until they reach the city of Oceanside where Alexis pulls off, turns left and drives back onto the north-bound onramp and back toward San Clemente. Sharing time is over.

Chapter 40

"General, the submarine is loaded and the crew is ready to get underway as soon as you give the order to set sail, sir."

"Thank you, Simmons. You are dismissed."

"Yes sir," Simmons says as he closes the door behind himself.

The General had had extensive cosmetic surgery over the last year and it has paid off, at least so far. He had walked through a hotel full of police and nobody noticed him. He looked like all the other tourists staying near Disneyland. Hiding in plain sight. He picks up his encrypted satellite phone and calls the captain of the submarine.

"Yes, General?" comes the voice over the phone.

"Captain," he says. "I understand you are ready to sail?"

"Yes, sir. All systems on the sub are ready and the drugs and weapons are packed in the water-tight containers for delivery. Our passenger is very anxious to arrive in America so he can carry out his mission." His voice gives away no trace of his Russian identity.

The passenger, Suhail Aziz, is a madman, driven by his belief that he will change history if he can kill the President of the United States. The General is being paid millions of dollars to deliver the lunatic. The General doesn't care what happens to the President of the United States. What he cares about, is that half of the money that has already been deposited in his bank account in the Cayman Islands. The balance will be transferred upon delivery of Aziz to a fishing boat off the coast of California.

"Excellent. You will set sail at sunset this evening. It's imperative to keep the submarine at a speed of no more than sixteen knots in order to prevent the Americans from detecting our movements.

259

You will remain on schedule at all times, Captain, regardless of any problems you may encounter along the way. I will check in with you during your voyage. Good luck, Captain."

Captain Yuri Popovich is a famous Russian submarine commander. The submarine itself was built by the Russian Special Services to transport an elite strike team in and out of any country that needed to be reminded the Russians still had teeth. But, as chaos and the loss of value of the Russian economy took its toll, General Sandoval was able to make a cash deal with the head of the Russian Special Services for the employment of the submarine. Captain Popovich agreed to come and work for The General, bringing the core of his crew with him, for a fee of five million dollars. The General considers this a small sum for the expertise he is getting. The sub itself was built from a metal compound discovered in Siberia a few years ago. When applied over the submarine's shell, the compound makes it essentially undetectable. The propulsion method is a radical system originally designed in the '70s, at the height of the Cold War, that virtually makes no sound. Between the composite skin and its propulsion system, this submarine is undetectable.

When the captain piloted the submarine away from Russian waters, he had shadowed a U.S. Navy L.A. class attack submarine. After three days of maneuvers, the captain was sure the Americans were not able to detect the Russian sub. Confident in the near invisibility of the submarine, The General's plan was for the boat to come into American waters and stay inside of San Clemente Island, a U.S. naval station with a submarine base. The location was within 36 miles of the California coastline and 20 miles of Catalina Island, where stupid Americans partied on their multi-million dollar yachts.

Once the sub had entered U.S. waters, the crew would begin off-loading the drugs and weapons, sealed in water-tight compartments, at selected sites along the route. The contraband would be shot out through the aft torpedo tubes at the designated locations, but only after the money from each buyer was deposited in The General's Cayman Island bank account. Once all the drugs were retrieved by the runners, The General would meet up with John Gomez and pick up his cash delivery. The General needed cash to pay off the Captain, his crew and the bribes that were required for his safety in his new country.

The terrorist Aziz would be dropped off right before The General met up with John G. From there Aziz would be picked up by gang members from East L.A. Sandoval would then ship that would deliver him to the Ivory Coast. From there he would disappear and make his way to South Africa where he had further resources. Once again, he would change his looks. He had plans to ship his drugs to South Africa. His drug empire would expand greatly as he would once again make millions from people's misery. He had less than one week to take care of all the loose ends, just five days.

Chapter 41

"Bobby! Prepare to tack! Is the chute set and ready to go?" DJ calls across the deck.

"We're set and ready, Boss," I call back.

"On my mark!"

As we pull closer to the marker buoy, I can see that DJ is going to over-shoot the marker and take a wider turn before he heads for the finish line. We pass the buoy and keep going. He keeps driving the boat, picking up clean air so when he jibes he'll have a great line and clean air for the downwind leg of the race.

"Now, Bobby, now! Pop the chute and drop the headsail!" he yells back at me.

Thomas and Dave drop and pull in the headsail as I raise the spinnaker and make sure it goes up without getting tangled. DJ makes the turn, now heading for the finish line.

"The spinnaker's up and the headsail is down below, DJ."

"Good job you guys. Now, Bobby, get back here and take over flying the spinnaker. I've set a lay line for the finish."

DJ steers the boat as I call the sail action.

"Bring her up, DJ, about five degrees."

DJ corrects our line and we are boat for boat with the leader, but have the advantage. From where we are right now, we can force the other boat to either tack or take a chance of getting forced up at the finish line. The other boat tacks away and is about to set another lay line for the finish, but DJ and I know the race is in the bag. We cross the line a good three plus minutes ahead of the other boat.

"Bobby, do the math. Did we beat these guys?"

Just because we cross the finish line first does not mean we won the race.

"We beat them by 4.5 seconds. We won!"

He lets out a whoop, "Great work, everybody. Bobby, break out the beer."

Delaney walks up out of the salon with a six pack and hands them out to the crew. If I'm not mistaken, he's just a touch green. Maybe it's wishful thinking.

"That was very impressive, DJ." he says, opening a beer for himself. "Your crew works like a well-oiled machine."

"Yeah well, thanks," says DJ waiving away the beer until he gets the boat back into dock. "We all raced for my dad when we were kids. With all that time spent together sailing we don't really need to talk that much. We just do what needs to be done."

Thomas, one of our racing crew along with Dave, has already started to clean up the deck.

"Dave, pull in the lines and after the boat is all packed up and clean, drinks and burgers are on me," says DJ with a smile. The crew cheers and gets to work.

We dock the boat, fold the sails, wash her down and cover the mainsail.

Delany stays out of the way on the dock and watches us work. The rest of the crew heads up to the yacht club as DJ and I lock up the boat.

Finally Delany says to us, "Thanks for the ride, guys. I really enjoyed it. Could I meet up with both of you tomorrow? I need to talk to people about getting you clearances."

DJ and I look at each other. We're still not sure we want to do this. When do we get to go back to being regular guys who don't get shot at anymore?

"Sure, I guess we can do that," DJ says. I can tell he's not thrilled. He looks over for my approval. I nod my agreement. "It'll have to be after work, though; we're just starting back up on the T-Street job that was shut down by Ricky's death. I'm way behind schedule and we'll be working late."

"How about we meet tomorrow night, let's say seven-thirty, at the Wind and Sea restaurant? Dinner is on me," Delany replies.

"Sure, that works for us," says DJ. "See you then."

Delaney walks toward the parking lot as DJ and I head toward the bar. DJ stops, opens his wallet and hands me his credit card. "Take care of the crew, would you? I need to call Maria and the kids. I miss them."

"Are you going to join us later?" I ask, taking the card from him before he changes his mind.

"No, I don't think so. I told Maria they could come home next week so, it'll take me that long to get the house back in order. Plus, I have to get ready for work this week. I want you back at T-Street Monday morning at eight a.m., okay?"

"You got it, Boss. I'll stay on the boat tonight and set the crew up on the job Monday morning."

"Thanks. The doors and windows are being delivered Monday; let's get them laid out when they get there so we can start installing them on Tuesday," he pats me on the shoulder. "Nice spinnaker set on that last leg of the race today. It felt so great to be back out on the water, racing. When this is all over I've decided we're going to race the boat a lot more. Talk to the crew and see if they're up for it. Tell them that lunch and beer will be on me after each race."

I don't have to think about it, "I'm in. I'll bet you that the other guys are, too."

"Thanks, Bobby. See you Monday morning at work."

I give him a wave as he heads toward his truck and turn to go into the Dana Point Yacht Club. I can hear the crew as soon as I walk in the front door. Thomas has always been loud – it comes from competing with his five brothers, Tim, Tony, Terry, Ted and Trevor – and he gets even louder with beer and the excitement of winning a race.

"Hey, Bobby," he calls to me. "Where's DJ?"

"He wanted to call his wife and kids, and then get set up to start work Monday. All is not lost, though," I wave the card. "He gave me his Yacht Club credit card, so he's springing for dinner and drinks."

Thomas and Dave raise their beers, "To DJ!" They shout and order another round.

We recreate the race over burgers and a couple more beers, and everyone is headed home long before dark. A sailboat race is hard work and we're all pretty tired. I walk back to the boat and find Murph and Alexis sitting in the cockpit, drinking martinis. Well isn't this cozy?

"Hey, where were you earlier? I ask as I climb onto the boat. "We had a killer race and could have used a couple more hands."

"I haven't sailed in years," says Alexis. "I used to be pretty good. Let me know next time you take the boat out."

"Sure thing." I bet she knows her way around a jib. "It seems odd to see the two of you casually sharing a pitcher of martinis."

Murph reaches for another glass but I shake my head. He gets right to the point. "We've come to the conclusion that the leak is deep in my department," he says.

"We don't know who it is, or how high up the leak goes," continues Alexis. "And, we don't know who we can trust. Sandoval is always two steps ahead of us. We're sure he's still hiding somewhere in Orange County."

"Do you have any guesses as to who the leak might be?" I ask. Shit. Maybe it's too soon for DJ to have his family come back.

"No," Murph replies. "Alexis and I have been talking about it and we think it's safe to keep Captain Sprague and Special Agent Delany in the loop, but no one else. Our unit is small, and Delany only answers to one person."

"We can't rule out that the leak might be coming from there," Alexis says.
Murph says, "We can't rule out the rest of the Sheriff's department either." He looks down at his watch, "Well, it's been real folks, but I'd better get myself home. My wife will have my head on a platter if I miss another family dinner."

He gets up and says, "Crap. I came here with Alexis. Hey, Bobby, let me borrow your van. You can have Alexis drop you off at my house later on to pick it up."

"Sure, Murph," I toss him the keys. It's got to be safe to lend your wheels to a cop, doesn't it? I don't feel like explaining anything else to my insurance company after getting the glass repaired.

"Just leave the keys under the driver's side mat. Have a good night Murph."

"Goodnight, I'll catch you two later," Murph says as he jumps off the side of the boat onto the dock.

Well. Here I am alone with the lovely Alexis as the sun begins to set. "Can I pour you another martini?" I ask her.

"It's so peaceful here. Yes, and thank you, Bobby," she replies. I grab a glass for myself and fill that, too. I've worked with a hangover before and I can do it again.

We talk until late into the evening and when I'm pretty sure neither of us is going to drive anywhere she says, "I'd like to spend the night here. On the boat. With you."

It's a good thing it's dark because I wouldn't want her to see my jaw hit the deck. She leans toward me and kisses me, gently at first and then with more passion than I ever thought I'd feel again.

****

I awake when I feel a shift in the way the boat sits in the water. Quietly, I reach over and touch Alexis on the shoulder. She opens her eyes with a smile and I put my finger to my lips.

"There's someone on the deck, near the front hatch" I whisper. "Have you got your gun?"

She nods, leans over toward her purse and hands me her gun. We quietly pull on some clothes and move toward the front hatch.

The movement of the boat indicates that whoever is out there was moving aft, toward the cockpit and the opening of the salon. I ease the hatch open, glad that I used WD40 on it last week, and slip out one side, as Alexis slips out the other. Barefoot, I work my way towards the shape, dropping down into the cockpit. I slide the safety off, move to the top of the cockpit and shout, "Freeze! Drop your weapon or I'll shoot."

"Bobby, don't shoot! It's John. I'm unarmed."

Alexis, looking angry, shouts, "Are you crazy? What were you thinking, sneaking around like that?"

"Bobby, will you please put that thing away? You're making me nervous. I tried to call both of you but your cell phones went straight to voicemail, so I decided to come down here. I figured I'd find Bobby here, but not the two of you, together." John G. gives Alexis a knowing look, but it has no effect on her. "Can we go down below, please, you never know whose watching. I need to talk to you both about what I've found out in the last few hours."

This is the first time I have ever seen him not one hundred percent in control, so I nod and we head down into the cabin, and I make us some coffee. Finally we're all seated, somewhat uncomfortably, and John G. looks at Alexis.

"You are very, very good at your job, Alexis," he begins. "It was extremely clever of Special Agent Delaney to help guide you into my home and into my life. If this whole situation had happened differently I would never have suspected you of being a government agent."

I look over at Alexis and her expression hasn't changed at all. I wonder if I should have held on to the gun rather than let her put it back in her purse.

"So Delany was keeping tabs on me through you and, at the same time, he was building a criminal case against me," John G. continues. "You were there to confirm I was telling him the truth and that the information I had provided was solid. I've been undercover for over twelve years, so I've learned a few things. I think Delaney might be the one who has sold us out to The General. I think Delaney is the leak you've been looking for."

I can tell Alexis is desperately trying to process what she's just heard. We hear a sound like a tin can being thrown on the deck. John G. stands up and walks to the stairs that lead to the cockpit.

"Grenade!" he yells as he turns and throws himself toward me and Alexis.

The explosion is loud, followed by a bright light – a flash bang grenade – meant to disorient, not kill. The flash was bright, blinding and disabling. And the last thing I remember.

Chapter 42

I start to wake up and see cops and paramedics standing around talking in whispers. One of them notices I'm awake and comes over to me.

"Can you hear me, sir? Sir? Can you hear me?" I can see his lips moving but I don't know why he's whispering.

I look up to see John G., with his head resting in his hands, and Alexis sitting across from me.

"I can hear you, but barely," I tell the paramedic. My ears are ringing. It sounds like church bells. I try and sit up, I barely make it, but I do.

"That's normal," he says, a little louder this time, "considering what just happened to you."

I see Murphy walking towards the boat, on his cell phone and looking pissed off. Great, just what I need. I'd been having such a nice evening with Alexis.

"What the hell happened here, Bobby?" he asks when he gets to me.
What is it with this guy? Why does he never ask me if I'm okay before he starts the third degree? I stand up, wobbly at first, and the paramedic steadies me.

"Give me a few minutes, Murph? I need to clear my head."

I walk up and look into the cockpit to check out the damage. I can see burn marks on the deck and down below, and some damage to the storage lockers. I don't see anything that would make the boat unsafe.

"Are you alright, Bobby?" John G. asks as he comes up to the top of the stairs. Finally, there's somebody who might give a shit about me.

"Yeah, John, I think so. Thanks for what you did down there, saving our lives," I say. My hearing is slowly returning to normal.

"If that had been a real grenade we wouldn't be having this conversation right now," he replies.

Alexis steps up onto the deck then down into the cockpit, and hugs John G. "Thank you, John.

He nods and she walks over to sit next to me.

"This is starting to really piss me off," she says. "The General is stepping up his assault on us, and we all need to be ready for any attack. He won't stop until all of us are dead. I'm sure of that now."

Murphy climbs up on to the deck, "I need to get statements from all of you," he says. "Let's get off the boat and let the crime scene techs do their job."

We all rise stiffly and make our way off the boat and over to the Coffee Importers café where we find a table away from everyone else. Murphy goes in to order coffee for all of us, before he comes back to take our statements. An hour later, and another round of coffee, Murphy has all the information he needs and stands up to leave, but not before delivering a stern lecture about not getting killed. Like we wanted to have our eardrums blown out? The three of us look over to see the crime scene tape blowing around on the boat.

"I guess I'd better bring DJ up to speed," I say, reaching for my phone. The call was not a fun one to make and I have to hold the phone away from my ear as he yells at me. Obviously my hearing has returned. Finally I say, "Why don't you get your ass over to Salt Creek? I hear that the waves are still good and I feel like surfing." I pause, and he finally lowers his voice a few decibels.

I take a deep breath, "Listen, all the whining in the world is not going to get us on the boat any sooner. My van is still at Murph's house. Grab a couple of boards and I'll get Alexis to drop me off at Salt Creek; then we can get all this out of our systems. It's early. We'll start the job tomorrow. One more day won't matter."

He finally sees the sense in what I'm saying and agrees to meet us at Salt Creek once he calls the subcontractors and explains that the job is shut down till Tuesday.

When Alexis and I arrive in the Salt Creek parking lot she says, "I need to make some calls. I'll get back to you later, Bobby"

I get out of the car and before I can lean in to kiss her, she drives away. As I'm thinking about what happened last night, DJ pulls into the parking lot. We don't talk much as I grab my board and we walk down the trail to the beach.

It's a great wave. A point break that's mostly a left, Salt Creek Beach, when the surf is big, is as good a wave as you would ever hope to surf. DJ and I look down at the point and see a large set roll through and watch a gal take off from behind the peak, make a big sweeping bottom turn and pull up into clean barrel, get covered and pop out of the tube at the end, blonde ponytail flying.

I look at DJ and say, "What are we waiting for? Let's go."

After a couple of hours in the water I take off on a set wave, make an easy bottom turn and pull up tight into a jaw-dropping barrel. After about five seconds, I come blowing out and head in to the beach.

273

I turn around and watch as DJ takes off. Suddenly, it looks like his board just stops and he's pitched face first into the trough as the wave crashes down on top of him.

"What the hell?" I mumble to myself, watching and waiting for DJ to pop up in the white water. I start to run toward the water as another set of waves starts to come through and I finally see DJ pop up and climb onto his board. He turns around, paddles into the wave at a sideways angle, drops down the face of the wave and does a slight stall maneuver then he pulls up into a massive tube. He's covered up for what seems like forever and comes blowing out of the wave, standing so casually on his board, that he looks like he's out for a stroll. He makes it look so easy when he's having a good day. He rides standing up almost to the beach, before he jumps off and calls to me.

"Did you see that asshole grab my leash so I'd eat shit on that wave?" he yells. "What a jerkoff. I could have really been hurt. He's lucky I caught that next wave or I'd have gone after him out there."

"Did he say anything?" I ask. "And why would he do that to you?"

"Yeah, he said 'Salt Creek is for locals only.' Then he called me a fucking kook. Me!" he continues to yell. Then he lowers his voice, "Hey, let's wait for that moron to get out of the water so I can kick his ass."

"Let it go, DJ, we already have enough trouble. We don't need to start anymore."

He stares out at the water, watching for the jerk. Finally he says, "You're right, Bobby. It just pisses me off that someone would try to hurt someone else for surfing here. You don't get any more local than the two of us. We've been surfing here since we were kids."

Localism, surfers trying to keep other surfers from surfing their home break, has been going on since the sixties. It's a turf war without the turf.

"C'mon, let's grab some lunch," I pat him on the shoulder. "I'm buying."

"Damn right, you're buying," says DJ with his first smile of the day. "I'm always up for free food. Besides you guys ran up a pretty good size tab at the Yacht Club yesterday."

We walk up the beach trail toward the car. I glance up at the Ritz Carlton Hotel, overlooking the ocean, and think back to when I was a kid and there was nothing around here. As we come around the truck, we see Alexis sitting on the lowered tailgate.

"I was watching you. You guys are pretty good," she says, getting up so we can slide our boards into the back of the truck.

"I saw you fall on that wave, DJ. That would have sent me home, but you made the next one seem so easy. One might even say, graceful."

I clear my throat, "Weren't you watching any of the other surfers out there?"
She turns to me and smiles, "You were pretty good, too, but you didn't do a face plant on the front of a wave. What happened out there?"

"Join us for lunch and I'll tell you all about it," says DJ. "The second best surfer in the world is buying."

"That's true," I say. "I am, on both counts. But you didn't just come down here to watch us surf, did you Alexis?"

"No," she says. "I called a friend at the agency and asked some questions that nobody wants to answer."

Chapter 43

DJ and I pull into Big Jack's, a Dana Point restaurant specializing in Italian and great seafood. At this time of the day it'll be quiet, allowing us some privacy. Alexis pulls up next to us in the parking lot, gets out of her car and locks the door. She looks wonderful.

"Did you go home and get all spruced up for us? You really look great." I ask. I'm so smooth.

"I did," she says. Do I detect a blush? "Thanks for noticing."

She's wearing white jeans, a dark blue blouse that sets off the color of her eyes and beaded sandals.

"Hey, Bobby, quit drooling. You're embarrassing yourself," DJ says, shaking his head.

I pull myself together and we walk into the restaurant. I can see Alexis hiding a little smile. Jack, the owner (obviously) looks up from the reservation book and comes over to greet us. Jack is about 6'8" and all Italian: Dark hair, dark eyes, handsome and charming. If he was younger than his fit sixty years, I'd be a bit more worried.

"DJ, Bobby, how are you?" he reaches out to shake hands before turning to Alexis. "And you, young lady, are you lost? Surely you're not with these two?"

"Jack, this is Alexis," I introduce her. "We found her stranded in the parking lot."

"Clearly you don't know who you're with. Just give me a signal and I'll show you how to escape through the back of the restaurant." He takes her hand and kisses it.

277

"Very funny," says DJ. "Jack, would we be able to get a table in the back where we can have some privacy?"

"Sure. I don't blame Alexis for not wanting to be seen with you two." Jack picks up three menus and takes us to a dark corner of the back room of the restaurant. "I just received a shipment of the Foggerty Pinot Noir from the Santa Cruz Mountains. Should I open a bottle?"

"Just water for me," says Alexis. "But you guys go ahead."

"I'll make sure you're not disturbed," Jack says with a slight bow, then leaves us.

Alexis looks around, "This place is gorgeous. I feel like I'm in Italy."

Jack had decorated the dining room in an Italianate finish: plastered walls, marble floors and wood beams that looked two hundred years old.

"Yeah, Jack had a vision when it came to decorating the old place," says DJ.

"Let's not forget the magnificent craftsman who did all the work, Mr. DJ," says Jack, returning with water and bruschetta.

"You're too kind," says DJ.

"Oh, I know how much time it took you to make it this beautiful, since I was the guy who paid the bill," says Jack. "But it was worth it. It feels like home."

"So, you and Bobby did this remodel?" Alexis asks DJ.

"I did all the trick work," replies DJ, reaching for some bread. "Bobby and Kevin did most of everything else during the framing and finishing sections of the project."

Jack returns with the wine and we order our meals. Once Jack's gone, we sit back to listen to Alexis.

"Prior to my going to work for my current employer," she begins, "I used to work for the CIA. I was recruited right out of college. They were impressed by the fact I spoke several languages and with my athletic abilities. My old handler, Harold White, ran me during my career at the agency. I won't bore you with what I did and where I did it, but I spent several years running around the world, dealing with this and that."

I take a drink of my wine, needing the fortification. I know Alexis's 'this and that' is very different from mine.

"I called Harry and explained our current situation to him," she continues. "He'd like to meet with us tonight. It involves using your boat, DJ, and Harry wants you to sail your boat down to the Swift Response Base at Camp Pendleton."

"Who is this guy, Alexis?" asks DJ. Alexis looks at us for a moment; then she reaches for her water and takes a sip before answering. "Harry White was a field operative with years of service abroad. When 9-11 happened, the then sitting-president formed a new division within the CIA to deal with domestic surveillance of terrorist suspects. Harry was appointed as the Deputy Director in charge of this new division. He answers only to the director of the CIA himself. That's all I can tell you. He called me while you were out surfing, and told me he needed you two and the boat."

Jack brings a tray of antipasto and leaves as quickly as he had appeared.

"That's all I've been told. He wants us at Camp Pendleton tonight at ten p.m., including John G. and Detective Murphy. Here's the

279

radio frequency he'll use to contact us once we leave the harbor."
She writes a number on the back of a Starbucks receipt and slides
it across the table to DJ.

"Let me get this straight, Alexis" DJ says. "You want me to turn
my sailboat over to the CIA so they can use it in some capacity to
possibly take down General Sandoval? What about my family?
Who'll protect them?"

"We're working on a plan to keep your family completely safe, but
to answer your first question, yes, we need you and Bobby," she
says, reaching for some bruschetta. "We think the agency I work
for, the DEA and the Orange County Sheriff's Department might
have been compromised in some way by The General. The plan
that White has is the best and fastest option that we have. We
know that we can trust both of you, based on the complete
background checks White has done on you. The CIA works fast,
and agent White makes decisions even faster."

"We have two conditions, Alexis," I say. "First is that DJ's family
is protected and second is that DJ and I want to be part of the team
that does the take down."

DJ looks at me like I've lost my mind. "Are you insane? I can't be
part of this! What about my business? I have jobs on the books and
crews that need me right now. And let's not forget that I've
invested tens of thousands in the restoration of that boat."

"I understand your reluctance and concerns, DJ." Alexis tries to
calm him, "but we're running out of options. We don't know who
we can trust anymore. I assumed that you both would want to be
part of the team, and you both have been cleared in full. Nobody
knows that boat like you do, DJ. We need it and you."

Our meals finally arrive, giving us time to pretend we're
concentrating on eating. This is huge and we all know it. We eat
mostly in silence, other than commenting on how good the food is.

Finally the bill comes and I pay it. We say goodbye to Jack and make our way to our cars.

DJ looks over at Alexis first, then at me and says, "We're in, Alexis, under two conditions. First, I need assurances about my family's protection. Second, if my boat is destroyed, the CIA will find me a replacement boat."

Alexis opens the door of her car and looks at us, "I have a few errands to run. I'll call White and express your concerns to him. I'll call you as soon as I get some answers. I'll meet you at the boat around seven p.m. Make sure you pack for the next few days. Stock up whatever food supplies you think we'll need 6 people for a week and the agency will reimburse you. We won't be returning here until this is all over."

We nod as she closes the door and watch as she roars down the street.

DJ looks at me. "I guess you'd better hit the grocery store." He says, "In the meantime, I'll go to the house and call Kevin and put him in charge of both jobs. I guess then I can give the sub-contractors instructions on what they need to get done on each job. I hope Kevin's ready to handle running my company. Once I'm done with that, I'll meet you back at the boat."

"I'm glad I'm in charge of provisions. We'll need plenty of beer," I reply, watching Alexis' car disappear up the road. "I hope she knows what she's doing. Can you drive me to Murph's house so I can pick up my van?"

He lights up a cigarette and blows smoke away from me. "Let's roll. I sure as hell hope we know what we're getting into."

Chapter 44

"Captain, there is a U.S. submarine off our port bow, bearing zero-five-zero, at five thousand meters. They're dropping sonar buoys on the surface. Are they trying to track us, sir?" the helmsman asks.

"Helm power down one-third and maintain running silent," Captain Popovich says into the ship's communications line. He knows that if they can elude the Americans' attack submarine and the sonar buoys, they will have no trouble moving on to their destination undetected. He orders the engines slowed to eight knots. He will push the engine speed back up to fifteen knots if, in the next two hours, the Americans do not detect the Russian submarine's presence.

Aziz walks into the control room and asks, "What's going on? Why are we slowing down? I must arrive at the rendezvous position on time or my mission will be a failure."

"Aziz, go back to your cabin, now. If the Americans are actually searching for us then we need to be cautious for the moment. If they do not detect us in the next hour or two, then, and only then, will we increase our speed. We will still arrive with more than enough time for your pickup in American waters. Now, leave my bridge and let me do my job," he turns his back on the terrorist as a dismissal.

What a piece of shit, thinks Yuri. In war, you do what you need to do. But Aziz's country uses women and children to carry out their terrorist acts, while the men stay behind the scenes professing their devotion to Allah. What bullshit. If you believe in your cause, you do it yourself. You don't hide behind your women and children.

"Steady as you go, helm," the Captain says. They hear a sharp sound. "They are actively pinging with their sonar. They are searching for something."

They hear the ping again.

Captain Popovich knows the next ten to fifteen minutes are critical. He afford can't to lose much time because of how long it will take to deliver the cocaine to General Sandoval's dealers. He had helped The General's men devise a tube-type container that was made of a composite material that could hold drugs, weapons, cash, or if needed, a man. When the submarine arrives at the designated drop site, the mock torpedo will be loaded into the torpedo tube, which is then be flooded with water and the container ejected out into the ocean. With mounted homing devices and buoyancy compensators attached to the containers, they will float at a depth of five or six feet under the surface of the water. When the drug runners arrive in the designated area in small fishing boats, they will activate the homing devices, find the containers and tow them back to the harbor. From there the drugs, weapons and anything else in the containers will be distributed to other dealers in the network. He doesn't care what happens once the packages are picked up. He will have done his part and been paid for each successful shipment. The General and the Captain are getting rich making the deliveries.

After an hour and a half of toying with the Americans, the submarine has still has not been detected. Popovich decides it is safe to proceed. "Helm, increase our speed back to twelve knots for the next ten miles. If there are no sudden moves by the Americans, increase our speed to fifteen knots after that. Notify me at once if there are any changes. I'll be in my cabin."

****

General Sandoval sits in his hotel room overlooking Newport Beach, planning his last attack. His plan is straightforward. After each container of cocaine is deployed through the torpedo tubes, the runners will pick up the containers, check the purity of the drugs and make sure the kilo count is correct. They will then wire-transfer payment to The General's private account in the Cayman

Islands. Once the process is completed, he will deactivate an explosive charge that is built into each container. If the payment does arrive, well, it's simple. Pay me with money or your life.

The General's aid comes into the room and hesitates before asking, "General, we have located the targets. What would you like us to do?"

"Nothing at this moment, they will be dealt with shortly. Now leave me and do not disturb me until I call for you." Yes, The General thought, his plans are falling into place very nicely.

Chapter 45

In the grocery store, I load up the cart buying everything I think will be needed to keep us going for the next few days. Back at the harbor I unload the van onto one of the harbor dollies to get everything down to the boat at one time. Murph and John G. are all waiting on the boat. No one says much as we load the provisions below and make sure everything's secure. Murph gives me a look when I hand him a case of Heineken in cans. "What? DJ told me to get whatever I thought we might need." We're finally loaded when Alexis and DJ arrive.

"Here, DJ." I hear her say, handing him a piece of paper. "These are the coordinates that White wants us to sail. We'll be met by a Marine swift boat escort that'll guide us into their training center. White will meet us there. We need to shove off soon if we're going to be on time."

DJ looks at the coordinates, then at me, "Bobby, will you type these coordinates into the SAT-NAV system?" He hands me the slip of paper.

I nod and head below as he turns to Alexis. From below I can hear him tell her, "I think we should motor down to the meeting point. That way we'll be there with time to spare and we won't have to fold sails once we get there."

"I think that makes sense, DJ," Alexis replies.

I come back on deck and look around at our crew. Alexis has told us she sailed in the past, and I know John G. has, so they both know their way around a boat. I don't think Murph has much sailing experience, but he's got the cop thing going for him, so that'll be helpful. I'm sure we can handle anything.

It's dark, windy and there's no moon as we motor out of the harbor. The entrance to the harbor is U-shaped and we feel the wind really hit us as we come around the breakwater. It's pretty choppy as DJ heads the boat south toward the Camp Pendleton Marine Base.

DJ and I are familiar with the coastline and we motor past the San Clemente pier in silence. According to Alexis, the rendezvous spot is a couple of miles off the coast where the base is located. Camp Pendleton is a beautiful stretch of land and the coast is unoccupied between San Clemente and the town of Oceanside, twenty miles south. We see the lights from the San Onofre Nuclear Power Facility, but for the most part, it is pristine California coastline. If California could sell this piece of real estate, it would wipe out our state debt. Instead the land is used for training Marines to defend our country and for military exercises. It's not unusual to see helicopters, aircraft carriers and Marine tanks and personal engaging in war games.

We chat a little, but for the most part no one has much to say. I can tell everyone is nervous, unsure of what we've volunteered for.

"Skipper, off the port bow," Alexis finally calls to DJ, "about two hundred yards, that's our escort."

DJ throttles down to about three knots and guides us alongside a low profile Marine swift boat. John G. and I toss a couple of lines to the Marines and they tie up beside us.

"Permission to come aboard," a familiar voice calls into the night.

"Permission granted, Delany," replies DJ.

John G. and I give Delany a hand up. When he gets close to me I can see that he's dressed in naval uniform with commander symbols pinned to his collar and a Navy SEAL badge on his chest. There might be more to this guy than I thought. He must have been sandbagging after that sailboat race. He's probably never been seasick in his life. I see two divers flop backward into the water off

288

the side of the swift boat.

"Thank you for volunteering yourselves and for the use of your boat for this mission," he says, shaking DJ's hand, then turns to the rest of us. "We have a lot of ground to cover in the next few days if we're going to be successful. We know that General Sandoval has moles inside my organization, so we're going outside of normal channels. Director White has been recalled to Washington and is returning as we speak. He has every confidence that we can pull this mission off with the crew we've assembled."

He turns back to DJ, "We're going to have to make some modifications to your boat."

DJ nods, "Don't touch any of the woodwork below, okay? Bobby and I worked our asses off getting that restored."

Delany smiles, puts his hand on DJ's shoulder and turns to us again, "For the next few days all of you will be trained to help us with our plan to capture Sandoval and shut down his operation. We have divers sweeping the hull of the boat for tracking devices. Once they're done, they'll sweep topside, too."
He barely has the words out when one of the diver's heads pops out of the water. "Commander, you need to see this," she calls.

She hands something to one of the Marines in the boat and he in turn reaches up to pass it to Delany. Delany gets down on one knee and leans over to take what the diver has found. He stands up and studies it for a moment. It doesn't take him long to figure out what it is.

"Let's get that team over here to sweep this cabin, now!" he orders.

Two men climb aboard our boat with hand-held equipment and quickly head below; Delany follows them. After about ten minutes, Delany comes topside, looking grim.

"We have a major problem, people," he says. "DJ, please start the engine and follow us into the harbor."

With that, Delany steps over the rail line and in to the swift boat. We cast off the lines and as the swift turns around. No one says anything as we follow them toward the Marine base.

Chapter 46

We follow the boats into the harbor the Marines had created for their Swift Boat Assault Unit. I let out a low whistle.

DJ says, "Holy shit. I've sailed past this and have seen it from the freeway, but had no idea all this was behind the walls."

The facility has a harbor set up with docks for the hovercrafts the Marines and SEAL teams use in there. There's a pier and a boat yard and off in the distance I can see what looks to be three of four small submarines tied up to the docks at the far end of the enclosed harbor. I look toward the shore and can see the grey outlines of three large buildings and some smaller ones.

"Bobby," DJ says as a Marine directs us to pull into a boat slip, "Tie us down, please."

I pull myself together and ask Murph to give me a hand. We drop the fenders, step off the boat and grab the lines Alexis and John G. throw to us. I tie mine off and go over to check Murphy's. Not bad for a land lubber. I tighten it up and give him a pat on the shoulder. Delany walks down the dock and over to us. "Alexis, will you come with me, please," obviously not a question but an order. She hops down off the boat. "The rest of you sit tight until I get back. Do not leave the boat, do you understand? This facility is classified top secret."

Murph and I climb back onto the sailboat.

Delany looks up at the four of us, "This is very serious, gentlemen. The motto at this facility is, 'what you see here, what you hear here, stays here or never leave here.' Look around you."

We turn and look at all the Marines on patrol, heavily armed. DJ goes a little whiter than he was before. Murph and John G.

maintain their stony expressions. I hope what I'm thinking – did I bring enough changes of underwear – doesn't show on my face.

"Don't think for one second that any one of these men or women will tolerate any sort of shenanigans. This is very serious business and they will shoot you if they have to. Understood?"

We all reply, "Yes, sir," at various volumes.

With that, he turns on his heel and heads down the dock with Alexis marching close behind. Even in beaded sandals, her presence is as military as everyone else we see. Delany stops and speaks with an MP, who looks over at us nods, steps back and salutes. Delany and Alexis get into a jeep and drive away as the MP positions himself at the foot of our dock.

"Well, boys," I say, "Since we can't leave the boat and we have no idea when they'll be back, I say we open a couple of beers until our host returns."

Murph looks around and says, "This place is amazing."

John G. nods, adding, "The Marines and Navy must have spent a couple of billion dollars on this place. A natural cove surrounded by high cliffs on one of the most secure military bases in the world."

I hand up four cans of beer from below, "Whatever Delany and his crew found can't be good. Did you get a look at his face when those divers came up from under the boat?"

"Yeah," says Murph, "He looked concerned and pissed off. Thanks." He opens his Heineken and sits down on the cabin top.

DJ waves the beer away, "Not for me. I might be driving. And, I hate to sound like an old lady, but I don't think we should get hammered. Just one beer guys. Who knows how quickly they'll be back and what other shit we'll be asked to do." He stands up and looks toward the buildings.

"This is bullshit, you guys," Murph says, agitated. "I hate waiting."

He stands up, nearly spilling beer on me. I look over at the MP, who has not taken his eyes off us since getting his orders from Delany.

"Murph," I grab his arm to get him to sit back down, "Calm down. We all agreed to help Delaney do this, so let's just sit and wait until we find out what the man has to say, okay? Have another beer."

"No more beer," says DJ, still looking at the buildings and the activity on the shore.

****

"Captain, you are needed on the bridge," the First Officer says, standing just inside the door of the cabin. "We have successfully slipped away from the American Submarine. However, we have lost a considerable amount of time and our passenger is making threats about being delayed. Some of the men are concerned about this man, sir. There are rumors aboard he may be crazy."

"Yes, I know," replies the Captain, lowering his voice, "I will first deal with Aziz and then I will plot out a new course and speed to get us back on schedule. Would you be so kind as to escort our guest to my cabin, then take your post on the bridge until I return?"

"Yes sir."

Once the First Officer has left the cabin, the Captain stands up and looks at his reflection in the mirror over his sink. He quickly washes his face and combs his hair.

At the knock on his door, he calls out, "Enter."

Aziz lets himself into the cabin, with the First Officer remaining outside.

"You wanted to see me, Captain?" says Aziz, sitting in the chair beside the Captain's desk, "Obviously to address my concerns, since your men have done nothing."

"My men have done nothing because I have given them no instructions. They answer only to me," replies the Captain, leaning against the hatchway. "Your pressure and endless questions threaten to undermine our entire mission. So, if you do not wish to spend the rest of this voyage confined to your quarters, you will stay off my bridge, not speak to any of my men and keep your threats to yourself."

Aziz rises from the chair, an expression of indignation on his face. Before he can open his mouth to speak, the Captain moves with so much speed that the terrorist does not see the gun until it's cocked and pressed against his head.

"The next time you disobey my orders, you oily little shit," says the Captain through clenched teeth, "I will pull the trigger and feed you to the sharks. Do you understand?"

"Yes, Captain. I understand. I was merely ..."

The Captain opens the door. "Escort our guest back to his cabin. Ensure he is locked inside and post a guard at the door."

"Yes, sir," replies the First Officer with a smile, "It will be my pleasure, sir."
Once they are gone, the Captain replaces this pistol in its holster and heads to the bridge so he can figure out how he can get submarine back on schedule without being detected. He would

have shot that bastard if he hadn't been afraid the sound of the gunshot would have given away their location.

****

Delaney and Alexis arrive back at the boat after we sneak in one more beer. DJ can be such an old lady.

"I apologize for my abruptness earlier," Delany says once they are both aboard, "We have a major problem. The tracking and listening devices we found on your boat, DJ, are brand new, state of the art and made for the United States government in Irvine. Right here at home, boys and girls. We are tearing their offices apart right now to find out how these devices ended up on your boat. Now, let's get you guys settled in to your new quarters so we can re-rig your boat. The changes will be very subtle but very necessary if we want to capture Sandoval."

"What changes?" asks DJ.

"We'll go over all of that in the morning, DJ. We need to keep all of you isolated from the rest of the base, so you'll be bunking in the barracks by the large repair hanger at the south end of the Swift base. Alexis will show you the way. Get a good night's sleep. You have a busy schedule for the next three days," Delany says and jumps down off the boat and walks over to speak with the MP.

I have the feeling this MP will be our BFF for the next three days.

"Let's go get settled," Alexis says.

She takes a quick look around and spies the empty beer cans. Uh oh.

"You bastards," she says, sternly, "Didn't you bring me any vodka?"

Chapter 47

I awake to the sound of a horn. It takes me a few seconds to figure out where I am. The sound is coming over an intercom system. I can see DJ swing his legs over from the top bunk across from me as John G. sits up from the bunk below him. Murph must be in my top bunk. I see the rest of the men in the barracks get up, and walk through the door at the end of the barracks. We follow them.

Everyone is heading into the bathroom, another huge room in typical military style, toilets on one side and showers on the other with a small partition wall between. I grab a towel and hit the shower. Who knows when we'll see one again? I can hear Murph grumbling about this reminding him of gym class. We all quickly pull our towels around us as we hear wolf whistles and Alexis walks into the bathroom.

"At ease, gentlemen," she says with a shake of her head, "Children. You're all the same."

She turns to look at us. Do I detect her giving me the once-over? Or is it just wishful thinking? I notice a stack of folded clothes in her arms. She's wearing a uniform like the ones she's holding.

"Delany wants all of us dressed in these uniforms. I'll drop them on your bunks. Unless you want me to wait here?" she says with a little smile.

"No, no," says Murph, a little too quickly, "Put them on the bunks. That'll be fine."

"Okay," she says, "If you're sure. Once you're dressed, meet us over in the building marked C-3, to the left of us, for breakfast. Delany wants us there in twenty minutes, so you'd better hustle."

She turns to walk into the bunk room amid more wolf whistles.

I dry off, go back to my bunk and dress in the fatigues marked 'Paladin' inside the collar. Just like at camp. I pull the shirt on and see my name embroidered in a patch on the front. I look over at DJ to see him looking down at the 'Frasier' on his.

Murph says, "What the hell is this shit? How many beers did I have last night?"

"Just put it on. You can complain about it to Delany," says DJ. "I'm starving."

I walk back to the shower area and call out, "John! We're supposed to meet Delany and Alexis for breakfast in ten minutes. Shake a leg!"

He comes out of the shower with his hair wet and slicked back, "I liked it better when she was working for me."

We look like every other Marine we see as we walk over to the building marked C-3. We stand just inside the door and look around. We see Delany and Alexis over on the far side of the room, off in a corner and Delany waves us over. There is a steam table along one side of the room and we see Marines lined up getting eggs, cereal, coffee and toast.

Delany says, "Good morning gentlemen. I trust everyone slept alright." He doesn't wait for an answer. "We have a lot of work to do today. Go grab some breakfast with the other men and we can get our meeting started while we eat. I'll be right back."

We follow the line to the end and grab metal trays. It looks pretty good. Maybe being in the military isn't too bad. Back at the table, we see packets with our names on them at places on the table. I sit near mine. It's sealed, so I eat my breakfast. I'm assuming we'd better wait for Delany to get back before we open them.
"What's in here?" DJ asks Alexis, holding his package up.

"We'll cover all that in a few minutes," she says, biting into a piece of toast. Delany returns followed by an officer in fatigues.

"I'd like to introduce you to your training officer, Command Master Chief Ferguson. The chief here will help you get ready for the mission which he'll help lead. Chief," He says and sits down at the far end of the table.

"Thank you, sir," says Ferguson. "Good morning. Please open the packets in front of each of you. This is our training schedule for the next few days. In that time, you will become familiar with me and the plan. The use of civilians is highly unusual, but Commander Delany is unusual himself and I've learned not to question his motives."

We all turn to look at Delany who is calmly sipping his coffee.

The Chief continues, "After this meeting, we will proceed to the shooting range to evaluate your ability with different firearms. Next, we'll advance to the village and see how you deal with identifying targets as civilian, or enemy. After that we'll take a quick run through the obstacle course in order to gauge your fitness levels."

I look around the table and figure we should all be okay with the guns, except for DJ. He's not used to shooting a gun and Maria would never let him have one in the house anyway. We're not GI Jane fit, but we're all in pretty good shape. We fill out forms in the packet, shoe size, blood type, home address, and next of kin. I'm pretty sure these guys know all this already, except maybe the shoe size.

"The last thing in the packet is a release form," he says, "It states that you have willingly agreed to help on this mission and you or your families will not sue the U.S. Government because of injury or death. You will not be allowed to leave this room unless you sign this document. Should you refuse to sign, you will be kept here, under guard, until the mission is completed. Understood?"

The Chief hands me a pen and I sign. I pass the pen to John G. He and I are the only civilians without families and so have the least to lose. Murph signs; he's a cop and knows what he's in for, but when the pen gets to DJ, he hesitates, reading the form very carefully. He looks across the table at me.

"You don't have to sign it," I say. "Just hang out here until we get back. I'll take good care of your boat."

He looks down at the paper again, "Fuck it," he says as he scribbles his name across the bottom of the page.

"Good," says the Chief. "Thank you. I'll work with each of you individually, starting with you, DJ."

"Yeah, sure," says DJ, pushing his eggs around his plate.

"After you have finished your breakfast, return to the barracks where you'll find boots and caps in your sizes. There will also be a set of dog tags. Please put these on. The rest of you can relax in the barracks until I send for you. DJ, please meet me back here in twenty minutes."

Delany, Alexis and Ferguson walk out of the mess, leaving the rest of us to finish our meal.

"What do you guys think? Those release forms make me really uncomfortable," says DJ. "I mean, if something happens to me, I don't like the fact that the government will throw Maria and the kids under the bus."

"None of us wants to die, DJ, but Sandoval has to be stopped," says John G.

"Yes, he does," agrees Murph, "He's a corrupt son of a bitch."
"He killed Ricky and Jeannie; he's hitting too close to home. We've got to do what we can to stop him," I say. "If there was

300

another way, I'm sure these guys would have thought of it by now."

DJ nods, "I just can't figure out how it all got so complicated. One minute I'm working on a job and the next minute my family, my business, my boat," he looks at me, "and my best friend are all on the line. But, I will not say no to my country."

John G. says, "So, we're agreed. Sandoval has to be stopped and we're going to do whatever it takes to do that."

We all nod.

"Fair enough," he continues, "Let's go finish dressing and see what they have in store for us."

Chapter 48

"DJ," the Chief says after they return to the mess hall, "I singled you out after looking at your dossier. Your background is neither military nor law enforcement, yet you've been involved in some interesting situations and have managed to stay alive and defended yourself admirably. Most of the others have weapons training with firearms. Have you?"

"Not really," replies DJ. "I'm more comfortable with a bow."

"A bow?" asks the Chief, "As in bow and arrow?"

"Yeah," says DJ. "I've been bow hunting for years. It just seems to be more fair. I've won a few archery contests and I can protect myself. That's what all this is about, isn't it, Chief? Protecting ourselves so we don't get killed on the government's dime?"

He ignores the jab. "Well, bow hunting wasn't in your dossier," says Ferguson, "After we're done at the firing range, we'll go to the archery range and see what you can do."

****

"Now, DJ, the object is to kill the enemies and try to not kill any civilians. Think you can handle that?" asks Ferguson.

"Yes, sir, Master Chief," says DJ, "I've got it. Shoot the bad guys, let the good guys live."

The village is a replica of any average small town that the Marine recon or SEAL teams might encounter in Afghanistan or Iraq.

The Chief raises his arm to signal the village operations officer that they are ready to begin. He drops his arm and shouts, "Go!" to DJ. DJ walks slowly through the village with his bow at the ready. He's impressed with the archery equipment they have here. He'd

303

thought these guys were all bombs and bullets. This 4' longbow with precision sight and night scope is much more high tech than the one he has on the boat. Maria won't let him keep it in the house.

To his left, a cutout of a young child pops up. He holds his shot, even though the sudden movement startled him.

"Watch for the IEDs!" the Chief yells to him. The Improvised Explosive Devices are hidden throughout the village.

DJ makes his way up the street, swinging the bow back and forth. To his right, a figure holding a gun pops up in a window. DJ fires off an arrow hitting the target square in the chest. He doesn't wait before re-loading and moving forward through the village. For the next twenty minutes, he stalks through the village, hitting all the bad guys and missing all the civilians. He only comes close to making one mistake. A woman with a child in her arms pops up in front of him, but he sends the arrow up and over her head as he realizes his error.

When he reaches the end of the village, he spots an improvised explosive device three feet to the right. He gets off a kill shot at the bandit standing in a nearby window. The device goes off with a loud bang, throwing dust up into the air, some of it raining down on DJ, who has crouched on the ground, covering his head with his hands.

The Chief walks up to DJ, extending a hand to help him up. "Nice shooting with that bow."

DJ looks over at the bad guy cut out in the window, an arrow through his forehead.

****

We all watch DJ from behind two-way glass, waiting our turn.

"Impressive," says Alexis. "I might have to get him to teach me how to do that some time. I can see where it would come in handy."

I look over at her, but I don't say anything.

The rest of us go through the village, doing pretty well. I'm the last to go, and I'm nervous. Alexis is watching and I haven't done anything like this since my days as a cop. I look at the choice of weapons and grab a rifle with a sound suppressor attached to the barrel. I walk into the village and crack a round into the chamber. The first figure to appear is a terrorist holding a cartoon bomb. I hit him in the chest. The rifle makes a spitting sound – very little noise. A nice change from all the kabooming we've been hearing all day. I jack another bullet into the rifle and keep moving through the village. I see the IED too late and it goes off. As I dodge to my left, I get off a shot before the concussion of the explosion hits me. I lie there dazed and disoriented. I roll over on my back and see the Master Chief standing above me, reaching out a hand to help me up.

"Nice shot, Bobby," he says, "You got the bad guy, but you would have been injured had that bomb been real. Shake it off and keep moving."

We go through the village numerous times until the Chief is happy with everyone's results.

"Good work," he tells us, "You sure none of you want to enlist?"

We all shake our heads and call out a chorus of, "No," and "No, sir."

"Fair enough," he smiles, "the Commander wants to see us now that we're all done. Let's do a nice two mile jog to back at the base. Follow me."

I let out a sigh as I fall in behind the others.

Chapter 49

"General, we have just received a transmission from the submarine. They are running late. They are asking what you want them to do," his aide tells him.

The General thinks about the possibility of the U.S. Navy finding the submarine. "Send a message to the Captain to increase his speed to twenty knots after he crosses into U.S. waters. Tell him to listen for any type of tracking from the Americans. It's imperative he keeps the appointed time of our rendezvous points. Did he say why they are behind schedule?

"No, sir," replies his aide, "They must have encountered trouble. The Captain is a cautious man."

The General thinks a bit longer before replying, "Contact the Captain. Inform him there will be a million dollar bonus if he can arrive on schedule. If he does not arrive on schedule, he and his crew will be executed. Then end the transmission. Do not give him the opportunity to reply. That is all," he says, dismissing his aide.

He stands up from his desk and looks out the window at the Newport Beach Harbor. If he does not deliver the terrorist Aziz on time, he may be executed himself.

****

The communications officer turns to look at Yuri, "Captain, we have received a reply from General Sandoval."

"Yes?"

"I – ah –," hesitates the officer.

"For God's sake man, just tell me what it says," barks Yuri.

"He says he will add a million dollars if we can arrive on schedule."

"Tell him I'm not sure that's possible."

"He says if we don't arrive on schedule, the entire crew will be executed."

"Ah."

"Should I still tell him it's not possible?"

"No, of course not, you idiot. Don't reply to the message," Yuri turns to his First Officer, "Have our guest join me in my quarters for a cup of tea, please."

As he makes his way to his quarters, Yuri knows what he has to do. If he fails in his mission, then the first person to die will be Aziz. Then he will scuttle the boat. He'd be taking himself and his crew to their deaths, but also cause The General's death. If not his death, at least he would ruin what was left of The General's life.

Chapter 50

When we arrive back at the barracks, Delany says, "Shower, get into some clean clothes and meet me back here in one hour. At that time, I'll lay out our plan. The Master Chief and I will listen to your input, but you will have to be prepared to follow orders."

Delany and Ferguson get back into the jeep and drive off toward the main base. I look over at Murph, Alexis, and DJ, but I don't see John G. Where did he get to?

DJ is looking behind us and says, "Hey, check this out."

We all turn to see the boat being towed out of the hangar.

"Holy shit," says DJ, "What have they done to my boat?!"

We start to walk toward it, but before we can get close, we're stopped by an MP, our buddy from yesterday.

"Commander's orders," he says, raising his rifle across in front of us, "You are not allowed near the boat until he returns."

"But..." starts DJ.

Alexis stops him by putting her hand on his arm, "Do as Commander Delany has asked. He'll explain everything when he returns."

Another MP joins the first and we know they mean business.

"DJ," I say, "It looks awesome from here. Let's give Delany the benefit of the doubt and let him explain the alterations when he gets here. It could make us the fastest boat in Dana Point Harbor." He turns on me, "I don't need any of this high-tech crap to win a race. I'm a good sailor with a good crew. That's all it takes."

"I know – that's not what I meant. Look," I say, "I don't know about the rest of you, but a hot shower sounds pretty good right about now."

We walk back to the barracks in silence, thinking about today and what lies ahead. Alexis waves to us as she heads toward another building, either a woman's barracks or some kind of VIP quarters. There's another set of clothes on our bunks. We shower, get dressed and walk back outside.

John G. is sitting on a bench looking at a pile of paperwork. I lean over him and recognize the pages Ricky had hidden in the puzzle box.

"Where have you been?" I ask him, "We haven't seen you since we got back from training."

"I've been going through the paperwork that Ricky stole from Sandoval," he replies, looking up at me, "With what Ricky stole and what new information I've uncovered, we might have a chance of getting Sandoval and shutting down a major drug cartel at the same time. If we can take the terrorist alive, we might even shut down a major terrorist cell. The boys at Gitmo are very good at finding out information from these Jihadists. Ricky unknowingly found the coordinates for the cocaine drops coming up from Mexico. We'll be able to guess his course by plotting his drop sites and find a place to ambush the submarine, Sandoval and stop those drugs from hitting the streets."

He stands up and puts a hand on my shoulder, "Ricky died a hero, Bobby."

I can't say anything I'm so overcome with emotion. Before I have to stop tears, Delaney and Ferguson pull up in the jeep and walk over to where we're standing. DJ, Alexis and Murphy have joined us.

"Well, the good news is John G. has found new information that will help us in the attempt to capture Sandoval," Delany tells us, "The bad news, we don't have enough time to go through normal channels to find support for our operation. We'll be on our own. Now, my question for all of you is; are you in or are you out? Now's your chance to go home. We won't hold it against you if you decide to stand down."

I look around at the group and one by one, we all nod to each other.

"We're in, Delaney," I say, "Now, tell us your plan."

Another Marine walks up from the dock toward us. He's young, blond and doesn't look old enough to shave.

"DJ, you and Bobby go with Sergeant Proffit here and he'll explain all the work his group has done to your boat. The rest of you get your gear together. When these two are done, we'll grab some chow and set sail. Once at sea, I'll tell you the plan."

DJ and I fall in behind Sergeant Proffit. I give our tight-assed MP buddy a little smile as we walk past him onto the dock. When we get to the boat, the Sergeant starts to explain the modifications to us.

"We did a major refit, starting with removing the lead from the keel and filling it with a new polymer that works the same as lead but cannot be detected by radar or sonar." Proffit starts in a Georgia drawl, "We also applied a special coating over the entire hull similar to that used on our stealth fighters. We installed a new carbon fiber mast and rigging. We've replaced the sails with a new type of material that is superior in strength and is much lighter than conventional sail cloth." He points to the areas of the boat as he tells us, and then motions us aboard.

311

"We installed a satellite link for navigations and a weapons bay down below," he continues.

"Weapons? What kind of weapons?" DJ asks. It's too late for him to get cold feet.

"Commander Delany will go over all that when necessary," Proffit cuts him off. "There is dive gear in the forward locker. Basically, your boat is now undetectable by radar or sonar, allowing you to sail up to any ship without being detected by their technology. She'll be more responsive and will sail better than she ever has before."

"She sailed just fine before," mutters DJ.

The Sergeant looks at him for a moment before continuing, "The Master Chief knows how to operate the new navigation station and you will be able to track your target once it acquires a lock on their signature."

We both look at him, "Signature?" I say.

"Their vessel, sir," he replies. "You should be able to locate the sub, but they shouldn't be able to detect you. The guns are loaded and the safety protocols are in place."

We spend another hour going over everything and finally Proffit asks us, "Do you have any questions, gentlemen?"

I do – are we insane? What have we gotten ourselves into? I keep them to myself. We nod and the Sergeant escorts us off the boat and into the mess hall where Delany and the rest are grabbing something to eat before we head out.

DJ sits down across from Delany, "So, the government has turned my sail boat into a floating stealth type weapon, do I have that right?" he asks.

Delany looks down at his coffee. "Yeah, DJ, I guess we did," he raises his head and looks DJ straight in the eye, "But if we make it out of this alive, you'll get to keep all the upgrades, courtesy of Uncle Sam. Now, you two get something to eat. We haven't got much time."

Ferguson stands up, "Sir, you and I should get the latest intelligence, then meet the rest of the crew at the boat."

"Agreed," Delaney stands up and we watch them leave the mess hall.

Chapter 51

I have the helm as DJ helps the others get settled below. I love sailing into the sunset on a beautiful night. It promises to be spectacular tonight. But, there are dark clouds on the horizon. As we navigate further out into the ocean, I start noticing boats appearing on the in the distance and I grab a pair of binoculars. I know what's going on; Squid boats. Giant squid must be running and these boats are carrying fisherman who will try to catch these deep water behemoths.

"DJ, you have to check this out," I call below.

DJ, Delaney and Murphy pop up and look at all the boats turning on bright lights that will attract the squid to the surface. They're followed by John G., who steps onto the deck with a troubled look. "What's up?" I ask him.

"We know where the original meeting place is and what time Sandoval is scheduled to meet the Russian sub, but the intel that Ricky stole from Sandoval has two other alternate sites," he says and turns to look at me and DJ. "Could you two look at these sites and give me your input? We only have one chance and if we get it wrong, Sandoval gets away."

DJ takes the paper from him and says, "Alexis, would you please take the helm for a few minutes so Bobby and I can look at John's map?"

DJ and I duck below where John has a coastal chart spread out on the table in front of him. I recognize the Dana Point harbor and see that the chart goes all the way past Los Angeles. John has taken a pencil and circled three spots, presumably the sites. DJ lights a cigarette as we both lean over to study the chart. After a moment, DJ looks up at me.

"Do you see what I see?" he asks.

"Yeah, deep water that goes into shallow coves. All of them are isolated but very accessible by boat. The submarine will have no trouble getting away."

Delany looks over my shoulder, "Where do you think would be his first choice to try to make the transfer? You guys are familiar with this coast."

I know what I think, but I want to hear DJ's opinion before I say anything.

"I think," he says, blowing smoke out the open hatch, "With all these squid boats out tonight, they're going to have to change their plans and go with site number three." He points to the chart, "The first two sites will be crowded, but site number three is off Crystal Cove. It's isolated enough to do the exchange."

"I think so, too," I agree. "Sandoval will be able to get into the sub and get away. It's out from a state park and no one will be anywhere near there at this time of night.

DJ continues, "I also think from there the Russian sub will be able to hug the coast as closely as possible to escape. No one would think to search for it close to the shoreline."

The Master Chief has been listening and steps up, pointing to the chart and tapping Scotchman's Cove, "If we can get here, three of us can be put in the water and have the boat sail out into the exchange site while we sneak up on the power boat Sandoval must be using for this. He sure won't be swimming out to the sub. If we can get close enough to place charges on the sub's propeller we can disable her, grab Sandoval, the drugs and the cash."

"Not bad, Ferguson," says Delany. "Let's put together two teams: one for the water and one for the boat. How much dive gear do we have on board and what's the weapon status?"

"Hold on," I say. "I'm not getting into a wet suit and handling explosives, in the dark, no way."

Delaney holds up his hand to stop me as the Master Chief continues, "During the training session we assessed the diving abilities of the civilians." He's talking as if we're all not standing right here, "All have some level of scuba experience, but Alexis, John, Delaney and I are the most qualified. I took the liberty of stowing the scuba gear for the four of us."

I hope the relief doesn't show on my face. DJ's probably the best free diver on this tub, but Ferguson must have taken his family situation into consideration before assembling the dive team.

"Excellent," says Delaney, "That leaves Bobby, DJ and Murphy standing by, waiting to move in on our signal." He turns to look at us, "DJ could you relieve Alexis on the helm so we can get her up to speed? You can start to motor us toward our destination. Under the cover of darkness, we should be invisible. We'll motor from here to within a mile of the site and sail in from there. The boat has been fitted with state-of-the-art black sails made of a lighter, firmer fabric," says Delany. "You won't even hear them in the wind."

DJ shakes his head. "These bastards really did think of everything," he says as we climb into the cockpit.

"Do you want to drive the boat for a while?" he asks me. "We can switch off every two hours or so."

"Thanks, DJ, I'd love to see how she handles with all the enhancements. If we make it out of this, your boat will be unbeatable. The interior, all the new instruments they've installed and the high-tech sails, we'll never lose a race again."

DJ sits beside me, gazing out at the squid boats with all their colorful lights. "I don't think the government will let me keep her, whether we're successful or not, no matter what Delaney says.

317

This boat is now a new, high-tech weapon that the military can sail into any hot spot and not be noticed. I'm pretty sure this is a shakedown cruise to test the equipment and the boat."

We're silent as we motor the boat into the night, headed toward San Clemente Island.

****

"General, the first drug drop has been completed in San Diego and the money transferred into the Cayman Islands bank account," his aide tells him.

"Good, very good. Things are still running behind schedule, but with all the problems we have faced, it's not unmanageable," The General responds. "Is there any word on the other operation? Have we located Frasier's wife and children?"

"Not yet, sir."

"Imbeciles!" The General slams his hand on the desk, causing his aide to jump. "I want them found right now, damn it. Advise them that whoever delivers Mrs. Frasier to me before one a.m. will get an additional five hundred thousand dollars, cash."

"General, we have teams looking for them here and in Oregon. We'll find them. It's just a matter of time."

"Enrique," says The General, in a much calmer tone, "This will give me the leverage I need to keep the Americans at bay. Once the last drug transfer takes place and we escape in the submarine I'll have enough to build another drug lab. One large enough to deliver drugs to any part of the world. The Americans must know the location of our lab by now and will be working with the Mexican government to destroy it."

The General looks down at his Rolex. In the next twenty-four hours his fate will be decided. Life or death. If it were only that simple.

Chapter 52

The dream. The dream has awakened me; or has it? I hear shouting from down below—Delaney and the Master Chief are going at it. I look over and see DJ still at the wheel.

"About time you woke up, you lazy bastard. It's your watch," he says.

I get up; stretch and walk back to take over the helm.

"Stay on this heading," he says. "We're about fifteen miles off San Clemente Island. I want us to swing a wide arc around it so when we head back in we can sail on a close reach. Then we can see how she really handles." He pulls a cigarette out of the pack he has lying beside the wheel and lights it.

"What are those guys arguing about?" I ask him, waving the smoke away with one hand.

"Sorry," he says, blowing his cigarette smoke away from me, "Who knows? We're not invited to that conversation. I've been told by Delaney that we're just the delivery system so they can take down The General."

"Well, they'd better settle this before we get close or the bad guys will hear them and make a break for it."

He stretches out on the bench in the cockpit, "Wake me up when we make the swing around the far side. Delany wants to be notified when we start the run to Abalone Point." He's asleep in minutes.

DJ can sleep through just about anything. Delaney and Ferguson have finally calmed down and are speaking in normal tones. With everyone else asleep, I have the helm to myself. There are squid dotting the ocean. I love sailing on nights like this: the air fresh and clean, a million stars above, and the boat slicing through the ocean below. It almost makes me forget why we're out here. As long as I stay on this heading and the wind doesn't die, we'll be on our way around the front side of island in a couple of hours. I pull my MP3 player from my jacket pocket, put in my headphones and find some AC/DC to keep me awake.

The new wheel stands about five feet tall with a compass on its pedestal base and is attached to an all new steering system so the boat now handles like an ocean racer—so much fun. I'm so engrossed in the music and keeping the boat on the right heading that I don't notice Murph walk up carrying a cup of hot coffee.

He taps me on the shoulder, "Bobby."

I yank the headphones out of my ears, "Crap, Murph, you scared the shit out of me!" I hiss.

"I didn't see the headphones, sorry," he says, handing me the coffee.

"Thanks," I say, carefully taking the coffee from him. "I guess I got caught up in driving this thing. This boat is officially certified Bad Ass now." I take a sip of the coffee, "It's pretty quiet down there. Did those guys get everything worked out?"

"They have a plan," he says, looking out at the ocean. "They're getting some rest. Delaney wants to be on deck when we get to the end of the island. How close are we?"

"We'll be there in about half an hour. We're about an hour ahead of schedule. If the wind holds tonight, we'll be on site by about three a.m." I say. "That's at least an hour before Sandoval's meeting with the sub."

"There must be something pretty special about this last deal, because he's doing it in person," Murphy says. "From what I

322

understand, that's not his usual style."

"I think you're right, Murph, but what can be so special about this one?"

****

The Russian captain walks up to Aziz, who is sitting on his bunk, sucking on a thin, brown cigarette. "We are about three hours from our meeting with General Sandoval. Please make your final arrangements."

Aziz opens the locker in the room and removes what appears to be a metal briefcase. He opens it and looks at the timer. He will set it when he is safely ashore. At night the virus inside the briefcase will be carried through the moist wind and spread through downtown Los Angeles, in time for morning rush hour. The U.S. President is making a speech at the Rose Bowl stadium. He's in Los Angeles to talk about his Employment Bill to rebuild the country's infrastructure, which he has pledged to start in LA. The briefcase contains a strain of the 1918 influenza virus that killed over fifty million people worldwide. With the stadium full of people coming to hear the President speak, there was an excellent chance of infecting not only the President, but a good portion of the population of Los Angeles. These people will infect others, and this weapon could kill as many as one-quarter of the population of the United States, perhaps more. The critical part is for the Russian captain to get him to The General, who would in turn have him delivered to downtown Los Angeles. It will take twelve hours to get to his site, hide the briefcase and get away. He knows if he doesn't get away himself, at least thousands of people will be exposed to the death he is unleashing upon the great evil of the world, The United States of America.

Chapter 53

Delaney and Master Chief Ferguson climb up on deck from down below. "How's it going, Bobby?" Delany asks.

"We just passed Wilson Cove and I'm sure that the Navy has eyes on us sailing this close. We're about six miles out from the island, in unrestricted waters."

San Clemente Island is owned by the U.S. Navy and is highly restricted because of the testing they do there. "Right now we're running little more than an hour ahead of our projected time frame."

"Hey you guys, shut the hell up. Can't you see that I'm trying to get my beauty rest," DJ says as he sits up and slips his legs over the side of the bench.

He lights a cigarette and climbs back into the cockpit. "I'll take it from here, Bobby. Where are we?"

I step away from the wheel and sit down across from him, "We're about six miles off Wilson Cove, making eight knots on a northwest heading. The wind is picking up and I think we'll have a lay line in about an hour. If we put up the star cut spinnaker with a full main and the wind holds true, we should be at the meeting site about an hour early. That is, if we have no problems. We should probably raise the headsail right now. We'll make better time with the wind picking up."

"That sounds like a great plan. Have you thought who you want to help you out when we tack?"

"Yeah," I tell him as I get ready to raise the sail off the deck. "I want Alexis on the mainsail and Murph on the spinnaker line. I'll drop the headsail and have Delany and the Master Chief pull it in while I pop the chute. As soon as I get the foredeck tight, I'll jump in for Murph and then it'll just be you and me driving the boat again." I raise the sail and DJ pulls the line in and ties it off to a cleat on the deck. I walk back to the cockpit, sit down and take over controlling the head sail. We're doing close to ten knots.

"What are you guys talking about?" Delaney asks as Ferguson ducks down below.

"We have to tack the boat," I say.

"Is that a big deal?"

"Well, when we tack, it's kind of like a controlled Chinese fire drill," DJ continues. "What Bobby said was that he'll set the spinnaker pole and sail at the front of the boat. I'll take the boat from the heading we're on now and change directions. When we're on the correct tack, Bobby is going to raise the spinnaker and the spinnaker pole will come up at the same time. After that sail is set, he'll drop the sail we have up now. You and the Master Chief will pull the sail up into the boat as fast as you can, and the spinnaker will fill. Murph will crank down on the winch holding the free end of the sail. Alexis will let the mainsail down and if everything goes perfect, we'll be on a straight line to where Sandoval and the submarine meet up."

"And if everything doesn't go right?" Delany asks.

"Just pray that it does, Delany. Worst case scenario is we have to tack again, but we'll cross that bridge when we get to it."

The Master Chief comes up from down below, "We have a problem."

"And that is?" says Delany. They look like they're ready to go at it again.

"We have a fog bank that starts about five miles out from the coast. We won't be able to see more than ten yards in front of the boat."

"We'll have to go in on instruments, then," says DJ.

Delaney looks at DJ and asks, "Frasier, can you get us in close to the drop site with this fog bank?"

"Yeah, I can put us where we need to be," replies DJ. "My dad taught Bobby and me to sail using only a compass. We'll be able to see the squid boats because of their lights, but it'll be tough for us to see anyone else."

"Can we use the radar they installed?" I ask.

"We can, but once we get close, I want to shut down all electronics," Delany tells us. "That way no one can track us."

DJ says, "We have about ten more miles to go before we have to tack. Bobby, start running the sheet lines then check the halyards and the chute."

"This is not my first rodeo, DJ. I do know what to do," I say pointedly. The tension must be getting to me.
"Sorry, Bobby. I just want this to go smoothly and we haven't done this with any of these people as crew before," DJ says. "The wind is blowing pretty good and it feels like it's building. This is hairy enough with an experienced crew let alone our crew."

I nod my agreement. "Sorry."

"Murph, give me a hand with this, will you?" I say as I tie off the headsail and reach into the locker where we store the sailing gear. I grab the inch and a quarter ropes that are braided with blue into one rope and red into the other rope. "The blue rope is for the starboard side and the red is for the port side," I explain as I hand

327

him the rope. "Attach the blue sheet line to that cleat on the bow and attach this block to the rail where the large blue marker is. Then run the sheet line through that block and lightly wrap it around the large winch at the front of the cockpit."

"Got it," Murph carefully makes his way to the bow. Walking on the deck of a moving boat is difficult—even more challenging to an inexperienced sailor. We run the sheet and blocks with no problems.

"Okay, Murph, I'm going to explain how this tack is going to go," I say. "Master Chief, Delany and Alexis, you'd better listen to this, too. What we're going to do is tricky and dangerous."

"Bobby, you have about twenty minutes to get these people in place. I need John G. in the cockpit with me to let the headsail loose when we tack and to winch it down when we set the chute," says DJ.

For the next few minutes I explain everyone's job to them and put them into position for the coming task, hoping it doesn't look like a Keystone Cops episode.

Chapter 54

"Prepare to jib!" DJ shouts. At the same time Murph lets the headsails sheet loose and I help the sail under the spinnaker pole as John G. grinds the winch, pulling the genoa over the port side of the boat. Alexis pulls the traveler guiding the mainsail boom to the starboard side. I raise the spinnaker pole to the height I want it and tie it down tight on a mast cleat. I then pull as hard and as fast as I can, pulling the spinnaker out of its sail bag and hoisting it to the top of the mast.

"Dropping the headsail!" I shout back to the cockpit.

"Headsail away!" yells John as he lets the rope off the winch.

I start dropping the halyard that holds the sail up as Murph, the Chief and Delany pull the sail onto the deck. John G.'s now pulling in the sheet line of the spinnaker when DJ shouts, "We've got an hourglass! Fix it now, Bobby, fix it now!"

"I've got it." I run up to the bow. The spinnaker is starting to fill and if I don't fix the sail now, we could lose the spinnaker. This is not the time for a problem, there is too much resting on the sailboat being in place at the correct time. I stand up on the bow and unfasten the sail clew. I quickly untangle the sail, but as soon as I do, the sail starts to fill. I finally get the sail reattached, but as I do, the spinnaker fills with wind. For a few scary moments, I hang in the balance. Alexis has raced up the bow to give me a hand and grabs my belt to keep me from being pulled up and off of the boat and into the water. She's finally able to pull me safely back onto the deck.

"Thanks," I say. She smiles and I turn to the cockpit and yell, "Crank it down, DJ. We're good to go."

DJ starts to set the boat on our course to meet The General.

"Good job, everyone," says DJ. "Thanks for not letting my first mate fall into the drink, Alexis."

I can feel the boat knifing through the water now. We're doing twelve, maybe fourteen knots.

"What's our speed?" I ask DJ.

"Fourteen knots plus. We're flying. I hate to admit it, but she handles like a dream. Whatever you guys did to her made a huge difference."

Delany and the Master Chief are seated, enjoying the ride. "Why don't you guys go down below and get into some clean, dry clothes?" I tell them. "Murph, I'll release you as soon as I get this jenny reset. We'll have to drop the spinnaker before we get into that fog bank."

Murph and I start straightening out the jenny and the sheet lines but after about twenty minutes I step down into the cockpit and say to Murph, "Why don't you go get dry, Murph? I'll take it from here."

Murph nods and heads below. I can tell he's tired. He's in great shape, but sailing is a whole different kind of workout. Once again, it's just me and DJ sailing the boat.

"If we weren't doing something so serious, I'd say this is a lot of fun, Bobby. This boat has never handled better. My dad would have loved to see that tack," DJ says, with a sad smile.

We sit there, together, lost in our own thoughts, the boat cutting through the water, when DJ's phone vibrates.

"Hello?" he says. I watch his face as my best friend turns white. He disconnects and turns to me, "They have Maria." His voice is strained and his hands are shaking.

****

The General doesn't know exactly why, but he knows his plan is in jeopardy. He knows that Frasier and Paladin are involved and if he can control them, he can control the situation. He disconnects his call and looks at Maria Frasier sitting in front of him. She's a petite woman with jet black hair and bright green eyes. His men had finally captured her in Dana Point Harbor. She'd left the kids at her parents' house and come to Dana Point to surprise her husband. Some surprise. What she found was no boat, no DJ, just a couple of thugs who had obviously been waiting for her. She stares at The General defiantly.

"Mrs. Frasier, let me assure you no harm will come to you if your husband cooperates. However, if he does not," he turns to look out the window and continues with his back to her, "I will not hesitate to have you killed. Perhaps even your children, just to make my point." He turns back to face her, "Do you understand me?"

After a moment, Maria Frasier straightens herself in her chair and looks General Miguel Sandoval straight in the eyes. She isn't frightened. She's pissed.

"Yes. I understand completely," she says with as much dignity and control as she can muster.

"Good. If everything goes well, you should be reunited with your family tomorrow afternoon."

The General's aide walks over and leans in close to him, speaking in a low, intense voice. After listening for a few moments, The General stands and looks at Maria, "Sergeant, I'm placing you in charge of Mrs. Frasier. Treat her well. However, if she doesn't obey you or she tries to escape, shoot her."

"Yes, General," The sergeant says as he salutes his leader, "I will take her down to the boat at once." The sergeant grabs Maria roughly by the arm and pulls her to her feet.

"Easy, sergeant, I'm sure Mrs. Frasier won't give you any trouble. She knows what's at stake."

The sergeant releases his grip a little and escorts her from the room and to the private elevator that carries them down to the parking garage. Before they exit the elevator he turns to Maria. "If you promise to cooperate, I'll let you ride up front with me. If not, I'll gag you, duct tape your hands and feet and throw you in the trunk, your choice."

"I promise to do as you ask," she replies without hesitation, "Please, don't hurt me."

He gives her a cruel smile and opens the passenger side door of a black Chevy Tahoe with tinted windows. They drive out of the parking garage. She hopes there will be a parking attendant she can signal, but the gate lifts without them having to stop. They drive down Jamboree Avenue and cross the bridge to Balboa Island.

They continue down into Balboa Island and turn left on a one-way street. The sergeant finds a parking spot on the street. He turns and says, "Mrs. Frasier, we are going to walk down the street here to a boat tied to that dock," he indicates a large power boat ahead of them in the water, "If you so much as make a sound, I will cut your throat right here. Do you understand?" Maria swallows hard. All she can manage to do is to nod her head.

After stepping out of the truck, the sergeant grabs Maria roughly by the hand and hauls her out of her seat. As she tries to pull away, he grips her harder, making her cry out in pain.

"Just a loving couple out for a stroll," he sneers as they walk down the street to the private dock. The sergeant pulls out a key, opens the gate and leads Maria to a one hundred foot yacht. He pulls her up the gangway and onto the main deck. She can't believe there is no one around to see or help her.

"I'm going to lock you in one of the staterooms," he tells her, opening a door and jerking her forcefully below. We'll be leaving soon. Behave yourself and you'll see your children soon." He shoves her into the stateroom, slams the door and locks it from the outside. As Maria hears him walk up on deck above she realizes she's trapped and alone on the boat. She knows where she is, which might help keep her alive.

Chapter 55

"What are you talking about?" I demand, not sure I heard him correctly. "Who has Maria?"

"The General does. That was him on the phone. How the hell did he get my cell number?" DJ replies, stunned into calm. "He told me if everything goes smoothly and there are no problems, I'll be told where I can find Maria. If anything goes wrong, he says he'll have her mailed back to me in little pieces."

"Son of a bitch!" I shout.

"Keep it down, Bobby." DJ hisses at me.

"Why? We have to tell Delany and John G. They'll be able to help."

"No, Bobby," he whispers, "I think we should get them to the drop site and then figure out what to do next. The General said he'd call me back in half an hour. I told him I wanted to talk to Maria when he did."

"Does he have the kids, too?"

"I don't know. I don't think so. He didn't say anything about the kids."

"Dude, this is too big for the two of us. We need help. We've got all these powerful people on board…" I whisper.

"No. He said he'd hurt Maria if I involve anyone else. I probably shouldn't have even told you."

We sail on in silence. Once we are on-site and the dive team is in the water, we're supposed to sail back off-shore and wait for them to call us to pick them up. DJ's phone vibrates and he snatches it up.

"Yeah?" I hear him say. He listens for a few moments before he says, "I want to talk to my wife." He listens a little longer before saying, "I can do that," and hanging up.

I look at him expectantly.

He shrugs, "He says he'll call me back in another fifteen minutes and let me talk to Maria. He says they've moved her to another location."

"Did he say what he wants you to do?"
"No. He just said if anything goes wrong, he'll give the order to kill her. Fuck. How am I supposed to make sure nothing goes wrong when I don't know what to do?" He slams his open palm against the wheel.

"Sit down. Let me take over."

We switch positions and DJ sits down, shaking, "What am I going to do?"

I open my mouth to reply, but close it again as Murph comes on deck. "How are you guys doing? Anything I can do to help?"

"No, thanks, Murph, we have it handled up here." I tell him. "Why don't you go back down and get some rest. We're going to need all hands on deck soon."

He nods and disappears below, leaving me and DJ alone in the cockpit again. DJ sits there, smoking and keeping everything inside. That's always been DJ's style: holding it in until he has it figured out. I sure hope it works this time.

A few minutes later his phone vibrates. "Hello? Maria? Are you alright?" I see him crumple in the seat as he listens. "Maria?" He takes the phone away from his ear and stares at it.

"DJ," I say, "Is Maria okay?"

We turn as we hear a voice come from below, "What happened to Maria, DJ?" John G. demands as he comes into the cockpit.

****

Aziz lies on his bunk and thinks about how much he hates being cooped up in this underwater tin can. However, the food is not bad and he has an area to pray to Allah in his room. There is running hot water and a flush toilet so, it is nicer than any home he had ever lived in, but he is among the infidels. Whether he lived or died, he is going to do his duty to Allah, the one true God. He wants to die because he knows what awaits him on the other side. The elders of his village say it is a great honor to do what he is about to do. He will strike a great blow against the evil American empire.

Aziz had learned English from the American soldiers stationed in the mountains of Afghanistan, who were trying to rid the country of the Taliban. When the village elders realized he spoke English, they approached him and cultivated his ability. They had him speak only English and wear only western clothes. They taught him the customs of the Americans. They told him of all the rewards that await him in Heaven when he has completed the mission they had planned. He will be remembered by his family and his countrymen as the man who brought America to its knees, and he won't even have to fire a shot. In heaven, he will live in a palace surrounded by virgins. He drifts off to sleep, dreaming of virgins.

****

"That was very good, Mrs. Frasier. Let's hope your husband will follow your instructions. Remember, I will not hesitate to kill you, your children and your husband if anything goes wrong tonight." The General says.

His aide comes in and whispers something to The General, who nods and stands. "Mrs. Frasier, I am leaving but my good friends from MS13 will be watching you. If anything goes wrong, these men have been instructed to make your death slow, painful and humiliating. If everything goes as planned, your husband will find you safe and sound in this stateroom. Your fate lies in your husband's hands, Mrs. Frasier."

The General closes and locks the door to the stateroom and nods to the armed guard standing outside. He walks up the stairs and into the main salon, where he sits down on the leather couch that runs the length of the Grand Salon. Sitting opposite him is a member of MS13, a transatlantic criminal gang. Mara Salvatruchi 13 started in the early 1980's, eventually growing into the largest gang of its type in the world. They are known for their violence and cruelty.

The man sitting across from The General, known only to him as Spike, is in charge of the Los Angeles gang.

"So, General, do you have our money?" Spike asks. "The deal was for one million dollars, up front, to get your man from here to downtown Los Angles. That didn't include the woman or killing her and her family, but what the hell? Maybe you'll give me a bonus at Christmas."

The General signals his aid who sets a briefcase on the coffee table in front of the gang leader and steps back to his position across the room.

Spike turns the case toward himself and snaps open the latches. He retrieves a pair of red, half-moon reading glasses from the breast pocket of his shirt and perches them on his nose, before lifting the lid of the case. He randomly picks up the bundles of hundred dollar bills and fans them out. After a few minutes of inspection, he closes the case and snaps the latch back into place. He removes the glasses and carefully places them back in his shirt pocket, then turns to speak to a man standing behind him. "It's all here, Julio. Put it in the car, please."

The General stands and says quietly, "If anything happens to my passenger while he is under your protection, it will be the last thing you will ever do for anyone. Do you understand me, Spike?"

Spike shakes his head and chuckles, "No need to threaten me, General. The fishing boats are picking up the last of the drugs right now. Your ecstasy and the passenger will be off-loaded from the submarine and on to the fishing boat we're using for the exchange. From there, we'll get him to his destination. Don't worry." He has no idea of who The General's passenger is and doesn't care.

The General nods. In a few days this asshole, Spike, will be dead, along with thousands of others, killed by the deadliest virus man has ever known. No loose ends.

Chapter 56

"DJ, tell me what's going on. Now! We need to know." John G. says. Delaney and the Master Chief have come topside.

DJ sighs, "The General has kidnapped my wife."

"How do you know that?" asks Delaney.

"He called on my cell. I don't know how he got my number. Maybe he made Maria give it to him. Anyway, he said that if there were any problems or interference during the exchange, he'll kill my wife and kids."

"Do you know for sure he has her?" Ferguson asks. "Could he be bluffing?"

"No way. He handed the phone to Maria and had her give me his instructions. It was definitely her."

"Fuck!" Delany explodes, "We don't need this shit right now."

"I think I might have an idea where she's being held," DJ says.

"How?" I ask him.
"Remember a few years ago we built those custom homes on Balboa Island? Well, Maria and I had a sort of verbal shortcut when we talked about work so she'd know where I was working. One of the homes looked like a great, big mushroom. We called it the Portabella House. It has its own private dock and can have as many as three large yachts moored there. She said they were keeping her in the dark, like a portabella."

"Let me get this right," says Delany. "You talked to your wife, who has been kidnapped by Sandoval. He lets her talk to you and in the span of a minute she tells you where she's being held captive without raising the suspicion of her kidnappers?"

"You don't know my wife, Delany."

"If DJ says his wife gave him a clue as to where she is then she did," I say, "The question is, what are we going to do about it?"

Delany looks at John G. and the Master Chief. Finally he says, "Look, DJ, I have gone way out of bounds on this. My career and possibly my freedom are on the line. We have been trying to take Sandoval down for years. It was my fault your friend Ricky is dead. I'll have to live with that for the rest of my life. But we are too close to catching General Sandoval to stop now. I'm sorry, DJ, I really am."

"Delany," John G. says, "What if, after DJ and Bobby drop us off at the dive site, instead of their sailing off shore and waiting for us, we let them go after DJ's wife? If they can rescue her before the deal goes down, it might throw Sandoval off his game long enough for us to take him down."

"I don't know…," says Delany.

"You can contact the base and have them send another ship to pick us up. We'll already be in, so it won't have to be as stealth as this one." John G. turns to the Master Chief and Delany, "Ferguson, take DJ below and see if you can figure out a plan for him to rescue his wife after he leaves the dive site. Make it a quick one, too, because as soon as this goes down, she's dead."

Delany sits down for a moment to think. Finally he says, "Alright, Master Chief, do as John G. asks."
"You guys better come up with something quick." I say, "We'll be on top of that fog bank soon. We'll have to drop the cute and get the headsail back up after we tack."

As DJ and the Master Chief go below, John G. says, "Bobby, I am truly sorry for putting DJ and his family in harm's way."

I hold up my hand, "Stop, John, DJ and I are big boys. We knew what we were getting into. We'll get you guys where you need to go and then try and save Maria. DJ, Murphy and I are more than competent and with our knowledge of Newport Harbor, I'm sure we can pull this off." I hope I can convince myself.

As though speaking his name summons him, Murph comes up top. "I just heard. This is so shitty. Alexis is down there helping with the plan."

"Since you're not part of the dive team, you'll be coming with us." I tell him.

"Bobby," he replies, "I have a wife and kids myself, but this is what I do for a living. I'll help you and DJ rescue Maria, but I'm in charge. If you don't follow all of my directions, I'll shoot you myself. If we piss off the local constabulary, it'll cause a shitstorm that only I can deal with."

"Understood," I say, "And thanks."

Murphy continues, "I know you were a cop and I watched DJ in action at the training, so I know I can count on both of you. Taking a hostage by force usually ends up with people being killed. I'm not worried about DJ; I'm worried about you, Bobby. If you don't think you can pull the trigger, I need to know and I need to know it now."

I can tell his concern by the look on his face. He's not wrong. I killed that kid—no, Dr. Summer says to use his name, so I say it out loud. "I killed Travis Lee by accident. I was cleared by the LAPD, the Police Commissioner, the DA's Office, and I was even cleared to go back on duty. I've been working with a shrink. You have to trust me. I can do this, Murph. I have to this, for Maria's sake. If I freak out or freeze, shoot me."

He gives me that piercing cop stare of his, "If you jeopardize this rescue Bobby, I will shoot you." Then a small smile crosses his face, "But I don't think I'll have too."

As a cop, it's important to trust the person who's got your back. I understand his concern. For the first time since shooting Travis Lee, I feel like I can carry a gun into the unknown again and pull the trigger if I have to. I owe it to DJ.

Alexis, the Master Chief and DJ, come up from below. DJ steps up to me and says, "I'll take the helm, Bobby. We need to start getting set up to drop the tack and get these guys to the drop site. Why don't you go below and get something to eat. By the time you're done, we'll be sailing into that fog bank and with any luck, disappear into it before anyone sees us."

"Do you guys have a plan?" I ask DJ. "Murph says he'll run the rescue to avoid local police problems."

"That's a good idea," he says. "Delany and Murph can put their heads together."

"Okay," I say with some hesitation. I really don't want to leave him alone right now. "I'll grab a sandwich and be back in fifteen minutes."

"Thanks, Bobby." He gives me a bro hug and says, "Let's go get my wife."

I hug him back, head below and pull a sandwich out of the cooler. As I eat, it occurs to me this could be my last night on the earth. If that's going to be the case then it's time to kick some ass and, if need be, kill us some bad guys.

Chapter 57

"Aziz," the Captain says, "You will be met by The General's men in fifteen minutes. Please be ready. I am only going to surface long enough to drop you off and to pick up General Sandoval. You will now hand over the five million dollar payment for getting you to your destination."

Aziz walks over to the locker and pulls out the black briefcase he was given when he started this mission. The Captain takes it from him, sets it on the desk and opens it. The case holds bundles of hundred dollar bills. The Captain picks up the stacks and, after checking them randomly with a money-marker, he is convinced they aren't counterfeit.

"Thank you. Ten minutes." He says into the intercom, "Prepare to surface."

Aziz, dressed in black with a backpack strapped to his back, picks up the briefcase with the deadly flu virus. The backpack contains money, a set of fake IDs that include a California driver's license, a social security card and a couple of credit cards, all real and active.

"Captain, we have surfaced in the middle of a dense fog bank," says the first mate.

"We will give The General's men five minutes to find us," the Captain replies. They must have been aware of this problem. It is their responsibility to find us. I will be up in the conning tower looking for contact. Please hand me the thermal scanner. That will help me locate The General's men."

Aziz follows the Captain up through the hatch and into the conning tower. They don't have to wait long. Within five minutes a fishing dory pulls alongside the submarine.

"Captain Popovich?" calls the pilot from the small craft. "General Sandoval sent us to meet you and pick up your passenger. Time is of the essence sir."

One of the men climbs up onto the deck of the submarine and walks to the conning tower to help Aziz, who hands him down the first briefcase, then the second.

"Good luck on your mission," says the Captain, extending his hand.

Aziz looks at the Captain's hand and shakes it hastily before climbing down onto the deck and following the man into the fishing dory. The small craft pulls away from the submarine and disappears into the fog bank.

"Prepare to dive," commands the Captain, securing the hatch.

****

The General sits in the salon on the yacht where Maria Frasier is being held captive when his aide steps in, interrupting his thoughts. "General, Aziz has been picked up and they are returning right now."

The General wishes he could be here when the terrorist arrives, but he has to be on his way if he's going to be on time to be picked up by the submarine. "Gentlemen, let's go," he says. "Spike, your people will kill Mrs. Frasier as soon as we complete our business and the submarine and I are on our way. Make it look like one of your rival gangs did the murder. Don't do it here, and make sure you wipe down the boat. I don't want the police to find any trail of you or your people being on board. Am I clear?"

"Yes, General Sandoval, I understand. Let's go," replies Spike as he turns to his men. "As soon as this guy Aziz gets here, load him into the van. Drop him at the address he gives you, then drive into south central and kill the woman. Drop her in the middle of the Grape Street Crips. As soon as I get this deal done with The General, I'll meet up with you guys at our warehouse."

Spike looks directly at his right-hand man, "Don't fuck this up. As much as I love you and your family, I'll kill all of you if you do."

Chapter 58

"Prepare to come about!" DJ shouts.

We drop the spinnaker and hoist the headsail. We all do our jobs and do them well. There's too much at stake to mess up. Delany, John G., Alexis and the Master Chief are already in their wetsuits and checking their dive gear. They're diving with the LAR V Dreager Rebreathing System, a closed circuit SCUBA device. It runs on one hundred percent oxygen where all expelled breath is recycled into the closed circuit where it is filtered for carbon dioxide. It has an operating depth of only seventy feet but there are no tell-tail bubbles. Delany tells us all branches of the Armed Forces use this system for their special teams.

I watch as Alexis picks up the M4 CQBR assault rifle. She handles it like she's used one before. It's a compact weapon, but has the stopping power of an assault rifle. She covers the gun barrel with a balloon to prevent water from entering the barrel.

"How much longer to our drop site, DJ?" The Master Chief asks.

"About thirty or forty minutes, Chief. We'll sail up to within one hundred yards of the site, drop the sails, off load you guys and then head to Newport Harbor," DJ tells him. He turns to me and says, "Bobby, take the helm, would you? I want to make sure we're still on course."

I take the wheel from him. It's so foggy that I can barely make out the bow of the boat. We had shut down the radar hours ago so The General's sub won't know we're out here.

Alexis sits down next to me. "You know, Bobby, you've really impressed me with your ability to stay calm under pressure."

I look over at her. She's barely said anything personal to me since we got on the sailboat.

"So," she continues, "if we get out of this alive, I'll go on that date with you." She stands up and lightly kisses me on the lips. Before I have a chance to say anything, she's back to getting her gear together.

"Hey, Bobby, pay attention or you'll run us into something." He lights a cigarette and takes a seat in the spot Alexis has just vacated. I wonder if it's still warm from her....no, probably not through the wetsuit.

He starts to talk, pulling me back. I can't afford to be daydreaming right now.

"As soon as we get these guys in the water," he says, "You, Murphy and I will go over our plan then set sail to where I think Maria is being held. I promised we'd do everything Murph tell us, but, if I see a chance to rescue Maria, I'm going take it, Bobby. Have you got my back?"

I don't hesitate to reply, "You know it, bro."

****

Aziz sits in the dory as it makes its way toward shore. The fog makes it impossible for him to know where he is or where he's going. He has a job to do and no one is stopping him. He has been ordered to kill everyone in the boat once he reaches land. He has a cell phone that has been pre-programmed with the number of a contact who will pick him up and take him to a safe house. He will sleep, get up, enjoy his last meal, then set out to place the briefcase carrying the virus. When the timer on the cases hits zero, the small charge will cause the containers to start releasing the flu virus. It will take seventeen minutes for each briefcase to empty itself of its deadly contents. Once airborne, there will be no stopping it. Aziz tingles with excitement for what awaits him in paradise when his deed is complete.

****

"General, with the exception of Spike's money, everything has been deposited into the Cayman Island accounts," his aide tells him. "You have five million dollars on the submarine and between the cocaine and ecstasy Senior Spike is purchasing, you will have ten million dollars." He looks at his notes, "You owe Yuri and the submarine crew their three million, plus their bonus. That leaves you with six million in cash and over a quarter of a billion in off shore accounts.

"Thank you." says The General, "Excellent accounting. If you would please excuse me now and send Spike down? We have one more piece of business to discuss."

"Yes, General."

When Spike steps into the salon, The General says, "Thank you for joining me. Please sit down. I have a proposition for you."

Spike sits down across from The General and sets his large case down beside him.

"What do you have in mind? I'm always interested in making money."

The General takes a slight pause before beginning. "Spike, right now I am sitting on ten million hits of ecstasy. I will front you all ten million hits for fifty percent of their value, plus a ten percent fee for the exclusive distributorship of the drugs. The balance of the money will be due to me upon completion of the sale. With your connections in every major city in the United States, and with your emerging prowess in Eastern Europe, you will make millions of dollars in profit each month. I can also ship you as much cocaine as you can handle. I will turn over all my contacts to you so you can be in charge. I will provide the submarine for delivering the drugs and you will deposit up front monies into my Cayman Island bank account."

Spike sits for a couple of minutes, processing. He looks General Sandoval in the eyes and says, "If you'll lower your distribution fee to five percent, lower the price a thousand dollars a kilo on the coke and lower the ecstasy to a dollar and fifty cents a tab, we have a deal." He sits back, "I'll also pay cash up front for the ten million hits of ecstasy and a thousand kilos of coke, if this deal goes off smoothly. How does that sound?"

The General sits there, stunned. He wasn't expecting this response from a gang banger. He stands and extends his hand. "You have a deal, Señor Spike."

Chapter 59

Alexis, the Master Chief, Delany, and John G. are dressed in their dive gear. The X460 Electric Sea Scooters they will share are sitting on the deck. The sea scooters can go as deep as one hundred feet, with a battery life of five hours of continuous use. They'd be in big trouble if they needed any more than that for their mission.

"Delaney," says DJ. "We're coming up on your drop site. Bobby, get up on deck and get ready to drop the headsail. Murph, you go with him and help him haul the sail down onto the deck. Make sure you keep it out of the water."

We get into position and DJ yells, "Everyone, ready? Bobby, drop that headsail. Murph, Bobby - you need to pull that sail down faster!"

The boat has almost stopped in its tracks. It's hard work to pull in that big sail with only two people.

"Great job, guys," DJ says.

Delaney looks at the crew and says, "This is where we split up. Murph, your team has two hours to get to your objective and get Maria back. If we can't take The General out in that time, I'm going to call the navy and have them send out a P3 Onion Anti-Submarine warfare plane. If they can find it, we'll sink that sub, everyone and everything on board. Good luck, everyone."

I stand up, walk over to Alexis and kiss her. She holds me for a few seconds before letting go.

"Please come back," I say, "After all this, I'm going to need that date."

The Master Chief is the first into the water and we hand him down the first sea scooter. The rest of Delany's crew rolls into the water and we pass down the rest of their equipment.

"God speed," Delany calls up. He slips on his mask and they all disappear into the black water.

Murph, DJ and I are dressed in black and ready to go. DJ goes through his bow set to make sure he has everything he needs. I slip on a shoulder holster and check my Glock. We're not just in black; we're wearing lightweight, black body armor, provided to us by the good old United States Marines.

"Let's get this show on the road," DJ says and Murph and I start hoisting the sails. DJ drops the boat back so the sails can catch the wind. Within minutes, we're back underway, making eight knots, heading in to the unknown.

"At this rate, we should make the harbor entrance in less than forty minutes," DJ says. "I think Maria's being held on a yacht toward the end of Balboa Island. We can sail up to the gas dock and approach the boat from the blind side."

A fisherman's dory appears out of the fog, swerves, barely missing the hull of our boat. It must be doing fifteen knots.

"What a fucking asshole!" I shout. "What kind of a jerk brings a small boat this far out on a foggy night?"

****

According to the Master Chief's calculations, they're close to the site where the submarine and The General's boat will meet up to make the exchange of drugs and cash. After that, The General will then get on the submarine. They have to stop him from getting on that sub and disappearing forever.

354

The Master Chief suddenly holds up his fist as a signal for all of them to stop. He speaks into his underwater transceiver. "We're about one hundred meters from the transfer site." He says, "Once we spot our objective, we'll split into teams and approach the boat from the north side. Alexis, you're with me. We'll take the stern. Delany and John, you take the bow. Do your recon before you try to board the boat. Delaney, remember your pneumatic weapon only fires one hundred rounds, so choose your shots wisely. John and Alexis, you need to take you weapons out of their dry bags once you're on the surface. Any questions?"

They all shake their heads.

"Okay. Watch your backs and we'll meet up on the boat. Alexis, let's go," the Chief says.

Delany and John G. swim off in one direction and Alexis and the Chief swim off in the other, slowly making their way to their objective. When they break the surface of the water, it's foggy and dark. They pause, waiting for any sign of movement on the boat. John throws his grappling hook up, catching the railing. Pulling hard against it to make sure it's secure, he slowly climbs up on board as Delany covers him from the water. John motions Delany to climb up as he covers him. They wait for a couple of minutes before Delany signals John to take to starboard side while he takes the port side. John takes his time making his way down his side. There are lights on inside the cabin but he sees no movement as he makes his way toward the stern. He stops and listens. Slowly, he looks around the corner and sees the Chief and Alexis standing in the stern. They motion him into the cockpit. They split up and search the boat below deck, finding nothing. The boat is completely empty.

"General, it appears you were right," the Captain says, "The American Special Forces are approaching the boat. What are your orders, sir?"

****

The General turns to the Captain and replies. "Sink it, Captain, then set a course for Cape Town, South Africa."

"Yes, General." The Captain turns on the intercom. "Weapons station, prepare to launch torpedo on my mark." He types the information into the submarine's weapons computer and speaks into the intercom again, "Torpedo room fire in five, four, three, two, one. Fire."

"Torpedo away, sir," comes back over the speaker.

"General, the torpedo will hit the target in approximately seven minutes. Do you wish to stay and watch or do you prefer for us to get underway?"

"I need to reach Cape town as fast as we can," replies The General. "I'll be in my quarters. Please let me know when our target has been destroyed." He turns and leaves the bridge of the submarine.

Chapter 60

We've dropped the sails and DJ silently guides the sailboat up to the gas dock on Balboa Island. I jump down and tie off. I climb back on board and go below. Murph is sitting with his vest on, gun in hand. DJ follows me below to check his bow and fill the quiver with his favorite Easton St. Axis arrows. Full metal jacket, these arrows are bad ass.

"What's our plan, Murph?" I ask.

He stands up. "Let's go get your wife back, DJ. Shoot first, ask later. We'll try to get near where they're holding Maria without being spotted. DJ, you'll need to take out the guards as quickly as possible. Since we don't have sound suppressors for our guns, the arrows are going to be our best bet at getting to Maria undetected. I'd feel a lot better if we had a SWAT team here." He turns to look at me, "Bobby, cover our rear and keep a sharp eye out."

I nod. None of us knows if we'll come out of this alive, but we've got to try. The life of my best friend's wife is at stake.

DJ looks at us and says, "Thanks, guys." He grabs his equipment, climbs into the cockpit and we follow. He says quietly, "The boat is about a hundred yards down the road. Stay close and I'll try to take out the guards. It's got a fly bridge and a spotter's tower. There will be at least one guard with a radio up top. I'll take him out first. Don't fire your weapons unless it's absolutely necessary, okay?"

We nod and are right behind DJ as he jumps off the boat and heads up the sidewalk. I let the two of them get ahead of me and keep a lookout for the Harbor Patrol and the Newport Beach cops. We'll likely be shot ourselves before we can even explain what we're doing here– not that they'd believe our story anyway.

I see DJ stop up ahead in front of a boat named 'Border Trap,' right next to the boat where we think Maria is being held. There is indeed a guard in the spotter's tower. Under the cover of Boarder Trap's stern, DJ positions his arrow in the bow, quickly stands, fires and drops back under cover, reloading the bow. A second shot isn't necessary. The guard is dead and has had the courtesy to fall silently where he stood and not down on to the deck or into the water where he could have alerted the others on the boat. DJ quickly dispatches two more guards, one each in the stern and the bow of the boat. He then motions me to come forward. Murph is shocked at DJ's accuracy, but I'm not. His years of bow hunting, plus his motivation to get his wife back, have honed his ability tonight.

DJ signals for us to move quietly up the dock, and check for any more guards. We move slowly, silently, climbing over the transom. Murph signals us to stay put while he does a quick once around the boat.

When he comes back he whispers, "The deck appears to be all clear. We'll need to clear each of the staterooms next." We make our way down below and silently assure ourselves each stateroom is clear until we come to the last one. The door is locked. This must be where they're holding Maria.

"What do you want to do, DJ?" I whisper.

DJ thinks for a minute, then whispers, "Murph, do you think you can kick the door in?"

Murph nods.

"Okay. Bobby, you stand here and cover us. Murph, kick that door open and I'll take out anyone who might be in the room with Maria." DJ raises his loaded bow and points it at the door.

I can feel my nerves jangle as I wait. As I listen to Murphy and DJ plan how they're going to storm the stateroom, I think I hear a noise from the front of the boat. I move quietly forward up and into the salon and come face to face with a giant. A man of epic proportions is standing next to a second man, much smaller and of Middle Eastern decent, holding a silver briefcase. I see a look of terror in the eyes of the smaller man as he clutches the briefcase to his chest. Before I can react, the big guy sees me, grabs my gun hand and puts his other hand around my throat. He picks me up by the throat and twists my gun hand, forcing me to drop my weapon. With both hands around my neck, he gives an extra squeeze and tosses me overboard. I hit the water, knocking what's left of the air out of me and I hear the Giant say, "Let's get out the hell of here," as I begin to black out.

****

DJ doesn't notice Bobby is missing. He's too focused. He signals Murph to kick in the door and follows behind, bow loaded. He almost runs into Murph who has stopped short, gun raised.

"Captain?" Murph says.

Captain Sprague stands, his hand on Maria's shoulder. Her hands are zip tied to the arms of the chair.
"Detective," Sprague says. "Nice to see you."

"Captain, what are you....?" Murph sputters. "Oh my God. You're the leak. You've been in on this the entire time. I don't understand. Why?"

Captain Sprague laughs, "You always have been such an idiot, Detective Murphy. I don't know how you ever made it out of uniform. Did you think I was going to settle for a cop's retirement when there's so much drug money for the taking?"

DJ points his loaded bow toward the Captain. "Could you two please have your reunion later? Step away from my wife, you fucking sack of shit."

Murph sees the Captain's gun on the coffee table, about an arm's length away. He dives for it at the same time Sprague does. DJ runs toward Maria as Murph and Sprague struggle for the gun. Sprague punches Murph hard in the solar plexus and winds him. He grabs the gun as DJ stands and aims the bow. Sprague ducks through the door as the arrow hits the wall above him. He runs out, down the hall and up onto the deck. Murph bends over on his knees, gasping for air. He struggles to his feet, grabs his gun and heads after Sprague. The Captain turns and fires once but misses as Murph slips into one of the unoccupied staterooms. Sprague heads up onto the deck, Murph on his heels. Murph balances on the deck railing, plants his feet and aims at the retreating back of the Captain. Out of the corner of his eye, he sees something in the water. He turns and recognizes Bobby, floating face down. He glances once more as Sprague leaps off the boat, down onto the dock, running.

"Fuck." Murph mutters as he drops his gun onto the deck, peels off his vest, kicks off his shoes and dives overboard to save his friend.

****

I don't remember anything else until DJ wakes me up. I'm sitting on the deck, gasping for air, coughing out water. I try to force out the words, to ask him what happened, when I hear a huge explosion somewhere outside of the harbor.

****

John G., Alexis, The Master Chief and Delany are on the bow of The General's boat when the barge explodes less than one hundred feet away from them. They're slammed against the bulkhead, showered in water, sand and shrapnel. The group litters the deck

360

of the boat, blood and carnage surrounding them, the last thing John G. sees before losing consciousness is Alexis slumped up against the bulkhead with blood oozing from her mouth, Ferguson attempting to cover her and protect her from the falling debris.

****

I try to clear my head and sit up. I look around and see DJ, Murph and – thank God – Maria. Murph has blood seeping from a crude bandage on his arm but everyone else seems okay.

"Another couple minutes in the water, Bobby, and you might not be sitting here," Murph says.

Maria shakes her head and says, "You have more lives than any cat I've ever met, Bobby Paladin."

DJ reaches down and I grab his hand as he pulls me to my feet. "I'm okay. Just a little bashed up. There were two guys standing in the salon and they caught me off guard when I came up on them. One guy was some kind of a giant and the other guy was a little Arab holding a silver briefcase like held his lunch money and he was afraid some bully was going to steal it."

Maria turns to her husband, "Honey, those are the guys I was telling you about. The Arab guy has some type of flu virus he's going to release near the Rose Bowl later on today. You have to stop them!" DJ looks at me, "Bobby, the Carroll's' house is two blocks down the street. They're in Hawaii right now. We need to borrow their car. Murph, can you get us clearance to break the speed limit on the freeway?"

Cradling his arm, Murph pulls his phone out of his pocket, "What kind of car are you going to be driving?"

"A Lamborghini 560, copper color, with vanity plates that read, *Piece of Cake*," DJ shouts over his shoulder, "Get on it!"

He grabs my arm and we jump off the boat and start running down the street. I stumble to keep up with him.

"Are you nuts, DJ?!" I yell, "Ken loves that car more than he loves his wife!" We stop at the Carroll's garage door. DJ punches in the access code, which he remembers from when we renovated the Carroll's home. The garage door slides open and there sits the Lamborghini. It's so beautiful.

"Bobby? Bobby!" DJ shouts as he opens the driver side door, grabs the keys from under the floor mat and starts the car. I jump in as the car roars to life, the sound magnified in the enclosed space, and DJ squeals out of the garage and accelerates up the street.

Chapter 61

"Don't try to talk. You've been badly wounded." John G. can barely hear the medic because of the ringing in his ears. He looks into the eyes of the young woman as she injects him with something for the pain.

"The team," he gasps, "Where's the rest of the team?" But before he can hear an answer, he slips back into the black void.

****

DJ and I are hauling ass up the freeway. "Maria described the car those guys are driving," he says, eyes intense on the road, "It's a dark blue Cadillac Escalade. She didn't get the whole plate number, but she noticed it had four fours in it."

"Great." I say, "I got a good look at both of those guys. If we can find the SUV, we can take them down."

It's dark, late and starting to rain, just like that night so many years ago that changed my life forever. We're coming up on the Pasadena freeway. This was the first freeway built in the United States, built in the 1940s and you can tell. It's narrow with tight concrete walls that feel way to close to this very expensive car. I look over at DJ and he has that look of grim determination. I turn to look ahead and through the thin rain and see a dark SUV further up. That might be might our bad guys. Its reflective paint makes it seem as though it changes color as it passes under the freeway lights.

"DJ," I say, "That might be them up ahead, in the right lane." It's so hard to tell in this rain.

He clenches his jaw and downshifts and the powerful car surges forward. I get a good look at the license plate; it has four fours in it. We pull up into the Caddie's blind spot. "You need to pass them so I can get a look at them." DJ pulls out into the next lane and passes them. "It's them. You don't forget someone when he throws you overboard by your neck."

DJ pulls into the same lane ahead of the SUV so we're about a hundred yards in front it.

"Hang on, Bobby!" he says as he slams on the brakes.

Suddenly, everything is happening in slow motion. The Caddie swerves to the right and starts climbing up the embankment. The driver over corrects and the Caddie starts to roll over, again and again. It's late enough that the light traffic on the freeway is able to swerve and get out of the way of the accident. Horns are blaring and people start to pass and pull over on to the side of the road. We pull onto the shoulder and get out of the car in time to see the Caddie roll over one more time and come to rest on its roof, the wheels are still spinning. I grab my gun and we slowly approach the car. I shout at the other drivers who are pulled over to stay back. I watch as DJ makes his way toward the driver's side of the car and leans down to look in the window.

"This guy's toast, Bobby," he calls to me, "His neck is broken." There's karma for you.

We're so concerned with the driver that we don't notice the passenger climb out of the window until he's running up the embankment, carrying the stainless steel briefcase.

"Stop!" I shout, running around the car and raising my gun. "Stop!" I shout again. "If you give yourself up now, you might have a chance."

The man stops running and turns to face me, the hugging the silver case to his chest. "The General's long gone," he shouts. "He'll never be caught and you won't shoot me. I know of your past Bobby Paladin. You will never shoot anyone again. You are a coward! If you'll excuse me, I have a flu virus to release." He turns and starts to run up the hill.

I look over the barrel of my gun and see that my hand is shaking.

"Bobby!" I hear D.J. call my name as though from under water.

I take the shot.

Epilogue

For hours, the sheriffs, police and an alphabet soup of agencies have asked us the same stupid questions over and over and over again. Delaney finally shows up and takes the agent in charge aside. Fifteen minutes later, we're alone with Delaney in the interrogation room. He walks over to the two way mirror and presses his ID against the glass.

"A little privacy guys, please?" he says into the mirror.

The lights come on in the observation room and we see half dozen men and women open the door and leave the room. Delaney sits down at the table, facing us.

"You both look like shit," he says.

"Have you looked in that mirror today, Delaney?" I ask him, "Your career as supermodel is over, dude."

He reaches up to touch the place on the side of his head that's been shaven and stitched.

"It wasn't paying me much anyway," he says, with a slight smile. He turns serious as he looks at me, "Don't worry about the shooting, Bobby. You did the right thing. There won't be any charges filed against you. That terrorist was trying to unleash a deadly flu virus at the Rose Bowl during the President's speech this morning. The canister in the briefcase is still intact and in a secure location. Your actions saved the life of the President and the lives of thousands of American."

I spread my hands on the table and look down. I give a slight nod. Dr. Summers is really going to have her work cut out for her now.

"Where's Murph? Did he tell you about Captain Sprague?" DJ says.

367

"I never did trust that son of a bitch," says Delaney. "As we speak, Detective Murphy's pulling together a task force to find him."

DJ asks, "What about the rest of the team? Are they okay? That asshole said The General got away. Did he?"

I look up. "Alexis." I say, "What about Alexis?"

"She's alive, Bobby." Delany replies. "You won't see her any time soon, though. She's going to need time to recover from her injuries. Her boss has had her transported back to Washington, D.C. for recovery, debriefing and reassignment when she's healthy again."

He pauses before continuing, "John G. sustained some pretty serious damage to his chest and face. He's in surgery now. The doctors are very optimistic. The bad news is the Master Chief. He didn't make it."

"Ferguson? No. What happened?" DJ asks, shocked.

Delany shakes his head, "He was killed by the explosion, protecting Alexis. He gave his life so she could live. He was a true Marine."

We're silent for a few minutes before DJ repeats, "And The General?"

"Gone," sighs Delany. "Not a trace of him or the submarine. They're just gone. But you can bet your last dollar, that we haven't heard the last of that man."

****

DJ and I finally are allowed to leave the Pasadena Police Headquarters.

"Let's get this car back into Ken's garage before anyone notices it's missing," he says.

"We'd better top off the gas tank." I say.

DJ tosses me the keys to the Lamborghini.

"You drive," he says, "I've had enough excitement to last me the rest of my life."

Author's Note

I would like to say thank you to Lori and Theresa all for their hard work. Without them this novel wouldn't have been possible. I would also like to dedicate this book to my best friend, Richard Paul Weaver, Jr., who left us way too soon. And to Ray Felix from the Red Fox Lounge. To the Nines, Ray, to the Nines.

Made in the USA
San Bernardino,
CA